PROPHECY ACCEPTED

BOOK 2 PRIME PROPHECY SERIES

TAMAR SLOAN

JESS CONNORS
PUBLISHING

1

NOAH

My heart slams my chest with the same thundering beat as my paws pounding the soil. Claws dig into the ground, chewing out clods of dirt as I propel myself forward. Lungs fill like bellows, stretching to capacity then rapidly deflating, keen to do it all over again. The trees become a blur, a camouflage of green on green, the scent of pine hitting me so hard I can taste it.

My head dips, dividing the wind that rushes at us.

Faster.

My whole body smiles as the legs gripping my ribs tighten. Who knew this quiet, shy girl of mine had an inner-adrenalin-junkie just waiting for the right Were to unleash it? Not that I'm complaining—there's no bigger, better rush than running with Eden.

She leans down, her head brushing close to my ear, breath tickling my fur. "Faster," she breathes, this time out loud.

I heard you the first time.

I glance back, at the reddish-brown wolf and larger black wolf who are already falling behind. Tara slows, having the competitive spirit of a sloth. Mitch, on the other hand, dips his head, black brows coming low.

Bring it on little bro.

I stretch eager muscles, suck in my essential fuel—Eden and oxygen—and run. I run like gravity is optional, like the sound barrier is just ahead; I run like this will never end.

Mitch slows, and although I can't hear my twin's growl of defeat, my victorious mind imagines it. Eden's laughter bubbles out, a natural sound of joy and freedom, the magical sound that has progressively lost its rough, unused edge.

But I don't stop; I can't help myself. Without slowing, I angle to the left, forging a new track past the trees. With Eden, I always feel like I can gain a little more speed, a little more strength, a little...well...more.

Because when we're running, nothing matters. It doesn't matter what time it is. As if four months haven't passed since I banished Kurt, that it's only weeks since the icy snow of winter melted. That graduation isn't looming on a very near horizon.

It doesn't matter who we are. Me, the Alpha heir; her, a human. Well, mostly human. Because it was Eden who called the bears and mountain lions—a surprising, unimaginable act that prevented a blood bath. And the average human certainly can't do that. But that guy, her male alter-ego, the one who appeared on the rock ledge, has never shown up again. The very same dude Eden won't mention, let alone discuss.

I head west, knowing exactly where I want to go. Eden leans forward a little more, like it will help us get there a little faster.

Yes.

I smile, feeling canines push into my bottom lip, the wind whipping up the exhilaration. It's just Eden and me and the miles falling behind us. The sun smiling down on us. Our feelings flowing freely between us. Bigger, more real, more doggone incredible than anything I could have imagined.

Because here, alone and together, it doesn't matter that I've carried a secret for four long months. That I've concealed the small circle with a five-pointed star within it, undeniably imprinted on my chest. A little mark with huge implications, implications that make my conflicted heart soar and sink, depending on which way my thoughts take me.

Because no one knows, not one person or Were, that we've bonded. An impossible, confusing dream come true. Not even the one it affects the most–Eden.

Impossible because it's never happened before, impossible because our laws say it can't be.

A dream come true because, well, because it's Eden. The heart-tripping, mind-blowing, soul-grabbing girl that already owns my heart.

But ultimately confusing because I have no idea what it means. I don't know how to tell her. How she's going to take it. Shoot, if she wants this. I don't doubt her feelings for me; I feel them every single day, but a never-heard-of-before-bonding to a future Alpha? That's big. Irreversible, life-changing, how-do-you-even-bring-that-up big.

A stand of rocks crests on the horizon, at the top of a rise, breaking the skyline with their stoic harshness. Every time we run, I find something to jump. First fallen trees, then rocks, eventually the odd monolith. Each jump a little bigger, a bit more of a challenge. I see the rock we jumped last time, all rounded greys and angled whites. But those six feet of granite no longer pose a challenge. My head tilts up, and I angle slightly to the left. The boulder's bigger brother next door does.

Or maybe it's a daddy, because it's almost twice the size.

Now that's a challenge.

Through the wind blasting my ears I hear Eden's intake of breath, sense the jump in her heart rate. I certainly feel her hands clench my fur. The smile grows to a grin as I scan the rock getting closer and bigger.

Paws concertina in and out, over and over, devouring the distance, bringing us closer. Eden presses her front to my back, hands deep in my fur.

With precision timing, I leap, hit its cold hard surface, and push. My front paws have barely landed when they're replaced by my back legs, and I push up again. A powerful thrust and we're on the top. Now comes the awesome bit. I compress down as I land, coiling the spring, loading the gun. And bam! All that potential energy is propelled into the sky. Eden lets go, leans back, and arches to the sun.

The air that was rushing past slows, lifting us, holding us in suspended animation as we defy the laws of physics, stalling the passage of time. There's just a white wolf, stretched and taut, and his gorgeous girl, arched and open. I can just imagine that mane of hers flowing behind like a mahogany sail. It's a beautiful, breathtaking image.

But all things that go up and over a boulder must come down and honor gravity. A breathless moment later I hit the ground, elbows and knees bending, absorbing the impact. Eden's body crashes into mine, for a split second blending us into one.

Making our landings equally as awesome.

Neither of us needs to say a thing; everything we feel is overflowing between us. Two bodies, even one as big as mine, can't contain such a whirlwind. I gallop over grass and gravel, giving us a bit of time, a little to get our breaths under control, but mostly to bask in the wild feelings our runs unleash.

Because I know. I know it's the freedom that Eden loves, that makes this so special. She's had so little choice in her life, so few opportunities to decide. Which is why I'm not landing the bonding in her lap. She deserves to choose, in her own time.

And that's fine; I really don't mind.

I've waited this long.

Eden's legs tensing around my ribs bring me back to the present. Her thoughts tickling through my mind suggest we should turn around before we end up in Canada. I slow, making a big arc. A rhythmic lope takes us back to the Glade.

Tara and Mitch are sitting in the middle of the grassy clearing. The pine trees that surround it like protective parents glisten with melted winter snow. Back in human form, they're both leaning back, propped on bent arms, chests sucking in lungsful of air.

Eden slips off, her hand running down my shoulder, making me shiver.

Thanks.

Anytime, I reply, my response as sincere as her gratitude.

I head over to the Precept rock, the mini mono-lith that has our four laws carved into it.

YOU SHALL NOT REVEAL THE BLOODLINE

YOU SHALL NOT BOND WITH THE OPPOSITE BLOODLINE

YOU SHALL NOT ATTACK ANOTHER BLOOD MEMBER

YOU SHALL OBEY THE ALPHA

I DON'T LOOK at the reminder of everything I've just pushed out of my mind. I slip around the back, doing my usual transformation away from the green eyes I can feel following me. I hate hiding, pretending, but the alternative stirs an uncomfortable feeling I've yet to name.

As I return, Mitch grabs a handful of wet grass and tosses it at me.

The green blades are caught in the breeze and swept toward us. I leap in front of Eden. "Hey, that could have hit my girl!"

Eden's forest green eyes peep up at me as she slips beneath my arm. That sense of connection that never leaves gives me a jolt. I love it. It keeps me anchored. It keeps me high.

"My hero."

Tara snorts. "Thank Galactus you were there. Eden, you're going to have to gain some weight. We need to slow this Were down."

"I won't if we keep doing this every week."

I squeeze her hand. "Although if Tony keeps making those cheesecakes…"

Eden's eyes light up at the mention of the chef who works at her mother's Inn. A chef that seems intent on spoiling her more than me. "A cheesecake challenge."

My girl's version of heaven.

"As your bestie, I should help."

Eden nods sagely. "Proving there is no such thing as the selfish gene."

Tara shrugs dainty shoulders, tilting her head in an unsuccessful show of modesty. "I'm a team player."

Eden's eyes squint as she stares ahead, her lips puckering just a little, just enough to focus my eyes on them. "We'll start with the raspberry white chocolate swirl."

"Or the triple-choc cheesecake with the salted peanut caramel."

"We don't want to leave out the baked cherry and hazelnut praline."

Mitch sits up a little straighter. "It couldn't be a pizza challenge?"

Both girls turn to him, shocked, a little stunned, looking a bit like Eden did after she witnessed the first time I changed. Come to think of it, I looked like that, too. I shake my head. Mitch has been with Tara long enough; they're bonded, for heaven's sake, to know better.

"Of course not!" Tara punches his arm. "They don't even start with the same letter."

Eden and Tara laugh as Mitch mumbles something about cheese fitting the bill.

Just as I plonk myself on the grass, bringing Eden down with me so I can rest my head in her lap, Tara decides silence is overrated. "So, guys, we have a double birthday coming up, and it's a significant one. I've already spoken to your mom about initial preparations."

I feel Eden tense in the legs cradling my head, but more so deep within. "How big is this thing going to be?"

"I'm defs keeping it low key this time. Some peeps, some dancing..."

I hear Mitch shift in the grass. "Can I do the music?"

"No!" Three voices chorus their horror.

Mitch grins as the girls laugh, and I look up to the sky, seeing the weak spring sun doing its best to warm us. It's all I need to expand my chest in a deep breath and squeeze out any residual doubts that I'm doing the right thing.

Sitting there, in this place where time seems to stand still, I look to the girl I want to spend the rest of my life with, a girl I'm not supposed to be able to. I suck in another deep breath, a breath full of hope, her wildflower scent...and patience.

I can wait.

2

EDEN

"A themed birthday party?" I hope my slightly higher pitch sounds curious, maybe even excited.

Noah gives me a squeeze, pulling me closer to his heated side. I don't look at him, hoping he hasn't noticed my anxiety. I focus on the dainty redhead doing a little jig before me. Mitch lets go, admitting defeat as he tries to contain a pepped-up cricket.

Tara's hands bunch beneath her chin. "Mythical Mayhem! It's going to be amazing—fairies, witches, goblins..."

"How many?" *Do curious, excited people cut their sentences short?*

"Oh, the whole year group!" In a town as small as Jacksonville, that means about forty. That's thirty-seven too many. "Then there's the Phelans." And the numbers just doubled, just like my eyes and my heart rate. I know Noah has sensed my feelings now. They're too close to the surface for him to miss.

Tara springs over to Mitch, wrapping herself around his arm. He lifts dark brows into dark hair, an amused twist to his lips. She smiles up at him. "Come on, mate-of-mine, let's go talk to your mother about a smoke machine!"

"Now?"

"Yes, now."

"But we were going to..." He glances at Noah and me.

"Oh, yeah." A look passes between the three. Some Were secret I'm not part of, that I pretend not to notice. Tara frowns for a second, before the furrows are washed away by her smile. "Don't go anywhere!"

She part walks, three-quarter drags Mitch toward the house. Out here on the open lawn of the Phelan backyard, I look over to Grandfather Douglas. The giant Douglas fir has been our protective canopy through so many moments. It's seen our beginning, my tears, our first kiss. Our love takes root and blossom until it is the living, breathing connection that binds our hearts, our emotions so closely that we can feel each other, sense what the other is feeling. I wouldn't mind being there now.

As Tara and Mitch round the house, I turn to eyes the color of a summer blue sky. Through the long winter months, they never failed to warm me. Either with tenderness and love. Or with passion and desire. Sometimes all at once.

"It'll be fine."

My head tips to his chest. Here at home, he doesn't need to wear a sweater to keep up the pretense. My words are muffled in his t-shirt. "I suppose you only turn eighteen once."

Noah's hands stroke up and down my arms; the warmth of his palms, his chest meaning suddenly I don't need a jacket either. "We'll have a good time, you'll see."

"If you say so," I grumble into his chest.

"Who will you go as?"

"The abominable snowman?" Something that covers me from head to toe, leaving me anonymous. Maybe the invisible man; nobody would care what he wears.

"Maybe you could borrow your mother's Wicked Witch of the West uniform."

I smile into the warm muscles in front of me. I take a deep breath of spiced sandalwood, my favorite smell in the world, then tilt back to regard his handsome features. My favorite sight, the one I never get tired of looking at. "What about you?"

"Isn't it obvious?"

He wouldn't.

Noah wiggles dark blond brows, that delicious mouth of his tipping up at the corners. He leans in like he is going to share a big secret. One I already know.

"A vampire."

A spluttering laugh slips from my lips. "A vampire?"

"Yep. Mitch and I both."

I realize my reclusive tendencies aren't normal for someone my age. For someone who wants to desperately fit in with this guy, his family, his life. I suck in a little extra oxygen. "You know what? It should be fun."

"Really?"

I can already see those two in black, hair slicked back, white canines peeking out. "Sure. I've never seen a shifter dressed as an overgrown mosquito before."

Noah looks like he just won a prize without the fight. He puts his hands up in a you-won't-get-an-argument-out-of-me gesture. "Great."

I smile as I snuggle back into that hot, hard chest. I'm determined to enjoy every moment I have with Noah. I've had four months of getting to know this patient-leaning-toward-stubborn, hunky-hedging-toward-jaw-dropping-gorgeous, strong-to-the-point-of-being-recklessly-brave Were. And the more I've learned, the more I've fallen in love.

Enough to know that I need to savor, memorize every moment we have. Enough that I know a life with Noah has crystallized as the dream I never let myself have. Enough to know that whatever comes, wherever this goes, there will never be any regrets.

Noah's hands slide back around my waist. "You'll just have to stick by my side…"

Which is pretty much what we've done for the past four months.

I lean in a little more, pressing myself up against him. "Like this?" I breathe.

Noah's breath hitches a little. I love it when he does that, like this is just as heart-stirring for him as it is for me. His strong arms tighten around me, pulling me flush up against him. "I was thinking more like this."

I don't answer as words, thoughts evaporate. Internally combusted by the heat that just spiked through my whole system. Because those chiseled lips are tilting down, heading south. Coming closer to mine.

My breath is caught in my throat as every cell waits, reaching, stretching toward him. The anticipation suspending my ability to breathe. But I don't care; I don't need oxygen right now.

I need Noah.

"Okay, peeps, let's roll out."

The anticipation train comes to a screeching halt as we both stop. Neither of us turns our head; we already know Tara is skipping toward us, Mitch probably not far behind. Noah's forehead comes down to rest on mine, those lips close, but not close enough, and no longer about to come through on their promise.

"She's small. I'd only have to dig a little hole." Noah growls.

"You can't kill your mate-in-law. I'm pretty sure she knows how to reincarnate."

Noah takes my hand as we turn toward Tara. "Probably," he mumbles

"Oh, I hope I wasn't interrupting anything." Innocent hazel eyes blink at us.

"I'm still tempted." He growls ever so quietly.

Tara gives him a cheeky grin, most likely having heard everything we've said. Unperturbed, she holds out her hand to Mitch, and once he takes it, walks past us toward the trees across the back lawn. As she strides with purpose and a little hop, I realize she's headed toward a gap between the trees. An opening that I soon realize is a small track, one that disappears into the pine forest. I look at Noah in question, but he gives me nothing other than an enigmatic grin.

I look back to the track, wondering where it leads. Surprises make me nervous. And when you're dating a guy who's only half-human, I've learnt surprises can really rock your world.

In no time at all we're swallowed by the trees; tightly packed trunks and tangled branches create a barricade of green and brown on either side of us. The silent walls watch us as we walk, each in our respective pair, to who-knows-where. It's only a minute or so when the trees begin to space out, their pine arms no longer crammed into each other, fingers of light piercing the gloom. Tara races around behind me and puts her hands over my eyes.

"Can you see?"

With my sight blacked out, the smell of acrylic paint tingles my nose. "I can certainly tell you've been painting this morning."

A bright, excited giggle tinkles over my ears. Tara is practically hopping behind me.

A few more cautious steps forward, my hand firmly clinging to Noah's, and Tara pulls me to a stop. So, this is what a horse feels like being led.

She whips her hands away and leaps to stand beside me. "Ta da!"

I squint through the bright light to see a clearing in the

pines. Lush green stretches in a natural circle, light dancing across the emerald carpet, the never-ending rows of pines surrounding it. I turn to my left to see a dirt track zigzagging down to a wider dirt road. The road to the Phelans' house.

"What do you think?" Tara hops from foot to foot; beside her Mitch beams a proud grin. It's like they've just shown me the eighth wonder of Jacksonville. Which they planted themselves.

"It's...lovely."

Noah leans over, whispering. "Correct response."

I turn to him, wondering what I'm looking at. He wraps his arms around me, his chin resting on my shoulder. "This is where Mitch and Tara are going to build their house."

Tara rolls her eyes. "Obviously."

My stunned lips twitch. "Obviously," I whisper back.

Tara skips, practically cartwheels to the center of the clearing. "Our house will be Mitch's first big project as part of his apprenticeship."

"Mitch is going to help build it?"

Mitch crosses his arms, I think to keep down his swelling chest. "Uh huh."

Tara takes several steps forward. "Front door here." Then a few to the side. "Dining area here." She frowns for a moment, tapping her lips in thought. "Kitchen next door and master bedroom over there."

Mitch's arms drop to his sides, and he walks over to stand beside her. "Ah, we discussed the master bedroom. It's going over there, to make the most of the view."

A window there would certainly frame to majestic mountains that loom in the distance, dusted with what's left of the winter snow.

"But what about the nursery?"

I expect Mitch to blanch at the talk of kids like any almost-eighteen-year-old guy would. But he wraps his arms around

Tara and spins her ninety degrees. He points over her shoulder. "Right there."

Tara's eyes widen, and she smiles a gentle smile. "Oh, yes. That's perfect."

The two quickly lose themselves in their plans, their dreams. They step one way, then another, talking to no one but each other.

I turn in Noah's arms, my own going around his neck. "This is a great idea; they'll be close to your parents."

"My parents subdivided their block to allow some land for both of us. My mom's ultimate plan to keep us close to the nest."

So, Noah has a parcel of land nearby, too. Just waiting for him to bond and settle down. I turn in his arms again, my back against his front, taking my quiet face with me. "That's a wonderful idea."

"Yeah, it is," says Noah, his own voice a little quiet.

I wait to see if he'll say more. Something. Anything. But Noah seems just as lost in thought as I am. In the still, warm body behind me, I can feel a jumble of emotions, all too conflicted and confused, still too new for me to disentangle.

It sparks my own internal war. Curiosity encourages me to ask. Fear keeps me quiet.

We stand and watch as Tara and Mitch plot out bedrooms and bathrooms, backyards and front gardens, dining areas and living areas. Feelings, hard and tight, twist within me. A wrench of envy. A spasm of hope. A brief, fleeting impulse to turn around, maybe speak up.

But blanketing them all, like these feelings are bigger than me, is the wishing. And the wanting. My heart desperately searching for some indication, just a little sign this could be possible with Noah.

The impossible feat of an Alpha heir choosing a human.

Choosing me.

But nothing happens. Noah remains still, almost like he's waiting, too. The breeze moves around us, and in the shadow of the trees, I shiver a little. Noah's arms tighten, and I sink into the comfort of his warmth.

Maybe I should say something? I'm formulating some light-hearted question about his own piece of paradise in the pines, hoping to test these uncertain waters, when Noah's arms loosen, and he turns to look over his shoulder.

"Noah." I see what Noah heard before I did. Adam, Noah's father, is walking toward us. He seems to slow as he gets closer, but I tell myself I'm being paranoid.

"Ah, Eden, lovely to see you again."

"You too, Adam."

"What's up, Dad?"

"I need to talk to you about something."

"Yeah?"

Adam shuffles, "Ah, something private."

I flush crimson. "No problem Mr. Phelan. I was going soon anyway. I've got a pile of books waiting to be summarized."

"You don't have to go, Eden." Noah is frowning at his dad.

"Eden, I've told you to call me Adam. Sorry, I didn't mean to scare you off."

I force a smile. "Not at all. Unfortunately memorizing how DNA replicates doesn't happen unless you're reading the textbook."

"You sure?" Noah says.

I nod, the smile starting to hurt.

"See you next time, Eden."

"Sure, Adam."

Noah sighs, "I'll walk you to your car."

Noah takes my hand and leads me back to the little track in the woods. I wave to Tara and Mitch, but they're lost in their planning.

Noah's lips are tight as we walk back through the pines. A gentle breeze ruffles his dark blond hair, and I wouldn't mind my fingers doing the same.

He looks at me and catches me staring. "Sorry about that."

"It's fine. I understand." The truth that I'm human is never far away. I opt for a change of subject. "It's great to see him up and about again."

"Yeah, Were healing kicked in. The physiotherapist is touting him as the poster boy for her patented exercise regime."

"He'll be dancing with the wolves in no time."

Noah chuckles. "Dad wants to strangle her." The atmosphere warms a little, or maybe it's because we are out in the open with the spring sun overhead as we approach my car.

At the car, I turn to Noah. Summer eyes catch mine, tripping my breath, trapping my heart.

His hand comes up, tracing across my cheek, fingers moving into my hair, his palm cupping my cheek. A tender, captivating gesture that holds me just where I am. Not that I'm going anywhere.

"Now, let's do a little quantum physics and rewind time..."

Is it only an hour I've been waiting for this kiss?

We don't pause this time; we don't need to build the anticipation. I'm bursting with the feeling.

Those hot, soft lips are on mine in an instant.

Heating me. Melting me. I press all of me against all of him as Noah's hands band around my waist, securing the tight embrace. I'm all hot and heavy, all burning and bright, happily combusting and evaporating. Someone groans; maybe we both do. The hoarse, hungry sound just fans the flames.

Desire and passion detonate, my ability to think collapses. My hands go to his hair, pulling those heavenly lips closer, anchoring him to me. Trying to brand him as mine, so he can never leave.

Noah is the first to pull away. I pretend I'm okay with this.

I disentangle my fingers, then arms, but my heart doesn't want to let go. "I love you."

"I love you, too."

"I'll see you tomorrow."

Noah grins. "You can bet on it."

I climb into my car, my pulse pounding, my breath a little too quick. Kissing Noah is an exercise in losing control then grappling to regain it. A passion that gets so hot, so quick, can be hard to rein in.

As I head down the dirt road that leads to the Phelan house, I slow when I see a dusty intersection I'd never noticed before. The driveway that leads into the trees, that I now know opens to a grassy clearing, a clearing that will soon be filled with a house, two bonded Weres, and their bright future. It's a happily ever after that Mitch and Tara deserve.

I bite my lip as I wonder where the second driveway is. I don't see it as I head toward the highway, meaning it must be past Adam and Beth's house. I realize Noah never suggested he show me. That I didn't ask to see.

I know why I didn't.

Which leaves me wondering why Noah never offered. I accelerate again as I desperately try to ignore the images my mind is painting as inevitable.

Images of endings rather than ever-afters.

3

NOAH

"Well, that was rude." I cross my arms, going for the ticked-off-Alpha-heir look.

"We need to talk, son."

"After everything we've been through, there's little Eden can't hear, Dad."

Dad is shaking his head. "She's human, Noah."

"She's far more than that, Dad."

"She's not Were."

I consider telling him, for all of a nanosecond. But I know what he would want me to do, and I've already decided. Eden deserves the right to choose.

I take a deep, deep breath. "I know that. But she's the girl I love. And she's done far more for our pack than some Weres have."

Dad's arms fall to his side. "And I'll always be grateful. But you're the Alpha heir Noah."

My hand twitches, wanting to go to my tattoo. I shove it in my pocket and say nothing. I can't.

"Your decisions will always affect your pack. And you've already learned that can mean some tough choices."

He has no idea.

"And things are happening."

Finally, something I can respond to. "What things?"

"The Channons want an Alpha."

"I guess that was inevitable. Every pack needs an Alpha." Particularly the Channons.

"Well, Kurt didn't leave a direct heir." Meaning a male heir. "It looks like it's leaving things a little contentious."

"Oh?"

Tara and Mitch come to stand beside us, and Dad quickly fills them in on the phone call he just received.

Tara doesn't look surprised. "They've been unsettled. Weres need a leader, a direction."

"Seth has put himself forward as a candidate."

I frown, struggling to put a face to the name.

"He's the guy who got hot and bothered that night at Riley's."

The scene that night rises in my mind, two young males, drunk and fierce. My dad, the Alpha, stepping in before things got out of hand. And dangerous. They'd been acting like the Precepts were optional.

I remember Seth, the brown haired, angry young man.

"Oh."

"Seth can't be Alpha." Tara's little body is hard, determined.

Dad nods. "I agree."

Silence settles around us as we consider the issue.

I look to Mitch, who nods. We both turn to Tara.

She freezes, hazel eyes jumping from Mitch to me, then back to Mitch. The two newly bonded hold each other's gaze. They must reach a consensus, because Tara squares her shoulders. Mitch moves over to grasp her hand.

With the two of them standing there, hand in hand, Tara speaks. "I'll do it. I'm the firstborn."

Dad nods. "Very well, the Channons will vote within the week."

WITH THE MOOD ruined and Eden gone, we head back to the house. Dad strides up ahead, massive shoulders tense. Stash, his chocolate Labrador sidekick, comes barreling through the trees, leaping and wagging without a care in his doggy world. Tara walks with Mitch, her head down, shoulders hunched. I walk alone, wishing and wondering.

I wouldn't mind going for a run.

Dad enters the house, calling out to Mum. Tara says she has some phone calls to make before following shortly behind. Our sensitive Were noses pick up the scent of dinner. I think it's chicken, but it's hard to tell over the charcoal.

"Charcoal chicken?" Mitch suggests.

I chuckle; thank goodness for the twin bond. "Wanna sit outside for a bit? Let Mom finish dinner."

And psych ourselves up for crunchy, cauterized poultry. We have quite a bit to digest as it is.

Mitch and I sit on the thinking chair, staring out at the pine trees. I wonder if all those years ago when Mitch enthusiastically nailed this bench together he realized what it would become — Dad's place for contemplation. Or that it would start a little legacy of Phelan thinkers.

That Mitch would one day use it himself.

Stash sits between our feet, either needing to think himself or not ready to face the smell of the kitchen.

"So..." I know some people hate the unifying concept of twins. And believe me, being called 'the twins' got old some days, but on the whole, I love being a twin. I love the bond, the trust, the spare set of everything across the hall...the redundant need to complete your sentences.

"Yeah."

Silence settles between us just like Stash has.

Stuff the twin bond, some things need to be said aloud. "But you never wanted to be Alpha."

"Technically, I'm not."

I snort. "We both know that's splitting Were hairs. The Alpha mate has all the responsibilities the Alpha does."

Mitch pauses, his fingers scratching his collarbone. "It was the Phelan Alpha I never wanted."

Wow, I'm glad Dad's not here to hear that one. "Right."

Mitch's hand drops, bringing his shoulders down with it. "Yeah. So much baggage came with it. The expectation of being a cop, what it represented." His blue eyes catch mine. "It was you that was always meant to be the Phelan Alpha."

"But the Channon Alpha?" I don't need to point out the obvious. Alpha or not, Mitch is a Phelan.

Those shoulders drop another inch. "There's no rule about who the Alpha mate must be. And Tara needs me." With eyes straight ahead, Mitch delivers the punch line. "And it's way too dangerous for Seth to take the helm."

"True dat, bro."

Mitch's lips quirk, lifting when his shoulders won't. "Thanks, homey." Hopeful eyes turn to me. "You gonna be there?"

I rub my lip, wondering how we can make that happen. "Well, I'm the one who banished Kurt, so I think I get to see what happens next."

It will certainly make a statement, my presence there. But there's another reason for gatecrashing the Channon vote. Weres are the keepers of great strength and a whole lot of responsibility. The Channon pack seems unsettled, and what

Kurt was fighting for makes me nervous. Being there means I get to see where this goes.

Mitch nods, rubbing his own finger across his bottom lip. "That makes sense."

I wonder if the twin bond is working its magic and he knows what I'm thinking. I don't want to voice something that is nothing but a weird heebie-jeebie feeling, but he doesn't say anything else.

Possibly because he's put his hand up to lead them.

I slap his knee as I push myself up, and for some reason the gesture makes me feel way older than the seven minutes I have on Mitch. "Well, let's go find out when the big night is."

4

EDEN

Reaching the T-intersection that will take me home, I pause for a second. The indicator clicks out the passing seconds. Now that I'm away from Noah, distance muting our connection, I think of Adam and what he said. Adam is a wonderful man. A committed father and husband. A strong Alpha.

But he knows what I won't say, what Noah seems to be ignoring. He knows there is a ticking time bomb hanging over my relationship with his first-born son. I press my hands to my temples, watching the unmoving odometer needle, the indicator flashing siren orange, trying to pretend old insecurities aren't starting to gain strength again. For some reason, I feel like a counter's just been tripped.

I return my hands to the steering wheel—I'm not ready to go home. With a flick, I change the indicator and turn right. I need to be somewhere I belong.

The Soshoni Vet Centre rests on the south edge of town. A squat brick building perched in front of concrete kennels and chain link pens. I park the car in my usual spot, shaded beneath an aspen tree, and head for the door.

Emily, the vet who hired me for a part-time job within weeks of starting my voluntary placement, doesn't look surprised to see me, despite it not being my usual day. Thursdays are usually spent with Noah. Studying, hiking the moment there is a hint of warmth, or on the couch at my place, all whispery laughs and breathless kisses. But I've stopped off before, on days I'm bored or overflowing with physics equations or needing an animal fix.

"Three times a day, Mrs. Penrith, and Fifi should be back to nipping Norman in no time."

I smile at the elderly lady who pushes her Pomeranian in a pram. Fifi sits proudly in the seat, golden fur puffed out like a caramel marshmallow. Poor Norman doesn't stand a chance.

Emily, brown hair in its perpetual ponytail, still looking tanned after a snowbound winter, practically hugs me with her smile. "This is a nice surprise. Isn't this your day with Noah?"

I sigh, not sure how to answer that one. "He had something he needed to do."

Emily's smile gets a puzzled, maybe concerned, slant. "Something up?"

I look at Emily, thinking I haven't heard her mention a guy in her life in the time I've been working here. "I'm hoping not."

Emily's smile disappears. "Relationships are tricky, huh?"

"Yeah." I sigh again, sensing she understands. I glance away, tempted to ask, but knowing it's none of my business.

Gaze unfocused, Emily turns to the window. "I'm probably the wrong person to give advice, though. I fell pretty hard for the last guy, but in the end, I wanted kids and he didn't." She looks back at me, and it's the first time I've seen her sparkly brown eyes dim and dull.

I think of how Emily practically adopted me like any of the other wounded souls coming through this door, and images of kids and puppies rollicking on a grassy lawn come to mind. Emily was meant to have children. "I'm sorry, Emily."

"Yeah, well, you and Noah are different, and that's nothing you have to worry about for quite some time." The rumble of a car engine means I don't get to process whether her statement is true, and Emily's smile lights up her eyes again. "Either way, I'm glad you came. We've had a call for another injured animal. The rangers said a hiker is bringing it in shortly."

I think of the pika we saw last week, the beaver from last month, even the lizard that had trapped its head in a soda can yesterday. I wonder what frightened creature is on its way and whether I can help.

Emily's brown eyes twinkle in her suntanned face. "This one's special."

Her smile grows, and we head out front to see a tall, broad-shouldered guy hefting a large cage out of the back seat of his car. *It's a bird?* As he turns toward us, I see that it is indeed a bird, but not a run-of-the-mill feathered friend. A golden eagle watches us approach.

I turn to Emily, excitement and amazement making me smile, only to see Emily's is gone. Instead, her face is frozen in a frown as she watches the guy walk toward us. I look back, noticing how his eyes take her in.

It couldn't be...

He sets the cage down at our feet. "Hi, Em."

Emily straightens, like something has shot down her spine. "Where did you find her?"

The question almost has a sharp, accusatory tone. Like she's asking him what he's doing here rather than inquiring after the bird's history.

I glance down at the cage. The massive bird is perched in the center, not cowering at the back, seeking the shadows. Golden Eagles are one of the few birds of prey where the female is larger than the male and judging by its size, this one's a female. Coarse brown plumage, dull and rough, instantly shows the poor state the bird is in. Even the tawny yellow feathers on the back of her head lack any golden glow.

The guy swallows, and I'm trapped in the tension that's growing between these two. "I was hiking. She was on the ground when I found her. Barely moved when I picked her up."

Emily's frown deepens. "That's unusual."

"Yeah. Reckoned you'd figure it out."

Emily's eyes fly to the guy's, and I consider stepping back from all this emotion. There's been no introductions, but they don't have to state the obvious. This is the one that stole Emily's smile.

"Let's get her inside, Eden."

The minute Emily says my name my invisibility cloak disappears. The guy's eyes spin to me, all of a sudden taking me in. I'm not sure why he studies me, but I register he's a good-looking guy, and I wonder why so much emotion is swirling around us considering it was him that couldn't compromise. Although his scrutiny makes me uncomfortable, I throw him a small smile, knowing sometimes we can't change things, no matter how much we want to.

His hazel eyes narrow before turning back to Emily. "I know you'll take good care of her."

Emily picks up the cage and turns, no goodbye, no backward glance. Anger and hurt keep her back stiff as she takes the golden eagle into the building. I turn to follow, but the guy's voice has me turning.

Those narrowed eyes are trained on me. "Some differences can't be overcome."

I feel my eyes widen, the words that aren't supposed to be relevant to me hitting a vulnerable place in my chest. Why is he looking at me like he knows?

I spin on my heel; I haven't spoken during this whole exchange, and I don't have anything to say now. If I can't believe the impossible can be possible, then what hope do I have?

Emily has already headed past the kennels, the concrete pens, to the aviary at the rear. Inside she places the cage on the floor, opens the door and steps back. When nothing happens, she comes to join me looking in. The eagle has her massive wings hanging loosely and her body crouching over her feathered legs, like she doesn't have the energy to hold anything up.

"Poor girl," I murmur.

"She's underweight and in pretty poor condition, but I can't see anything obviously wrong with her."

"Parasites?"

"Yeah, I'll give her a dose of wormer. It could be some viral flu, but there's no other symptoms." Emily holds out a piece of red meat, dropping the cold chunk into my hand. I wrinkle my nose at the feeling of flesh, the metallic smell of raw meat. "Right now we need to get some nutrition into her."

I look at the lackluster feathers, the unblinking eyes. *What's up girl?* The eagle simply stares at me, giving me nothing. Odd, I would have expected agitation, withdrawal, even aggression. Not...nothing.

I don't have to hum anymore, that special melody that was gifted along with my eye color, my too-long second toe, and my tendency to avoid conflict just plays in my head now. I realized, all those months ago I didn't need to give it voice when the man appeared—I never said a word and the animals came. I push away the confusion that memory always evokes, not knowing if I should feel elation that the one person with my hair and eye color showed or rejection that he left.

For now, I just breathe and let the melody flow through my mind as I enter the aviary. I hold the piece of meat out to the eagle, showing her. Her brown head twitches, one golden eye turning directly toward me.

"That's a good sign," Emily whispers behind me.

I gently reach in, slowly extending my arm. The eagle's eye follows my movements. I think soothing thoughts, take calm regular breaths, and let the notes rise and fall. My arm creeps closer to the eagle, the raw meat dangling from my fingertips. The massive bird of prey simply takes a step away. Her lackluster feathers ruffle, and she hunkers back down on her perch.

Nothing.

I leave the meat beside her and retract my hand. The eagle doesn't even glance at it. If anything, she seems to shrink into her solitude.

Emily crosses her arms; I can practically see her running through the vet index in her brain, searching for possible causes. I'm pretty sure every veterinary journal and text is filed up in there. The bird doesn't twitch a feather, as if she doesn't really care whether Emily will solve the riddle or not.

Emily's arms unfold on a deep inhalation then fall to her sides as the frustrated breath puffs out. "We'll just have to keep an eye on her and see."

From inside the building a bell jingles, signaling someone has just entered reception. Emily glances at her watch. "That must be my five o'clock. You joining me?"

Emily knows it's a rhetorical question. I sit in on any consults I can, watching and learning, learning and helping. She's a wonderful vet to see in action, calm and gentle with the animals, warm and friendly with the humans, accurate and efficient with her treatment. The guy knew what he was doing when he brought the eagle here, despite the ulterior motive.

We enter through the rear door, pass through the surgery, and into the reception area. Emily goes through first, hand extended in welcome for her next appointment. I paste a smile on my face then freeze.

Bianca rises from her chair, along with a woman with

matching platinum hair, which they simultaneously flick over their shoulders. I'm guessing the woman with the cat carrier in her hand is her mother. The mother of the girl from my psychology class, the one who barely disguises her desire to sink her claws into Noah. The one who poorly conceals what she thinks of me.

Great.

A guttural hissing slips from the bars of the cage; Bianca leans down and whispers into its depths. She slips a finger through the metal bars, only to pull it back quickly when a white paw swats at it.

"Naughty, Fantasia."

Fantasia?

"Come on through, Mrs. Farrer."

"Ah, Emily, lovely to see you."

Bianca takes the cage with Fantasia and follows her mother into the examination room to my left. Within two steps she sees me, standing still by the door.

"Oh, hi, Eden." A false smile lights up her face as her free hand comes to her hair, brushing it forward to rest on her shoulder. "I didn't know you helped out here."

"Hi, Bianca. Yeah, I work here most afternoons." I don't know why I make a point of that, but I do, and I even do a little hair flick of my own when I say the word 'work.'

Bianca whisks past me, placing the carrier on the metal bench in the center of the room. A wail, one that would compete with an ambulance, howls around the room. It seems Fantasia has a pretty good idea what is coming up.

Bianca's mother stands back from the cage. "He's just here for his annual shots, Emily."

Fantasia is a he?

"We have a show coming up later this month. We're hoping to make it a trifecta this season."

Bianca steps forward, opening the cage. She peers into the back, cooing and whispering. Her head jerks back, her chin sucking into her neck, her hands pulling into her chest, when the wailing becomes hissing and spitting.

I hope he doesn't act like that with the judges.

Bianca straightens and fixes her hair. She turns to Emily with an isn't-this-your-job look. Emily just smiles her I've-got-this smile, and I know what is coming next.

"Eden, could you hold him for me?"

A teeny, tiny frown creases Bianca's blonde brows. I don't think she expected me to do anything but observe. Although this time, I was quite happy to watch.

"Eden?" Emily looks up; I don't think she's ever had to ask twice.

I really, really don't want to. "Sure."

I step up next to Emily, who moves over to the stainless-steel bench holding drawers of medical paraphernalia. She opens one to get the syringe, another to get a needle.

I step over to the carrier, bending at the knees to look inside. A white Persian, frosted fur spiked along an arched back, thick ivory tail speared into the roof of the carrier, tense white body scrunched into the back of the cage, hisses at me. Fantasia's mouth is pulled back to show pointed angry teeth, his eyes are wide open and a little feral.

Bianca isn't frowning anymore, she's actually smiling a little. "He's not too keen on strangers."

From what I can see, he's not too keen on humans.

Bianca watches me as I look back at Fantasia. I no longer want to have the little hair flicking competition; I just want to step back and blend into the cream walls. Because I'm not sure which is worse, proving her right and getting scratched, or proving her wrong. And publicly and irreversibly showing her I am the odd one out.

Fantasia lets out another grumbling hiss-growl, grabbing my heart. I know that helping him is my priority. I bend back down, blocking Bianca out.

It's okay Fantasia. It's going to be fine.

I can feel Fantasia's anger, his indignation, but underneath I feel his anxiety and confusion. He knows this cream room with its shiny bench means two things. Fear and pain. For the second time, the melody swirls through my head, filling me with music and peace.

I don't blame you. This wouldn't be my favorite place either.

Fantasia's lips come down over his pearly teeth. He looks like he is weighing his options. The music continues to flow through my mind, calming and reassuring the two of us.

Why don't we get this over and done with, then you can take your humans home?

When a white ball of fur launches at me, Bianca doesn't even pretend to hide her smile. A smile that quickly slackens into an open-mouthed stare when Fantasia lands in my arms and just sits there. Not moving, certainly not purring, but not scratching my eyes out either. I can feel his fluttering pulse, and I know his agitation is just beneath the surface. All the others see is a wide-eyed ball of fluff sitting in my arms.

He hisses at Emily.

Bianca stands back just watching. *Please don't come over.* I don't want to see if Fantasia will hiss or welcome Bianca. I could never explain why her cat would choose me over her at this moment. But Bianca doesn't move, and I keep up the soothing music in my mind.

Emily steps forward, and Fantasia tenses. I hold him a little tighter, a reassuring hug, one that means I'm not likely to have to chase him around the room. With the efficiency of someone who has done this a thousand times, the needle is in and out of Fantasia's shoulder before he has a chance to sheath his claws.

Good job, boy.

I put him back in his carrier, and Fantasia takes his white furred body to the back and sits down, his back to me. He throws me an indignant glare over his shoulder.

"Well, that was better than last year," says Mrs. Farrer.

Emily disposes of the syringe, then washes her hands. "Yes, it's nice to have my eyes intact."

Bianca says nothing, and I don't look to see where her gaze is.

Emily leads Mrs. Farrer to the reception desk, giving me a grateful smile over her shoulder. "Thanks, Eden."

"Sure. Lucky snap, huh?"

Emily gives me a puzzled look as I'm looking for a quick, silent retreat.

Bianca hangs back, bursting my hopeful bubble. "So, where's Noah?"

"He's at home, I'd say." I grit my teeth. We do spend some time apart. Like when he has to be a Were...

Bianca titters an artificial giggle. "It's just that you two are joined at the hip." She flicks her hand at me. "Does Mitch mind that Noah has found a new twin?"

I would never come between Noah and his family. "No, we love double dating." Artificial sweetener drips from my tone.

Bianca narrows her eyes at me for a hateful second before spinning on her heel, blonde hair billowing in an artful arc, and leaving the room.

Any sense of victory evaporates in an instant. Why does everything have to be a reminder that I don't belong? I'm certainly not Were, and it seems I'm not entirely human either. Now the one girl who sees me as competition has witnessed my inexplicable oddities.

I head outside to have one last look at the golden eagle. She hasn't moved, the meat remains on the perch, and she doesn't seem to care that I am standing there watching her. Wild animals don't like to be watched, it usually makes them nervous. But this girl simply stares at nothing, feeling nothing, doing nothing. I frown as I turn back to the building; this bird has something seriously wrong with her. But until we figure it out, we can't help her.

I'm just getting in the car when my phone tweets, telling me I have a message.

What time tonight?

I smile, from my toes to my head, from my heart to my soul. Our Thursday night is still happening. Noah has chosen to come.

Thirty minutes?

Can't wait. Got heaps to tell you.

Hope, and the order for a pizza and a cheesecake, swirl through my mind.

5

NOAH

The Channons are keen to get their leader voted in, because it's only three days later that I'm driving to the Glade. Mitch and Tara have gone ahead, Tara trying to look calm and composed like a future Alpha should. But the tips of her shoes bobbing up and down as her toes compulsively flex says otherwise. She's done that since we were kids. It was cute when we were eight and she stood by watching Mitch prove he could hammer a nail blindfolded. Hopefully, it will be less obvious when she's standing in front of the Channons.

As the truck rumbles up to the intersection, I get an idea. I glance at my watch. Yep, I've got enough time. I take a quick right, accelerating with a smile on my face.

In a few short minutes I'm at her door, knocking a happy little rap. Eden opens it, surprise, then pleasure, then a frown trading places across her face. "I thought you were heading to the Glade."

"I am." I shoot out an arm, pulling her off balance so she falls against me. Her soft curves smash up against me, and my already high body temperature spikes. "But I missed you."

A smile, a buoyant glow, lights up her face, from her tilted green eyes to her rose red lips. And it's those lips that snare my attention and don't let go.

With my own heart smiling, I kiss her. I trap those beaming lips with my own, aiming for a quick, sweet moment. I start on target as laughing lips touch then pull apart. But I quickly lose sight of my objective when they are drawn back together, and this time stay together. Man, she feels so good, so right, just where she is.

I almost forget that that I'm supposed to be elsewhere.

I'm all set to pull away when her arms ride up my shoulders, then drive into my hair. And I'm done for. With a groan, I throw up a white flag and toss out the half-hearted attempt to rein in this passion.

My arms band around her, hauling her as close as possible. All her soft curves meld against me, increasing the contact, multiplying the heat. I tighten my hold even more. Not because we need more contact or heat, but to keep my hands where they should be.

A thought almost evaporates in this sweltering passion as it clings to my consciousness. There's somewhere I'm supposed to be.

With a great show of reluctance, I pull back, and Eden smiles a rueful smile. She leans back a little, but the flow of cool air makes no difference to my heated skin. Her hands slip down my shoulders to grip my upper arms. I loosen the Herculean hold I have on her waist.

I sigh. "I'd better get to this vote. Who knows where this is going to go."

Eden's eyes hold something my passion-muddled mind can't quite decipher. "I know. You should be there for Tara and Mitch."

And I wonder if she wants to be there, too. Does she know that I hate doing this on my own? I know I hate not telling her.

But what girl would want to be told she is irreversibly the mate of a leader, of a bunch of Werewolves she barely knew existed, after only six months of dating?

So I smile, and Eden smiles. I wave and jump into the truck, and she waves and goes back into the house.

THE GLADE LOOKS like it always does, a magical arena surrounded by whispering pines. Subdued conversation creates a low hum as I skirt around the Channons. As I head to the front left, there's the odd hello, one or two smiles, a few closed-off scowls. I choose a spot close enough to the front to get a good view, far back enough to fade into the shadows of the trunks, and separate enough from the pack that is supposed to be an ally to the Phelans.

Silence settles on the Glade, and everyone turns their focus as four Weres step forward, all with their serious faces on. I got here just in time.

An older man stands at the head, Seth to one side, Tara and Mitch on the other, the rock with the Precepts carved into it stands between them. The old man is a Channon; that I can smell. But not of the Alpha line—no red hair. This guy will be the adjudicator, the mediator of the vote.

He steps forward into the silence. A light breeze brushes the small crowd.

Old dude puffs out his chest. "Welcome all. On this day, you will choose a new leader for our pack. Before you stand two candidates. Both Channons, each looking to become your Alpha." He steps over to Seth. I wonder if he will lift each person's hand, as if they are opponents in a boxing ring. "Seth. A member of your pack. A young, strong male."

Another step and he's beside Tara, whose toes stay still in her shoes. "Tara, daughter of Kurt, mated to a Phelan."

Short, sweet, and factual. And everything he said was true. Except for the slight omissions, like never mentioning that Seth is not blood-related to the Alpha line or that Tara is Kurt's firstborn. The slight emphasis on their genders, on Tara's choice of mate. Each point makes my stomach clench, because each calculated piece of information reeks of propaganda.

I'd like to cross my arms, but that wouldn't be a wise move here.

"You all know how this works. They will say a few words, and then we vote."

Without waiting for an invite, Seth steps forward. Showing eagerness and poor manners.

He struts forward a few steps. "Weres are gifted with strength, power, superiority. As a strong and powerful pack, the Channons are the ones who can represent, uphold this honor, this duty. To do this, we need to acknowledge that patience is not always a virtue. Nor is silence always golden. I know the Channons are a pack that is destined for..." Seth stops, surveying the Channons before him.

Destined for what?

"Destined for more. With me as your Alpha, we will fulfill our potential."

A handful of Channons nod. I try to note which ones agree with Seth's charismatic, clichéd, but concerning sentiments.

Seth holds himself there for a few more seconds, head slowly scanning the crowd. The guy thinks he's got it in the bag, and I'm worried that he's right. He takes several steps backward, never taking his eyes off the audience.

Tara and Mitch step up hand in hand, united. I feel my chest swell a little. She's making a strong statement. That she's proud of her bonded mate, that our alliance is real and valuable.

Tara releases Mitch's hand and takes another step, her little body solitary and strong. Her clear voice carries through the Glade. "Weres are unique. We span both the animal and the human world. A part of us rests in both. This does give us unique power, but you all know that with power comes responsibility, and the Channons are a pack that stands for what is right. The strength we possess we use to protect. The power we wield we use to safeguard the rights of all—friends, neighbors... allies. Our responsibility is to our kind—both Were and human. That will be our purpose and our direction."

I want to clap so bad. She just rubbished Seth's pseudo-Aryan sentiments, without once rubbishing him. And in those few sentences, summed up the rights and responsibilities of Weres. Man, it was practically the Were Bill of Rights.

The Channon crowd is silent. Holding their paws close to their chest.

Tara takes Mitch's hand again, and I see him squeeze it. He's tall and proud beside her. They turn and step back to their place beside Seth. Seth doesn't acknowledge their presence. Or the awesome speech.

Now comes the very public vote. Weres are not averse to putting each other in their place. The winner publicly victorious. The loser openly displaying their defeat. It's a bit like National Geographic meets the presidential election.

I shift from one foot to the other. Which way will it go?

Tara is a Channon, a first born.

But she's female. And bonded to a Phelan. Although we've lived side by side for generations, a strong alliance keeping us peaceful, friends even, Weres still have their roots in the animal kingdom. Where there's us, and there's them. Survival DNA dictates you look out for your own first.

And although Seth has no Alpha blood whatsoever, he's a strong, young male. We all know that counts for a whole lot in the animal world. And Seth represents a potential leader selling a whole new direction for the Channons. One independent of the Phelans. A worrying one.

The adjudicator steps forward, "And we vote." The crowd shuffles as he turns to Seth. "Those of you who vote for Seth raise your hands."

I stare straight ahead as those who nodded, and a few more, slowly raise hands into the air.

The adjudicator nods. "And those of you who vote for Tara raise your hands."

Once again, my head doesn't move as hands rise into the air above them.

It's undisputed, a clear gap. Tara and Mitch look at each other, their chests deflating as their breaths escape. Seth comes forward to silently shake their hands. Now Tara's toes can be seen doing a jig, the tips of her shoes dancing in the grass. The crowd swells forward as friends, cousins, and happy voters congratulate the victor.

Tara and Mitch are swallowed by a horde of celebrating Channons.

I want to applaud the voters. Those who knew what Weres stand for. Who didn't want to see someone like Seth at their helm.

Seth scans the crowd, narrowed eyes and hard lips telling them what he thinks of their decision. He turns on his heel and strides into the trees. My stage-left vantage point means I'm the only one to notice a handful of men and one or two women follow him. Their square shoulders and stiff-legged gait mean they never fully blend into the shadows. Like tense, angled pegs trying to blend into shadowy round holes. Not one, especially not Seth, looks back.

A hint of metal hits my nose, and I know the Channons are getting ready to run–with their new Alpha.

Mitch looks over to me, blue eyes shining. I smile and nod, acknowledging the subtle, but justified twist to his lips.

Because after all we've been through, after all the rejections and retractions and ribbing, Mitch became an Alpha before I did.

6

EDEN

"Okay, where do I set up?"

Set up? What sort of production is this? "Ah, I suppose my bedroom is the best place."

"Then lead away."

I head down the hallway, Tara skipping behind me, pulling along a small suitcase. Caesar, his big German shepherd body brushing mine, ears pricked backward to the sound of the wheels bouncing along with her, knows something is up. I open the door to my room and let Tara through.

"Eden, I think this room is the size of our lounge."

"Now that's an exaggeration. There is no way you could have fit all your brothers and sisters in here."

The minute I say it, I regret it. Tara hasn't heard from her family since Kurt was banished. Although she grumbled about being the eldest of the Channon menagerie, I'm guessing the Phelan house sounds like a school on summer break compared to her old house.

Tara's hazel eyes look to mine. "It's fine. I'm the one who started it. I keep forgetting that it's not home anymore. It just takes some getting used to, I suppose."

"I'd say it takes a lot of getting used to."

"Yeah."

"How is it going at the Phelans?" Having her bonding brought forward means Tara and Mitch, newly mated Weres, have to live with Mitch's parents. Not the most romantic of honeymoons.

Tara sits on the bed, her deep red hair matching the earthy tones of the bedspread, then flops backward, arms flying out. "There's no privacy for starters, and no one at school can know that Mitch is forever mine, that I'm his. I'm a bonded mate, living like I'm on a permanent sleepover."

I sit beside her. "Sounds tough."

She turns her head to look at me, her arms coming to fist together over the center of her chest. "I'm the happiest I've ever been! I wake up with him, I eat with him, I go to school with him."

That does sound pretty cool. Tara is where she is supposed to be—with Mitch.

Her eyes and chin drop. "And..." Her voice dips like she's coming to the best bit. "I get to go to sleep with him."

I shoot off the bed. "So, where do we set up?"

Tara's giggle tinkles behind me. I head over to her abandoned suitcase, hoping it gives me enough time for my flaming cheeks to settle.

Thankfully taking my lead, she spins to the center of the room. "Right, make up over there"—she points to the timber dressing table—"wardrobe here." She clicks the handle of her suitcase down with a flourish over by the bed. A full-length mirror, standing proud on its own wooden stand, reflects the sparkle in her eyes.

"Where's your costume?"

"In the wardrobe." I don't want to mention the fact it's a walk-in, so I just open the door adjacent to the bathroom.

She follows me in, giving a little whistle. "You could fit at least five of my siblings in here."

I grab the hanger and indicate we can leave. But Tara steps in, surveying the right side of the wardrobe. The one full of my mother's purchases. She doesn't even glance at the smaller left side. I suppose denim and cotton are not nearly as eye catching as the kaleidoscope of jewel colors she's gazing at.

"Oh, girlfriend, we are going to have some fun now that summer is coming up."

"I don't think so."

I grab her by the shoulders and propel her back out. She peers over her shoulder, hazel eyes calculating, one set of fingers tapping her lips. "The blue top is going to go great with that skirt."

"No," I say this louder, more forcefully.

Her other hand comes to clasp her elbow. "Although there were those cute little shorts..."

I don't think she's aware I'm in the room. I'm not going to be Tara's doll, getting primped and dressed in my mother's designer costumes. I am not...

Please don't let me be subjugated to that.

I sit on the bed, crossing my legs beside Caesar, as Tara does a real-life Mary Poppins and pulls out countless items from her magical suitcase. Her outfit, still on its hanger, is hooked over the bathroom door. It's all purple satin and puffs of tulle. She unfolds a large set of glittery violet wings, and places them on my desk.

She glances around. "How's your dress?"

I think of the bag now hanging on the wardrobe door. I didn't even try the thing on when it arrived. I have a teeny, tiny hope it might not fit, meaning I can arrive in jeans and a top. Knowing I can say in all honesty that I tried.

I wave toward the door. "Great, I think. It only arrived the other day."

Tara rolls her eyes. She leans into the suitcase and comes out holding a flat iron. An assessing hazel gaze measures the unbound mass flowing down my back. "We'll do yours first."

My hand pulls up a strand, bringing it before my eyes, my eyes crossing as I focus on the brown lock. "But my hair's already straight."

Tara lets out a long sigh, shaking her head as she delves back into Pandora's Box. Next, comes a large silver case. It's metal and shiny and intimidating.

"What's that for?" I squeak.

She puffs out another long-suffering sigh. "Makeup."

"Oh. Is that really necessary?"

I get a pointed look. "Yes."

"Are you sure?"

Tara's hand comes up to her hip. "Yes."

Although I know I am being bullied by a tiny soon-to-be fairy, I remind myself that her little body can multiply exponentially into an intimidating red wolf. My lips want to smile. "Do you want to use one of your words right about now?"

Her own lips twitch a little. "Yes."

"Which one?"

"Phooey fudge nuggets."

I open my eyes in mock shock. "Can an Alpha use that sort of language?"

Tara juts out an arrogant hip. "Alphas make the rules."

Not all of them. I smother that insidious thought with a smile. Tara is so excited and nervous at her recent rise to leadership, she doesn't need my personal issues muddying her waters. "Right, what's first, fearless leader?"

Tara giggles. "Hair," she says, pointing at the chair sitting in front of the dresser.

I certainly don't hop, skip, and jump toward the wooden contraption.

"It's not electrified, you know."

But that is." I point to the ceramic tongs that are flashing an evil red light at me from the dresser.

"Sit."

I sit on the chair like it is electrified—cautiously and gingerly.

Tara doesn't seem to, or pretends not to, notice and starts brushing my hair. She pulls out two duck-bill-looking clips and takes the top half of my hair, halves it, twists it, and clips it in place. She repeats the process on the other side with short, sharp movements. In three seconds flat, I'm staring back at my mouse-eared-reflection.

"Impressive."

"I have five younger sisters, remember? It was always a production line every time we had a social engagement." She pauses in brushing the bottom section of my hair. "Dana would ask me every morning."

I remember Tara's sister. Only a year behind her, Dana had been a pretty, vivacious, gob-struck-if-Noah-was-around girl. The last bit I recollect empathizing with.

"You miss them."

Tara's hazel eyes meet mine in the mirror. "Most of my life, I was hanging to leave." She leans over to grab the hair straightener. "I just never thought they would."

"And now you're Alpha."

Tara brushes a section of hair then sprays it with some chemical based, artificial flowery stuff. I tense as the heated flat iron heads toward my scalp then sizzles as the fake flower stuff is vaporized, rising to the roof. But all I feel is the radiant heat against the back of my skull, and then it's gliding down, maintaining a constant pressure. I wonder if it's time to change the subject when Tara speaks up, eyes still focused on my hair.

"Yeah. I'm the Alpha of a divided, unsettled pack. Meaning Mitch also inherits that bundle of joy." Tara nibbles her lip uneasily, eyes catching mine in the mirror. "Do you think I've asked too much of him?"

I turn on my chair, meaning Tara has to meet my gaze. "Tara, Mitch would go vegetarian for you"—a slow red tint slips up Tara's cheeks—"and he'd do it with a smile."

Tara sucks in her bottom lip as her cheeks brighten to match her hair. *Whoa, I just made Tara Channon blush. It could be time to buy a lotto ticket.*

"Besides"—I turn back to face the mirror—"all that Alpha training would have gone to waste."

Tara smiles as she grabs another piece of hair. Spritz. Clamp. Sizzle. Pull.

I admire how nothing keeps Tara down for long. She would have to be the most resilient material known to man. "I hope I don't get on a roll."

"Oh?"

She snaps the flat iron like a crab claw. "I might do Caesar next."

At the mention of his name, Caesar's eyes dart to Tara then me. He must see something that concerns him because he whines then buries his head beneath his paw.

We both giggle, and I realize how unexpected life can be. It feels so normal, so natural to have Tara over here. To talk about girly things. To giggle. Even though just a few months ago I doubted this was a reality I could be part of.

Spritz. Clamp. Sizzle. Pull.

Showing how unpredictable the future can be.

It's a full forty-five minutes before all my hair is done. Tara patiently and competently scalds each and every hair into smooth submission. When she's finished, she steps back, critically eyeing my hair like it's one of her artworks. I stand and turn, noting that my hair is a little bit longer, brushing my hips, but what's more, it's now a sleek, shiny, brown waterfall. I shake my head from side to side, and my eyes widen as the sheet of hair ripples and rolls.

Tara crosses her arms. "Well?"

"Fine, I'll admit it. It was worth all my hard work."

Tara sputters in indignation, spins, and grabs a cushion from my bed and throws it at my head. It bounces off my cheek, catching a few strands and separating them from the thick, glossy mass.

"Hey, careful of the hair," I warn as I do a very Bianca-like sweep of my hair back over my shoulder, only much slower and more exaggerated.

"I knew there was a diva in there somewhere. Now, my turn."

Uh oh. I look at the heated tongs, wishing I'd paid more attention to the fine art of hair straightening. "Sure, where do I start?"

"I don't think so. Besides, mine will take twenty minutes, tops."

Relieved, I could already see trusting red locks falling to the ground, smoke curling from the singed ends. I sit on the bed.

"Here"—Tara passes me the big shiny box of intimidation—"have a look at what colors you think would work."

I flip through the palettes and polishes crammed into the box. Absentmindedly, I run my fingers through the surprisingly sleek strands down my back. Maybe makeup won't be so bad.

"What color's your dress?" Tara spritzes and sprays the last sections of her hair. She's gone with a gentle curl at the bottom, the layers gently framing her face. I'm just thinking how pretty it looks when she starts pulling it up into a high ponytail. A purple ribbon is sitting on the dresser in front of her.

"Blue."

Her eyes light up. "That'll work great. Blue eyeshadow is so in right now."

What? Even Caesar perks his head up when he senses my alarm. Words can't come out of my mouth fast enough. "It's more of a pale blue, ice blue really, actually it barely has any color at all."

Tara bursts into a fit of laughter. "You should have seen your face!"

I look around for a pillow of my own. But Tara is quick; she jumps up and dives onto the bed, covering the cushions with her body. Caesar jumps back, unused to sharp movements from small bundles of energy.

I narrow my eyes. "You're lucky I don't sic my attack dog on you."

Caesar looks at the perky redhead clambering off the bed then me. With a very male snort, he leaves the room.

"That was close. I could have lost a leg!"

I tilt my nose up. "It barely would have made a meal."

Another cushion hits my back, followed by a round of slumber-party giggles. It seems getting ready for parties can be a lot of fun.

Tara glances at the clock beside the bed. "Right, makeup and then we get dressed."

Makeup, right. If I hadn't have been so nervous at the thought of preparing for this party, I probably would have gone on the internet to research the whole makeup thing. But I didn't. So, when Tara passes me a big brush and a pot of pale power, I take it. And just stand there.

Tara leans toward the dresser mirror, she swirls her brush around the powder, then starts brushing it on it circular strokes. Just like you see on TV.

I should be able to do that.

I dip my brush in the loose powder so I can copy what I just saw. Circular strokes start at my forehead, down over my nose, then around my cheeks. Dip, dip, and I fan the brush down my neck. Maybe, just maybe, I can succeed at being a girl.

"So, how're the house plans going?"

"We're in negotiations." Tara pauses, and I look over. "We can't decide between four or five bedrooms."

My eyes widen a smidgen. "How many kids are you planning on having?"

Tara smiles then chuckles. "We're still deciding. I want five. Mitch wants two."

It appears big families beget big families.

"You've got plenty of time to decide." Although judging by the chuckle, what I really mean is Tara has plenty of time to bring Mitch around to her way of thinking.

"Not really." Tara now has a little black pencil, and with small feathery strokes her eyes are outlined, making them wider, more striking. "Weres bond young, have their kids young. One foot in the animal kingdom and all that."

I think of Beth and how young she is. I think of the parents I see at the Phelan gatherings, and yes, they all seemed young. And happy.

"But what about college?" Elementary teaching was inevitable for Tara, thanks to her brood of younger siblings, but mostly because she has a heart that will be forever young.

Unlike me, who was old before my time.

Tara shrugs, unconcerned, before leaning back toward the mirror. A little pot of violet glitter is now in her hands. "I'll defer, do it part time. Beth will be there to help."

She strokes the colorful glitter across one eyelid. "Besides, we have to keep the Alpha line going." She never drops her voice or tone, but I know she just quoted Kurt.

I flick through the metal box, pretending I'm looking for just the right shade of whatever it is I'm supposed to be getting, keeping my voice just as casual. "Do you guys, you know, ever hook up with humans?"

Tara watches me in the mirror, but I keep my head down, in the box. "Sure. It can be a pretty small Were pond otherwise."

I shrug, picking up a compact of my own. "So, humans are more of a casual fling."

Tara turns, eyes wide and earnest. "That's not what Noah thinks or feels. You know what you have is special."

It feels like it is.

"But what about the Precept...?" The one that is carved indelibly into the twists and knots of my grey matter, far deeper than it's etched anywhere else. *You shall not bond with the opposite bloodline...*

"That's nothing you need to worry about," Tara says with the authority of her new Alpha status. As if just by saying it, she makes it so. She leans forward, focusing on painting the other eye. "You know, I broke a precept to be with Mitch."

"Oh," I say, wondering how I could ever ask Noah to do the same for me.

"I'll tell you the story one day."

"I'd like to hear it." Hoping it might give me some reassurance. But doubting it.

"Are you actually going to do your makeup?"

I look down at the pale powder in my hand then back up to my reflection. "I thought I was."

"You've got as far as foundation."

"That fits my definition of makeup."

Tara huffs again and pushes me back into the chair. She stands between me and the mirror, flitting, dabbing, flicking, and dusting. I stay very, very still throughout it all. When she steps back, I'm surprised at who is staring back at me in the mirror. Pale eyeshadow with a hint of sparkle has opened my eyes, pink shiny lips are slightly parted. Add that to the shiny hair and I look...good.

"See? It's not that bad."

Tara grabs her costume and disappears into the bathroom, wings whacking the doorframe on her way through. I head over to the bag hanging from the top of the wardrobe door. When Tara said we should both go as fairies, I'd spent some time online cruising for costumes. But all the tulle and glitter and short little skirts had me spending more time clicking the back button. Until I found this one. It wouldn't show off more leg than necessary, I wouldn't catch pneumonia, and I wouldn't poke anyone's eye out with a stray wing. Whilst still technically a fairy.

I'm just pulling on the matching slipper-like flats when Tara springs through the bathroom door, waving a glittery, trident-shaped wand. Purple tulle springs out like a tutu; violet wings with silver detail frame her shoulders. But after that, Tinkerbelle goes to the dark side. A black corset cinches Tara's little waist enough to push the rest of her torso upward, and black knee-high boots with purple laces hug her legs. Tara juts out a hip, showing just how much attitude this fairy has.

I whistle. "I want you to be my fairy godmother."

Tara curtsies, the tutu brushing the door frame. Then takes in my costume. I stand a little awkwardly, knowing it's nothing like hers.

"I like it." She claps her hands under her chin. "It's totally you, and you've stuck with the fairy theme. We're practically our own set of twins."

I laugh at that one. With our opposite heights, contrasting hair, and vaguely related outfits, we're barely in the same species.

Tara grabs my arm and pulls me to the door. "I can't wait to see our vampires. They are going to look haaawwt!"

"Have you seen my teeth? Whoa, what the —"

I'm just slipping my shirt over my shoulders, hands at the collar, when Mitch walks in the room — without bothering to knock. Admittedly, we've never really knocked, but this time I could have used a knock.

He freezes at the door, staring at my chest.

Where a mark that shouldn't exist is bare and exposed. I snap the two halves of my shirt closed, two seconds too late.

Because what has been seen cannot be unseen.

He points to my chest. "Interesting ink, bro."

"Keep your voice down, will you?" I step around him and shut the door.

Mitch looks confused then disturbed, the emotions scrunching up his face. "That's not a Were mark I've seen, anyplace, anytime...ever."

"Not, it's not."

"What's going on?"

"You can't tell anyone. Not Dad, not Tara, and definitely not Eden."

Understanding unfolds across his face, opening everything up with the dawn of understanding. "It's hers, isn't it?"

I deflate, my butt sinking into the end of the bed. "Yeah."

Mitch flops next to me, eyes wide, dark brows high. "Huh."

"Yeah."

"When?"

"Months ago, but I only realized the day Dad came out of the coma."

"How on earth is it possible?"

I throw up my hands, empty hands that have been grasping for answers for months. "It's not supposed to be possible."

Mitch is quiet for a while, his eyes scanning the carpet, like each pass of his eyes is turning some page over in his mind. After several seconds, whatever it is has given him nothing. "And you haven't told anyone."

I shake my head.

"And you haven't told Eden." His tone clearly says, 'why the heck not?'

I push myself up, walking over to the desk before I turn to Mitch. My hand jams into my hair, and the shirt gapes open. Mitch's eyes are instantly drawn to the black wolf outline, and the five-pointed star held within a circle sitting alongside it. Stupid mark is practically shouting, 'look at me!' I quickly close the curtains on my chest.

"Her life will never be the same again."

His eyes narrow, blue becoming just a glimmer of suspicion. "Do you want this?"

I look at Mitch, eyes unblinking, showing him just how ready I am. This is Eden we're talking about. "None of this would be possible without Eden."

Eden was the one who changed me. After two years of being a freak, it was her fear that was my catalyst. And it was her connection with animals that quite probably saved my life.

"Maybe you should tell her."

"And trap her? To a life that will never be normal, not even by Were standards? She deserves better than that."

My head drops, and now I'm doing the scan of the carpet thing. But even on the other side of the room, no answers can be found within its woolen loops.

All I get is the emotion that is never far away, just waiting for me to acknowledge it.

I push off the desk, hands coming up to my collar. With rapid flicks of my fingers, I do up the buttons. With lightning speed, the mark is curtained again. "She deserves to choose."

"But, how can she?"

"How can she what?"

"Choose. How can she make the right choice without knowing the full deal? You need to have all your cards on the table, so she can know what she's getting into." He zeroes in on me with intense blue eyes. "Otherwise you're just gambling."

That emotion moves again. Rising, demanding some air time.

I walk to the door quickly, hoping movement will rock it to sleep. "She needs more time."

"Does she?"

And in those two words, Mitch demonstrates how the meaning of a sentence changes depending on which word you put emphasis on. Because the stress that gets put on 'she' gives his little question a sucker punch of significance.

One that shifts that awful, uncomfortable feeling, making it multiply.

I stare down at the shiny new tops of my shoes. Doing two years of growing in a few short months has practically meant a whole new wardrobe. Add that to eating to support this growth spurt and we're all probably going to have to eat the spam from my email account.

"It's too soon."

Mitch grabs his set of teeth, the reason he barged into my room, and heads for the door. He points to my shoes. "You're going to need those...now that you've dug your heels in."

CALL 911. I've forgotten how to breathe, and the absence of a heartbeat tells me I've gone into cardiac arrest.

The two girls walking toward us have Mitch and me stalled in the front yard. And struggling to stay alive.

Tara looks great in a bonded-mate-in-law kind of way, all sparkly purple and racy black. But if Tara is a goth-fairy of the future then Eden has stepped out of the history books. Possibly straight out of Middle Earth. Her flowing, pale blue dress is breathtaking. Shocked eyes try to absorb it all. The skirt brushing the ground, the sleeves that fan out like bells, the pale blue material hugging most of her tall, lean body. That long hair lush and shiny, those glowing evergreen eyes that grab me across the distance, her now-pink lips parted.

The heart that was trying to start again stutters when I register the belt that hugs her hips then falls down the center of her skirt. The dark blue band frames them, accentuating their gentle sway as she approaches.

She's doing that shy, head ducked into her shoulders turtle-like thing. But then she straightens, arches her head so that hair of hers moves over her shoulder, and walks toward me.

That's my girl.

Mitch is the first to recover the ability to speak. "We did something right in a past life." His words flow out in a rush of gratitude, a little like a prayer.

That means I was Gandhi last time round.

I cover the last few feet, reaching out, wanting to touch.

Forgetting about anyone else on the planet. "I think I flatlined there for a second."

"At least your heart restarted. I'm still waiting. Being a vampire suits you."

I grin, feeling those extra-long canines digging into my bottom lip. "I can certainly see the benefits," I say as I move in to nuzzle then nibble her throat.

She giggles, and I love the breathless sound of it. Her hands come up to my chest, over my red velvet waistcoat, to sit on my shoulders. "I see what you mean."

I'm plotting where to taste next when Tara taps me on the shoulder with a purple sparkly thing. "We should do presents before everyone gets here."

Mitch claps his hands together, giving them a rub. "I'm up for that."

"Let's go, girlfriend." Tara grabs Eden and they walk away with purpose.

The girls were apparently organized because they head straight for the garage. I can't help but be mesmerized by Eden in that dress when they come out carrying two big presents and two envelopes.

"Why don't we do it under Grandfather Douglas?" suggests Eden.

Once under the spreading arms of the old fir tree, Tara thrusts the biggest one at Mitch. It's clearly a painting, wrapped in black shiny paper, a big sparkly bow on the front. Her toes are very obviously dancing in those thigh-high boots. Eden, now tucked under my arm, smiles a knowing smile.

Tara's excitement is contagious because Mitch tears at the paper, shreds of black falling to the needle-covered ground. Then he stares down at the black frame in his hand.

I look over his shoulder to see Tara's painting, the one I only saw the outline of because once Eden arrived I was no longer needed as the cheer squad. It's amazing. Two wolves up close, one red, one black. The midnight wolf leans forward to brush the red with his tongue, her eyes closed in bliss. It captures Mitch and Tara's love with incredible, vibrant color.

"It's amazing." He breathes.

Tara's hands clasp beneath her chin, that dancing energy creeping up her legs as she does a little jig. "You like it?"

"I love it." Mitch leans in to give her a lingering kiss. Ugh, is that what they have to watch me and Eden do? No wonder they complain. Constantly.

Tara turns to me, hazel eyes all glowing and purple sparkles. "Now for yours."

I get a smaller, flat square, another painting, this one wrapped in white with a silver bow. She looks a little less sure about this one, and Eden looks surprised. I don't think she knew about this one.

I undo the tape, opening the folds, and remove the sheet of wrapping paper whole. Tara rolls her eyes at my slowness.

Inside is a landscape, a picture of somewhere close, by the coniferous greens that it depicts in thick vibrant strokes. It's a clearing in the foreground, tall pines in the background. A single pine stands to one side of the grassy opening, smaller than the others. I look a little more closely; it's a Douglas fir. A very familiar one. I look up at my surroundings. It's a painting of where we're standing, but before Grandfather Douglas was a grandfather, before our house was built. Back when it was just an embryo of what it would become.

I look to Tara, impressed with her talent, a little gobsmacked at her message.

She smiles, not needing to ask me if I like it, and when Eden takes the painting to have a closer look, I grab my childhood best friend and give her a hug.

Tara says ever so quietly, so even Mitch can't hear, "No one would have guessed the significance of this place, or this pine. But it birthed a great family, a very special pack, and a whole lot of love."

I squeeze a little tighter, still struggling to find words. She squeezes back, telling me I don't need any.

"Now for yours, Mitch." Eden has placed the painting, very carefully, against the same pine it captures then hands Mitch a white envelope.

Mitch's eyebrows hike up into his hair as he takes it. He tears it with the same enthusiasm as before and looks down at two slips of paper. In a split second, Mitch looks like he's holding Willy Wonka's Golden Ticket. All big eyes and a bigger grin.

"Forgotten Fire?" He uses the same tone you would use for the Holy Grail.

Eden shrugs a one-shoulder shrug. "My mom knows someone. They stayed at the Inn."

I wonder if Mitch knows the extreme lengths Eden would have gone to get these tickets. We're talking, like, talking to her mom. Whether he does or doesn't, he jumps forward and engulfs Eden in a hug. She smiles then laughs.

Mitch goes back to the ticket, eyes scanning his holy grail. "Two tickets!"

Uh oh.

"And it's next weekend!"

Next weekend, next weekend. Please let me be doing something next weekend.

"Noah and I will be busy."

I turn to Eden in surprise, not to mention relief. "We will?"

And find her looking nervous, biting her lip, one hand strangling her elbow. She passes me an envelope of my own, this one bigger and thicker. I lean forward to give her a kiss on those tense lips. I have no doubt I'll love it.

I take the envelope, feeling its mysterious weight, testing the padded thickness.

"Hurry up!" Tara is doing rapid pushups on her toes.

I pull out a piece of folded cardboard. On the front Eden's written,

You swept me off my feet, now I return the favor...

I open it, and out folds a little red helicopter. It's a pop-up card, handmade and hand drawn. I look at Eden, confused brows moving down to meet a puzzled smile.

Her teeth dig into her lip again. "Look inside."

I open a little flap, the door to the helicopter, and inside are two stick figures, one with long dark hair, the other with short yellow hair.

My eyes widen as I piece together the puzzle. "We're going on a helicopter ride?"

"I'm hoping it's the one angle you haven't seen the reserve from, yet." Eden watches me, eyes scanning my face, looking like she's holding her breath.

In a flash, Eden gets her second hug for the day. This time I spin her then kiss her. Then kiss her again.

"No way. That's gonna be awesome!"

Eden blushes, pleasure and pride creeping up her cheeks. "They'll drop us off up the mountain then we'll hike back down..." Then the red gets higher, brighter. "We'll camp the night then hike out."

"And it keeps getting better."

That glowing smile breaks out again, and we're smiling and happy, together. "It'll be amazing, just the two of us."

"Just the two of us." That smile tightens, my teeth tighten. My chest tightens as it hits me. Just. The. Two. Of. Us.

Camping. Overnight. Alone.

With a passion that needs nothing but a glance to spark it.

Who am I kidding? I could be blindfolded, and it would ignite.

I take it back. I was Darth Vader in a past life. Because spending a night with Eden, in the wild where we are most at home, most connected, totally ALONE, knowing she's my mate but not, is penance for a whole lot of bad.

8

EDEN

There are people everywhere. Witches in the house, goblins on the lawn, demons under the trees. It's a supernatural chaos zone.

The Phelans are all there, Adam and Beth hosting with flair, Aunt Mavis dressed as Cupid, short white sheet and all. All our classmates hold glasses of punch as they gush, sometimes laugh, at each other's costumes. Most noticeable are the Channons, though. Having them here doubles the numbers of Weres, and I'm not sure if they add to the festivity of the party or bring a level of tension that wouldn't have been present. But with Tara as their Alpha, and by a Bonding that includes Mitch, they were invited.

My attention is wholly dominated by the Were-now-vampire holding me tight against his side. One dressed in a claret red, velvet waistcoat, a black jacket that hugs those delicious shoulders then comes down to hug lean hips before ending mid-thigh. All below dark blond slicked back hair, blue eyes above long canines that flash each time he grins. It's the birthday that just keeps on giving.

Just like every other Phelan family get-together, tables form a dotted line between the lawn and the trees. Phelan women walk between the house and the tables in a steady train, delivering plates of food and returning to the house. Some of the Channon mothers and wives give them a hand. They smile and chat, like the friends and allies they are. Friends and allies who are now much more intertwined.

I spend a couple of hours initially pretending I'm at one of my mother's work parties, smiling and greeting everyone as they wish Noah and Mitch a happy birthday. But it might be the happy glow that radiates from the firm muscles and blue eyes besides me or the two Weres that constantly smile and touch on my other side, because I find myself relaxing. Even enjoying myself. Even Bianca, dressed as a sexy red devil, doesn't dampen the light, warm feeling that sets up residence within me.

We eat, and Noah, ever considerate particularly when today is his day, has prepared me veggie patties. Some goblins sit, some cupids stand with plates in hand, as the supernatural crowd devours meat and salad, then more meat and more salad.

That black shoulder nudges my own. "Enjoying yourself?"

"I'm here celebrating with friends, happy families, and a heart-stopping vampire. What more could a girl ask for?"

And it's true. All I want is a sense of belonging to match the love I feel for this Were.

Noah leans in for a sweet kiss. "I want you to be happy."

"You make me happy." I give him a kiss of my own, sealing the truth of my words.

Shining summer sky eyes look into mine, lips parted; I'm not sure if he's happy with the silent love we're basking in or if he's thinking of saying more.

A clearing of the throat breaks our love bubble. Adam steps up to the head of the tables, signaling he is about to make a speech. He waves to Noah and Mitch to join him. Noah squeezes my hand, leaning in to give me a surreptitious eye roll and signature grin. The crowd of Phelans and friends watch as they stand beside Adam.

The three make an impressive line-up. Adam, big and blond with Noah, now almost as big and just as blond, next to him. Mitch stands on the other side, his dark good looks a contrast, but Noah's twin in height and the size of their grin.

Silence spreads through the crowd.

"Having twin boys has certainly been a ride. There were days I didn't know if I would survive." Adam glances from Noah to Mitch. "There were days I didn't know if they would survive."

The crowd chuckles. Pride has my chest expanding and my mouth tilting up.

"But we've reached a milestone—eighteen years. So, it seems we managed to stop you from killing yourself and each other or putting us in jail when we'd finally had enough of walls painted with cheese, skunks in the lounge room, and floor omelets."

Adam's hands eagle out to rest on each of his son's shoulders. "And you've grown into two fine men. Two boys we adored have become two young men we love. Two mischief makers have become everything we could have wished for. Two strong young men to become leaders of the future."

Adam draws them in closer to his sides. "But most importantly, two sons we can be proud of."

A wave of applause rises from the men and women, boys and girls, Weres and humans in the crowd. The humans seeing a proud father, two beaming sons. The Weres acknowledging their future leaders.

I see the boy I love. A proud son and undeniable leader. My heart swells with the feeling as my chest clenches with the implications.

Those mesmerizing eyes catch mine across the person-littered lawn and make me forget everything, because you wouldn't think you can squeeze so much love into one glance. But Noah does, making it look easy and effortless, and it cocoons me as I let him know he's not alone in that feeling.

"And now, the night belongs to our future generation. Joe, lights, please?"

Uncle Joe, beneath the veranda, flicks some switches. There's a brief moment of black that has the odd girl squealing, then a colored disco lights up the center of the lawn. There's a puff and a hissing sound and proof that Tara did indeed get a smoke machine furls across the lawn. A white cloud bellows out then sinks, tendrils snaking along the grass, curling around legs. The Phelan backyard has been transformed into a primitive, amateur, underage nightclub.

Dance music starts beating through the smoke and lights. A foot tapping, hip moving beat pumps from the speakers on the veranda. Strobe lights, some angled from the trees, others from the veranda posts, pulse out colored beams of light.

Groups of girls filter onto the dance floor. The confident ones, who don't care what others think or know they can rock that grass, start some pretty impressive hip gyrating, waist twisting action. Intimidating hip gyrating, waist twisting action.

Tara turns to Mitch, eyes alive, feet already skipping to the beat. She tugs on his hand, pulling him toward the dance floor.

Mitch makes a show of resisting, pulling her back, but the grin shows this is a battle he doesn't really want to win. Tara grins wider then sashays up to him, a sultry fairy temptress.

Mitch watches her with raised brows, glowing eyes. "Well, it's no Forgotten Fire, but I'll see what I can do."

Purple tulle bouncing, Tara leads Mitch to the dance floor. Beside me, Noah's fingers tap against his black-clad thigh, the hand holding mine pressing out chords.

Bianca and Brandon are next. Brandon's dimple flashes in his demon face as they bop past to the beat. They disappear into the multiplying crowd. The smoke machine hisses another stream of smoke that catches blues, reds, and greens, making the light move and swirl.

I know what's supposed to happen next.

"No."

Noah turns toward me, because he never asked a question. Slow dancing at a Were wedding, with the guy you just found out chose you, is one thing. Busting a move at a party full of judging peers, hoping to heaven you have rhythm, is not happening.

"Just one?"

"I can't."

Noah shrugs like it doesn't matter. But our clasped hands communicate the flash of disappointment. The fingers strumming his thigh slow then stop. "Maybe next time."

That statement makes me pause.

Safe Eden would never get up and dance. The Eden who belongs with the Weres and teens would already be up there. She wouldn't question it. Being with Noah, doing what makes him happy would be a no-brainer.

How many more times will I have this opportunity?

The next song, courtesy of Tara's dance compilation on random, decides for me. *Surely I can't get the Nutbush wrong.*

I step forward, his hand still in mine, before I can change my mind and regret this decision. I don't look back at Noah; I can already feel his surprise then pleasure. I head to Tara and Mitch as the crowd naturally forms into a grid, lines of people already kicking and stepping as Tina Turner pumps through the people and smoke. With Noah on one side, Tara on the other, I join them.

The first four steps start off well, the beat and smiles around me contagious. Two sidekicks to the right, two to the left. Then I discover why Tina never wore long dresses. My shoes catch the flowing hem as I step to the back then the material joins me as I try to can-can out the front. The little hop, skip, and jump to turn ninety degrees has me completely tangled and falling. Falling sideways until two strong hands grasp me around the waist.

But this Eden-who-belongs doesn't care. She's living life and loving it. I laugh, and Noah laughs. I hitch up my hem and keep going. In a line, vampire, fairy, vampire, fairy, we all jump and kick and dance until laughing gets hard, my mass of hair sticks to my neck, and I feel like I have the body temperature of a Were.

With the last chorus, we clap and pant. Blue eyes alive with happiness capture mine before his lips capture my own. It's a hot, sweaty, happy kiss. My arms wrap around Noah's neck as the rain of happiness continues. We're laughing and kissing and smiling.

Eden-who-belongs is a wonderful place to be.

The music changes to a Justin Timberlake song, all short breaths and sexy beats, and Noah's eyes darken to a twilight sky. Becoming eyes full of hot promises and endless possibilities.

Eden-who-belongs. This Eden belongs.

My pulse spikes, trips a little, and finds a new excited rhythm. A little good-excited as that big, warm, hard body aligns with mine. A lot nervous-excited as I'm no longer performing a choreographed line dance.

All of a sudden, I churn out two heartbeats for every swaggering music beat.

But Noah knows. And his unending patience rises to the challenge. He steps back, creating a little space between us, then starts moving from side to side, step left, step right. We start slow, two steps for every sultry beat. I copy, finding the rhythm, letting it merge with my limbs. I know I look like a gawky giraffe that just discovered modern music, but I try not to care. I pretend it's just me and Noah. Just me and those electric blue eyes and the current that's pulling us closer.

Very quickly, pretense becomes reality. My awareness shrinks until it's just Noah and me, our little piece of nature's dance floor, and the smoke, the lights, the music.

Hips sway, side to side, the occasional down, the odd breath hitching forward. There's a whole lot of pulsing...alongside the music and the rhythm the heat builds, muscles tense, eyes hold, passion throbs.

This Eden pushes her fingers into her hair then spirals her arms into the air, back arching, hair tumbling. This Eden is rewarded with summer sky eyes opening a little wider, heating a little hotter, hands pulling her in a whole lot closer. All the Edens love every minute of it.

When the song fades away, we still. I step up to place a soft, chaste kiss on Noah's lips. He leans in slightly, keeping the touch feather light. We both know any more and something might spontaneously combust. Possibly taking all of Jacksonville with us in a spectacular mushroom cloud.

"Drink?"

"Yes, please." That sort of dancing gets you hot, sweaty, and thirsty.

Noah takes my hand, and we weave through the angels and demons and Aunt Mavis. Tara and Mitch throw themselves around and against each other in abandon.

As we head to the punch table, Jordan approaches. Noah has to release my hand to give our biology classmate the standard fist pump, this time followed by a macho shoulder bump.

"Nice party, Phelan."

"I'm having a blast."

"As the birthday boy, that's all that counts. Hey, Eden."

"Hi, Jordan. Love the costume." Jordan's ebony skin pulls off a dark angel like no one else could.

I disengage myself, my parched throat seeking moisture. It's only a few feet, and I'm at the punch table. As I'm trying to avoid scooping an orange slice in my cup, a witch comes up beside me. She's short, but then again everyone is compared to me, with a black pointed hat, black fingernails, and a hooked plastic nose.

She holds out a plastic cup of her own. "Nice costume."

I smile as I scoop up another ladle, now neatly avoiding the citrus slices. "You, too." I look a little more closely; there is something familiar about this girl.

An arm snakes around my waist, pulling me into a solid, heated side. I turn, holding my two proud cups of punch, smiling. "Here you go. It's not even spiked, yet."

The two cups sink when I see Noah's expression. He is stony, staring at the witch.

"What are you doing here?"

"Noah, it's good to see you..." The stilted sentence fades away. She drops her chin, black fingernails tightening around her cup.

I don't get a chance to ask the obvious question.

"Where is she?" Tara zig zags through the throngs of people like a purple pinball. A high-pitched squeal tells me she's found what she's looking for. Tara throws herself at the witch, knocking the black hat backward.

Freeing the matching red hair that tumbles onto her shoulders.

Dana.

The two sisters hug and jump before Tara leans back, holding Dana at arm's length. Her smile is the width of her tutu.

"What are you doing here? How? Why?"

Dana laughs, bouncing herself.

The solid arm around my waist hardens even further. "We

should talk somewhere else." Noah hasn't caught the girls' excitement and enthusiasm; his words are a quiet monotone.

Mitch joins us, surprised and smiling, but arms crossed. We head to Grandfather Douglas, the one place the lights and noise don't quite reach.

Tara is still dancing, that tutu bouncing out her joy. "Well?"

Dana grabs Tara's hands, the two red-heads look like bobbing apples. "I never wanted to leave. My friends are here; school is here. When I heard you were Alpha, that was the clincher. I could finish school; I could be with my pack and my sister."

So, Kurt knows Tara is Alpha. I wonder how he feels about that.

"Wow. What did Dad say?"

"That the minute I walked out that door I would be dead to him, too."

Tara's breath hitches. I'm pretty sure the same fragment is reverberating in everyone's head—*dead to him, too*. I doubt it will ever leave Tara's.

Beside me, Dana dances the dance of the oblivious. "But I don't care. What he did was wrong."

"Let's not worry about all that for now. Who are you staying with?"

"Uncle James and Aunt Steph. They're happy to have me, free babysitting and all."

Tara throws her arms around Dana again, her purple colors disappearing as Dana's flowing black sleeves and gown clasp around her. "It's so good to see you."

"This is going to be awesome, Tara; you'll see."

Dana looks over Tara's shoulder, even her younger sister is taller than she is, and her face lights up again.

"Here comes my lift. Maybe we should double dance..." Dana glances at Noah and me. "Ah, triple dance."

Noah has gone hard against me again. Now what? I look up to see a brown-haired guy approaching us. It's my turn to freeze. The guy from Shoshoni, Emily's guy, walks toward us, smiling one of those smiles that seems genuine at a distance, but the closer he gets the more strained it looks.

Dana dances over toward him then wraps robed arms around his own. This guy is conspicuous because he's not dressed as anything. His height, width, and t-shirt and jeans in the cool spring air all start to spell an impossibility. Emily's guy is a Were.

Mitch crosses his arms as Tara steps back. "Seth."

Seth. Emily's guy is Seth? Shock quickly dissolves as I absorb the significance of this. Noah gave me a run-down of the Alpha vote, never saying Seth made him edgy, but not needing to. Seth glances at me before looking away, dismissal clearly on his face.

Noah's arm softens a little, giving me a squeeze. He can feel my discomfort, not knowing its cause is far more complicated than he thinks. This isn't a girl being intimidated by a Were; this is a girl facing a truth she doesn't want to admit. This is the guy that fell for a human. That ended it with a human.

Seth's smile grows, seeming to feed off the tension. "When Dana invited me for the surprise, I wanted to be here to see the family reunion."

Tara smiles her own wide, strained smile. "Great to see you, Seth."

"Happy birthday, you two."

"Thanks." Noah is the only one to reply.

Dana finally picks up on the tension; she smiles a bright smile. "Why don't we go celebrate?"

I don't know how the Grandfather Douglas' branches haven't collapsed under it. The weight presses down on my chest; I can see the strain between the Alpha and the one pack member that wants her position, the tension between the Phelans and the Channons. Tara and Mitch caught in between.

Seth looks at the four of us, but his eyes spend the most time on me. "It's certainly something, seeing so many humans and Weres together. Having a good time."

I stand very still, making a conscious effort not to shift my feet over the dry pine needles.

Noah's eyes narrow; I think he'd cross his arms if my hand wasn't firmly wedged in his. "The way it should be."

Seth's eyes leave mine to look at Noah, serious hazel not matching his smile. "Of course. It's wonderful when we can connect."

"The way it should be and will be," Noah says the words, and they ring with the authority of the Alpha he will one day be.

"I think we should join the party." Tara steps forward, pulling rank, showing that size doesn't matter when it comes to being an Alpha.

Seth looks toward the pulsing lights. "I don't think I will dance, Dana." He turns, throwing another smile over his shoulder, now looking at everyone but me. "See you guys at the run tomorrow."

The one I won't be at.

We head back to the thumping, smoky party. Tara and Dana show the same genetic resilience, bopping and bouncing by the time we reach the punch table. Mitch has no choice but to be caught in the updraft.

I know what will get Noah's spirits up. I grab his hand and head back to the dance floor. Some pop song that has held on doggedly to number one is thumping over the lawn. Noah's eyes light up, those broad shoulders already moving in a sexy roll as he follows me. I decide I'm more than willing to risk looking like an uncoordinated doe if I get to watch Noah moving to music.

It's rock poetry in action. No one is going to let Seth ruin this day.

Tara and Dana have a reunion to celebrate.

Noah and Mitch have a birthday to celebrate.

And this Eden is going to celebrate their milestones with them.

9

NOAH

The Glade on a full moon steals my breath as surely as Eden in a dress. Or Eden in jeans. Or even thinking of Eden for that matter.

It's night time, but the moon's white glow lights the arena like a silver stage. Phelans and Channons filter in, preparing to run like they always have on the night the moon is at its most impressive. We've done this for generations, and we will for many more to come. But this time is more special than the ones that have been before, more significant on so many levels.

To start with, the Phelans have their Alpha back. Dad is finally well enough to run. This is the first time since he recovered from his coma. I wonder what his physio would think of this little exercise. He steps into the clearing with Mom, looking big and broad and proud. But not only that, his Alpha heir will run with him for the first time. And I'm right there beside him, not quite as big and broad, but certainly just as proud.

Also significant is the new Channon Alpha. Tara joins from the east side of the Glade, her own pride making her look almost normal sized. Mitch is beside her, the two making a striking pair that I would follow in a heartbeat. Representing a decision that begins to blur the line between two packs that are neighbors and allies but have always remained separate.

No one needs to say anything; this is as natural and normal as nature itself. The shifting happens quickly, quietly, fueled by anticipation. The Glade fills with the metallic scent of so many humans becoming wolves.

I face forward, being at the head of the pack has the advantage of no one seeing your chest when you change. In a split second, I've gone from upright to four paws on the ground, from dulled human senses to sharp animal perception. From stationary to speeding through the trees.

And I finally experience what it's like to run with your dad, your mom, your brother, your pack. There is a chorus of paws hitting the ground, creating a low muffled rumble through the soil. Panting breaths surround me, the occasional excited yip penetrating the glowing black air. Canine and conifer sting my nostrils, spearing deep into my lungs. There are wolves everywhere. Each running and howling until our legs want to fall off and our hearts want to fly.

We all merge into a whole, running close, running hard. A pack of individuals, working as one. It's amazing, and I wish Eden were here to experience it with me. To see the wave of wolves moving through the forest. Dividing among the trees, coming together again when out in the open.

But Weres have been the only one to witness this since we began.

I slow a little, looking at the massive wolves around me, browns and reds, dark and light, shades of grey all outlined in silver.

Could Eden ever be part of this?

A grey shoulder slams me to the side; Dad's blue eyes zoom in close, exhilaration making them shine. I falter to the side, and as I right myself, Mitch shoulders me from the left, his breath coming in short, excited puffs.

Bring it on boys.

We run, overtaking the pounding animals around us. The three of us spearhead to the front of the pack, all thunderous paws and lightning speed. I dip into my reservoir, adding a sprinkling of speed, taking myself to the forefront.

Overtaking all but one.

A chocolate brown wolf rounds a tree and falls beside me, matching my thundering pace. Hazel eyes catch mine as wolfish lips tip up, before stretching forward and giving himself another burst of speed. Seth just issued a challenge.

He has no idea.

I release the pent up tension that had been coiled, waiting, and sprint forward. Seth expected this, and he picks up momentum besides me, his head once again level with mine. But he doesn't expect me to become a silver streak of speed. His heaving breaths fall behind me as I maintain the momentum, like I can do this all night. He tries, he really does. But he's no competition for the burning fire that has been kindled in my soul.

Up ahead I see the stand of boulders, and I wonder if I unconsciously led our packs here. To the place where I've already been, with the one that made this possible. With the one I want here.

Without thought, I execute the double jump to the top of the tallest rock. First Seth, then Dad, Mitch, Tara and the others reach our destination. They mill around, panting with exertion, leaping with abandon. And standing there, on that rock, I can't help myself, I howl long and hard. I appeal to the glowing moon. I call out to Eden.

I free the divided desires tearing me apart.

BACK AT THE GLADE, the Phelans and the Channons naturally divide. Leaving Mitch with a tough call.

He makes the decision I knew he would, following Tara to the east side of the Glade. The Channons need a strong, united front. And an Alpha without her mate isn't going to instill unification among anyone.

I change, my back to the Phelan crowd, and turn to see Dad watching me, a micro-frown catching the moonlight. I grin and come forward to slap him on the shoulder, ignoring the barely perceptible darkening of his features. "That was awesome. Thanks, Dad."

"Nice running."

I squeeze that shoulder. "You knew I was fast."

He opens his mouth then closes it, because jostling Phelans surround us, and Mom wraps me in a hug. Relief broadens my smile; I wasn't sure if I was going to have to explain the overtaking the whole pack thing or the weird show of modesty.

Just like they would have always finished, we stand in the clearing, facing the Precept Rock, chests heaving, hearts celebrating.

And that's where the similarities to the past end.

Because there is a gust of wind, a groan of trees.

And the rock grows. I mean, literally rises from the earth like a fist punching through the soil.

Some people gasp, a few shift, others, like me, are silent. Somehow knowing this giant rock is heralding big change.

The Precepts start to glow, their letters taking on a red-silver shine, making the words glitter in the silvery darkness. Laws we all know, all follow, are being emphasized with magical red highlighter.

You shall not reveal the bloodline
You shall not bond with the opposite bloodline
You shall not attack another blood member
You shall obey the Alpha

And before the eyes of every Werewolf, more words, another line, begin to form. Carving slowly and undeniably into the rock.

It's a short sentence, straight to the point like all the Precepts are.

He who is above the law is the law

Simultaneously, something rises as something sinks inside me, deep in the part that knows this has something to do with me.

I look at Dad, but he's doing the strong-silent-leader thing. He crosses his arms and nods. I look over to Mitch. He's looking at me with burning intensity.

Yep, this has something to do with me.

"Yeah, it seems that way."

Dad hangs up the phone. We're almost home, having driven through the bumpy, bushy track to the Glade, and Dad's cell started ringing the minute we hit the highway. There won't be any online posts, no hashtags, no emails about what just happened at the Glade. This will never be recorded.

But there will be a lot of talk.

All the Alphas talking to the other Alphas about the new Precept. Most calling Dad, because the Phelans are such an old pack and ours was the first Glade. Thanks to Were hearing, I hear the voices on the other end of the line, some reaching from other countries. There's all sorts of statements –

'At yours, too?'

I grit my teeth. Yes, everyone saw it. EVERYONE knows.

'This means big things...'

I cross my arms as the unsettled tones hang in the cab of the truck.

'Who?'

I hunch my shoulders. The one-word question every Alpha has asked.

Weres who are going to want answers.

Dad drops the phone into the console, a big sigh leaving his chest. Mom pats his arm, her strained eyes never leaving the road. Mitch has been listening as intently as I have, his hot, fierce gaze watching me the whole time.

The tension is driving me crazy.

"I wonder what it means," I muse aloud, hoping to lighten the mood.

Three stunned faces turn to me, the truck blatantly losing miles per hour.

"You don't know?" Dad sounds like I just asked if the Easter bunny will be coming this year.

"He doesn't know." Mitch is just as gobsmacked.

"No, I don't know," I say, feeling a little exasperated and a lot out of the loop. This is probably another example of the two-year gap in my Alpha education.

Mitch's burning gaze is back on me. "It's the Prime Prophecy."

I look to Dad, not being able to hold those hot blue eyes anymore. Hot blue eyes that hold something significant. Dad nods. "Yeah, the Prime Prophecy."

"Okay." I draw out, waiting for something more than the repeated statement.

Mitch grabs my shoulder, and I have no choice but to look back at the blazing blue. "It's like the ultimate Alpha. An Alpha to rule all Alphas."

Oh.

Dad nods again. "It seemed more of a legend. One day an Alpha would be chosen to lead all Alphas."

Oh. "But what for? Each pack already has a leader."

Mom turns to look at me in the back seat. "We don't know." She turns to look at Dad. "Everything seems to happen for a reason, though."

Dad grunts an assent. Their easy acceptance doesn't sit well with me. There are other questions that need to be asked.

"Why now?"

Dad drums his fingertips on the steering wheel. "Another valid question, but one that I can't answer."

The last question I don't say out loud. It's the question that has Mitch's face hard and focused and his eyes trying to punch a hole in my face.

Another question that won't have an answer.

Why me?

I look at the dress lying across my bed, mouth tense, brows low, arms crossed.

Why would she think I would wear that?

I wonder if I can still be angry at Noah for getting me in this situation. It had been a Wednesday study afternoon when Alexis had come home, all surprised to see us. Despite the fact she was home two hours earlier than any other day of the week.

Grey eyes had turned to me, the steel in them making me wary. "I have some good news." The ability to say those words without a smile is a talent few people have mastered. Alexis has a black belt in it. "I'm receiving an award for our winter marketing program."

"Great." I didn't bother smiling either.

"There will be an awards dinner." Those steel eyes held me still.

Oh no.

"When?"

"Saturday."

My mind had scrambled for a valid excuse. The helicopter trip was booked for the following weekend. Could I move it forward? I'd looked to Noah, hoping for a get-out-of-jail pass. His eyebrows had hiked up in question. I hadn't told him about these functions I get dragged to, playing happy family. How much I hate them. But I could see he registered the panic in my eyes, felt the sinking of my stomach, realized that 'no way' was about to come out like a nuclear projectile.

"We'd love to come." Noah's arm slipped around my shoulder, his blinding blue-eyed, teeth-glinting, breath-sucking smile bedazzling my mother.

I'd been wide-eyed. Did he just say I'd go? *And invite himself?*

My mother's practiced perfection was almost shattered by her own round-eyed shock. But she's an accomplished perfectionist and recovered quickly. She'd crossed her arms, and I could almost hear the papers shuffle as marketing trends were shelved and she weighed her options. Look rude and un-invite Noah? Be smart and admit defeat?

"Sounds lovely."

Or go with the opportunity presented her.

"Great. It sounds like a fun night. And congratulations." Noah's smile never budged.

Mine was buried, possibly never to surface again.

"Thank you. I'm looking forward to it."

Alexis's eyes had scanned me from head to toe then come to rest on my face. "I'll get you something to wear."

Then she'd spun on her heel and headed back out the door.

Noah's arm had come back around my waist. "I think I just scored some brownie points with your mom."

"But you're now in the negatives elsewhere."

His summer sky eyes had widened, the smile slipping a little.

"You have no idea how awful these things are. Why would you do that?"

His arms pulled me to him. Apologetic eyes looked up beneath dark blond lashes, his mouth pulled into a goofy droop. "Your mom looked like this wasn't going to be very negotiable."

"It's not, usually. I was working on an escape plan."

"Well, I figured if I gate crashed, maybe it wouldn't totally suck lemons."

I'd stared at his collar, not willing to admit defeat.

Noah bent his knees, chin tilting down to catch my begrudging gaze. "It might just suck cumquats."

Despite being the worst joke ever, my smile rose from the dead.

Although its resurrection was short-lived as I head for the wardrobe several days later, my mouth a straight line. Surely there's something else I can wear. I flick through the long dresses I've never worn, barely look at the short dresses I'd never consider wearing. Surely some women would wear slacks to an awards dinner? Sinking shoulders acknowledge I have no idea what other females would throw on for a night like this.

Shoulders that practically scrape the timber floor acknowledge the dress waiting on my bed is my best bet at appropriate attire.

I glance at the clock, knowing I have to get ready for the dreaded evening. I pick the dress up by the thin straps; the soft black material hangs in midnight folds, never reaching the floor. I sigh. My mother has essentially bought me a little black dress. One thing is certain; I'm not going to be comfortable in that.

I change quickly, slipping out of jeans and t-shirt into the dress. The stretchy material hugs me from my chest to hips then flares out gently down my legs. Thankfully it's not as short as I thought, although it's still not long enough for long-limbed me. I tug at the hem, but it doesn't quite reach my knees. I put on the stockings next, quickly realizing I may have done things the wrong way around as I have to hitch up the skirt. The kitten heels come next, all of a sudden making my exposed legs feel too long.

I grab the brush, looking at myself in the mirror. With Tara's help, I'd put on a light layer of makeup, some pale eyeshadow, a little nude lipstick. I bite my lip, belatedly realizing I'm now eating the stuff. With the black dress and dark hair, the black stockings and black heels, my serious eyes and somber face, I look like I'm going to a funeral.

Caesar sits up, tongue hanging out. I lean over to pat him. "You can smile. You don't have to go."

As I head for the door, he barks from the bed. I turn with my hand on the door. "Stop gloating," I admonish. I get another canine grin in response.

Alexis is waiting in the living area. My mother looks lethal in a tight red number, killer red heels, and gold accessories. Her grey eyes scan me from head to toe and back again, those chili-red lips puckering slightly.

"Good." It looks like the cattle passed muster. "Try to smile." Except they're meant to smile as they get led to their doom.

I keep my face in the land of the serious. Alexis sighs, looking at me for a second longer before glancing at her watch.

Creating the best time to bring something up. A time-limited time. So I say casually, quietly. "I'm going camping with Noah next weekend."

Alexis is much more interested in the ticking diamonds on her watch. "Okay."

"We'll leave Saturday morning."

Grey eyes flick to me then back to the gold timepiece. "Okay."

I smooth the soft black material. "We'll be back Sunday."

Silence.

I look up, grey eyes, ringed with flawless makeup, are well and truly honed on me. "Do we need to see Dr. Welch?"

Dr. Welch? The middle-aged man with the bedside manner of an angry mule? "What for?"

"To talk contraception."

Did she just say what I think she said? I want to bring my cold hands to my hot cheeks. I want legs, frozen in shock, to take me out of this room.

"Well?"

"No."

"We don't want any regrets."

I don't need my hands anymore; my cheeks are cold. All the blood sucked deep into my painfully beating heart. She's always acted it, but never actually said it.

"It's not a problem," I choke out.

Those smoky grey eyes flicker for a moment. "You know that's not what I meant." She glances around the room then back at me, frozen on the timber floor. "I just don't want you to go through what I did."

I don't want you to repeat my mistakes.

"It's not a problem."

Red lips open then shut. Alexis looks back at her watch as her shoulders drop on a sigh. "Where is he?"

Just as the doorbell rings.

"I'll get it." I go to rush and then remember the heels. It's a wobbly, noisy dash to the door.

I open the door to a hunk in a dark suit, the conversation I just had evaporating. Noah, in a classic suit, sucks all the air from my lungs. My eyes don't know what to devour first. They feast on long legs in black slacks, the chest I know is muscled and defined, now covered in a white shirt divided by a black tie. They scan and consume a cleanly shaven jaw, smiling lips, almost-tamed blond hair, summer blue eyes.

Eyes which darken as I connect with them, a look I've gotten to know well over the past few months.

Noah likes what he sees.

Alexis's heels clack toward the front entry. "Hello, Noah. I appreciate you being on time." Gravel crunches on the driveway. "Excellent, as is our ride."

I look over Noah's shoulder to see a black limo pull up in front of the house.

"You look lovely, Mrs. St. James."

"Thank you." Alexis grabs the clutch that was sitting on the hall table. "Let's get going."

Noah steps back as fire-red breezes past. His glinting grin comes back to me. "You look good."

I don't have anything to carry, so I close the door behind me. I lean into Noah, whispering. "I hate it." I point to the stretched transportation as we follow Alexis down the driveway. "I hate that."

His eyes rake me from head to toe. "Well, I love it." Then he leans in, his beautiful face filling my vision, his sandalwood scent filling my senses. "And I love you."

Those words stop me mid-stride. An unwilling smile softens my face. "I love you."

Noah grabs my hand, giving it a squeeze. "Let's go own this thing."

I feel my smile stretch my lipstick. With Noah, I can do anything.

In the limo Alexis takes one side, glass of wine already in hand, whilst Noah and I sit on the other.

"So, Mrs. St. James, what are these awards for?"

Alexis smiles her first smile for the night. "It's a national marketing award. The Inn's winter promotion was nominated then shortlisted. It was one of our most successful campaigns. We had record numbers over the winter season."

"Sounds like you've got it nailed, but good luck anyway."

"Thank you." Alexis takes a sip of wine before speaking again. "I've been informed you're going camping this weekend."

For the first time this evening I feel a little jolt of nervousness from the hand wrapped around my own. "Yes, Eden gave me a helicopter ride for my birthday. It should be amazing."

Contemplative eyes turn to me. "Did she?" Then return to Noah, developing a hint of steel. "I trust you'll be safe."

I don't know how Noah isn't shifting on the tan leather seat there's that much nervousness churning through him. "Eden always comes first, Mrs. St. James."

I can feel the protectiveness that overrides the nervousness beside me, and I squeeze Noah's hand, my leg brushing his as I infinitesimally move closer.

Alexis looks out the tinted limo window. "I hope so, Noah."

I can't decipher the tone in my mother's hard words. Could I detect a trace of doubt? A warning? A little part of it almost sounded protective.

The rest of the limo ride is quiet. The only time Alexis's eyes leave the window is to line her wine glass up to her lips. I study Noah from the corner of my eye, tapping into the little barometer I have within me that senses the emotions in the black suit beside me.

Noah is still. Still and quiet. The sharp line of his jaw tilted to the window, lips resting together, his breath steady and slow. Looking as cool and composed as my mother. But I can feel something beneath the surface, an edginess, a slight uneasiness. I can feel Noah is nervous...about an awards night? I don't think Alexis is on his Christmas card list, but she's never made him nervous. Maybe it's my nervousness overflowing, having a contagion effect.

Noah turns from the window, catching me watching him. He smiles, squeezing my hand, and the feeling settles. That must have been it. I will myself to relax over the remainder of the trip. Noah's right, this won't be so bad with him here.

We arrive at the Stanton Hotel, multiple stories of long, narrow windows, a well-lit entrance that has its fair share of limos pulling up and dropping off expensive cargo. I suck in a fortifying breath and climb out, Noah not far behind. He looks up at the daunting building then looks at me. He mouths two words, 'own it.' I squeeze his hand in return. There is one thing that Noah already owns.

My mother's stilettos clack out our approach across the marble foyer, as if she knows exactly where she's going. Inside, there are more men in dark suits and women in dresses that scream money and power. I haven't been to one of these things for a while, and certainly not as formal as this, but I know what I need to do. So I climb back up on that bicycle, adjust my posture, and arrange my painted lips.

Alexis is smiling, too, a glass of champagne in her hands, as a grey-haired man clasps her, kisses one cheek then the other.

"Alexis, lovely to see you. Big night for you m'dear. Ah, I see you've brought her with you."

"Thomas, this is my daughter—"

I stretch out a hand, smiling like I love riding, wondering what he's talking about. "Eden, lovely to meet you."

"And this is Noah, her...partner for the evening."

For the evening?

Noah shakes Thomas's hand. "Nice to meet you, sir."

"Oh, Alexis, you are a clever woman, bringing your campaign to flaunt before your competitors." Thomas quirks a brow, leaning in close. "I see where she gets her looks from."

Alexis flutters a hand over the man's wool jacket. "Oh, Thomas, stop it."

Although her tone says the opposite.

"The Everetts are here."

My mother's smile takes on a hard edge. "I expected they would be." She shrugs a bare shoulder. "I felt their campaign didn't quite...capture the audience."

I take Noah's hand when a woman walks up this time, dressed in silver, air kissing my mother on both cheeks. I once again get the look over, but I introduce myself, turn my grimace into a smile, and almost find a rhythm. Underneath it all, I'm glad Noah invited himself to this thing. I don't remember Alexis's associates paying this much attention to me before.

As we cross the room I smile, shake hands, smile some more. I talk about veterinary science; I act like marketing is interesting. It's as if I've learned from the best. We finally make it to our table, and I sink into the chair the waiter is holding for me. We're right up front near the stage, where a handful of glass trophies stand, one three times the size of the others.

Alexis sashays and schmoozes her way through the crowd, taking her time arriving at the table. I turn to Noah, one eyebrow raised, saying 'see?'

He leans in. "When I said, 'let's own this,' I didn't know you planned on being the CEO."

That brow comes down to join its mate in confusion. "What do you mean?"

"You're the hostess with the mostess. I've never seen you so... owning it."

I pull my chin in surprise. I suppose shy, timid Eden isn't here. "Alexis has made me attend these things since she could dress me in frills. I suppose I just got into character."

He kisses me lightly on the temple. "I love that you keep surprising me."

I flush a little, wishing I'd put on a heavier layer of foundation. I nudge him with my shoulder. "Never underestimate an introvert with a mission."

Noah's index finger comes up to stroke his bottom lip, that thoughtful, sexy Phelan thing he does. "Noted."

I look around to see Alexis heading to our table, a red ribbon merrily winding through the tables. I'd forgotten how happy these things make her. I smell the sandalwood, feel the heat at my shoulder, before I hear Noah speak again. "Can we talk after?"

It's a simple question, an innocuous one. But there's something about it that has me pivoting to face him. Maybe it's to see the little smile, just an excuse to find the summer blue pools. Maybe it's the nervousness that I can sense. Maybe it's because he thought he had to ask.

"Sure, we'll go back to yours?"

A quick kiss, I don't want to call it a nervous peck, and he smiles a little. "Is it too cold for Grandfather Douglas?"

Maybe it's because it's a talk beneath Grandfather Douglas. "Never. What about?"

A soft shrug of those black, broad shoulders, and the smile grows. "Nothing urgent."

"Now, you two, I have sodas and hors d'oeuvres."

Alexis slides into the seat next to me, all smiley and motherly, as she places two glasses and a crystal bowl with an assortment of nuts before us. Maybe I got the acting abilities from her, too, because I don't pretend her interruption is annoying.

"Thank you, Mrs. St. James, this is a great looking hotel."

"Isn't it? These awards are quite prestigious, so they had to find somewhere that reflected that."

Alexis sips her champagne as she turns to face us both. "So, Noah, you and Mitch are twins."

My back stiffens a little at this unexpected social opening. Aren't there some exec types she needs to wheel and deal with? I glance at the glass, wondering how much she's had.

"Yes, ma'am. Somehow my parents survived, although I think my mom used some pretty intensive anti-aging cream."

"Handfuls, were you?"

"You have no idea." Noah pops a nut in his mouth then grins a little. "We learned that garbage bags don't make good parachutes. That the average response time for the fire brigade is fifteen minutes. And I'm pretty sure we now have a chocolate Labrador because the last one got dyed blue and pink. On separate occasions."

Alexis smiles a little, tipping her glass toward Noah. "I may need to get the brand of this miracle cream."

I sit there between Noah and my mother conversing, completely unsure whether this is a good thing. I do know it makes me uncomfortable, and I'm glad the topic seems to have run dry.

Noah grabs another nut, winks at me, then turns to Alexis. "So, what did Eden get up to as a child?"

What? I turn to Noah in shock.

"Oh, nothing like that."

"What? No plastic toys in the oven, no haircuts when you weren't looking?"

"No." I'm sure that's a shutdown comment from Alexis, since when did she talk about me as a child? "For her, it was always animals. The first was a mouse"—grey eyes turn to me—"What was its name?"

I flick the edge of the fan napkin on the plate in front of me. "Twitch."

"Yes, that right. Although Twitch brought relatives. I don't know how we didn't have a plague."

They never figured out how to open a jar of peanut butter, so we were safe. Luckily, by the time I had to release Twitch his leg had healed.

"I thought we were past it, only to discover she just went

underground. I got suspicious one day when I caught her harvesting dead flies off the window sill."

Where is this coming from? I look around, certain that some mogul is watching us put on a happy family show. But there's no one.

Noah quirks a brow at me, asking the question.

I flick the napkin again. "Legs."

A delicate shudder shakes my mother's shoulders. "A spider."

Alexis releases her glass for a moment—I mean, releases her glass! Then points with a fire engine red nail at Noah. "Then there was the kitten. It certainly raises eyebrows when your vegetarian daughter asks for a can of tuna."

"Nor does cat litter totally absorb smells," I grumble beneath my breath.

Noah nudges me with his shoulder. "False advertising, huh?" He turns back to Alexis. "I wonder where she got those tendencies from?"

I resist the urge to turn shocked eyes to Noah. *What did he just say?*

"Indeed." Coolness creeps back into Alexis's tone, the wine glass coming back up.

I don't know if Noah doesn't care, or doesn't see the shutdown, because he keeps prodding. "What about Caesar?"

I almost fall off the shiny brocade chair when Alexis keeps talking. "That one was the most impressive. She kept him, how long?"

Impressive? That's not my definition of her response when she discovered a German shepherd in my room. "Five weeks."

"Before I realized. By then I was told it was too late."

Noah's arm comes around my shoulder, and I think it's the first time it doesn't prompt a lip tighten. "She's certainly connected to that dog."

"He's been a wonderful companion for her."

This time, I actually look at my mother. Since when did she pay attention to any of this? Alexis's eyes are looking at me, grey and indecipherable. I'd like to say something, but I have no idea what.

"Ladies and gentlemen, we've now come to the part of the evening that everyone is waiting for." We turn to see Thomas at the podium.

Alexis straightens and turns, one hand gripping the back of her chair, probably wishing it had something else to hold, like a glass of wine.

"As you all know, marketing is a highly competitive industry, one where excellence will give you the edge. It is this commitment to quality that grows marketing as an industry, encourages innovation, and powers our economy. And it is this excellence that should be recognized."

Noah's hand creeps under the table and takes mine. Thomas's voice blends into the background as that warmth graces my palm then starts to wander up. I lean toward him, finding his shoulder just where I need it.

"Your mum let you keep Caesar," he whispers into my hair.

I glance over my shoulder, wondering what he's getting at.

"She didn't have to. A lot of parents would have made their daughter get rid of the dog, no matter how many weeks had passed."

I turn back to the front, where the crowd chuckles at some witty marketing pun Thomas just made. I suppose Noah's right. Alexis never insisted I get rid of Caesar. *Why would she do that?*

Sandalwood tingles across my senses again as Noah's lips brush my hair. "Because she cares."

I stiffen, because Noah just responded to my unspoken question with an answer I hadn't considered.

"The runner-up for the National Marketing Excellence

Awards is Everett Luxury Eco-Lodge, for its sustainable but innovative campaign. Congratulations, Charles Everett."

A round of applause follows Charles, immaculate in a dark pinstripe suit and perfectly combed black hair as he walks up to the podium. The screen behind Thomas lights up with a lush rainforest shrouded in mist then zooms into log cabins nestled in the ethereal light. An airbrushed, happy couple sits on a flawless timber deck. Colorful birds and cute furry animals eat from their manicured hands. Alexis claps along with the crowd, a small smile curling those red lips.

Charles takes the frosted glass trophy and steps up to the microphone. "Thank you, ladies and gentlemen." Cultured tones instantly show Charles is English. As does the reserved, classy acceptance speech.

As Charles returns to his table, Thomas grabs the mama trophy and turns back to the crowd. My mother has gone very still beside me. "And for the winner. This campaign exemplified excellence in the marketing industry. It grabbed your attention with its quality, but more importantly, it never let go once it grabbed your heart. Who didn't want to go to Clear Creek Inn after you saw this?"

A round of applause erupts as Alexis rises to her feet, a huge, genuine smile lighting her face. I clap, too, feeling confusingly pleased and strangely proud. The screen lights up again as my mother approaches the podium, a panoramic shot of a snow-covered vista brightening the screen in dazzling white.

The picture fades, changes, and my hands sink down, silent and numb. Because a dark-haired girl, looking out at the rugged white mountains, a gentle smile gracing her face, is dominating the screen. A mosaic of scenes scroll before my unblinking eyes. Her hiking, flushed, and smiling. Alone in a sea of white, tilted eyes closed to the sun. Standing beneath a white frosted pine, hair a little wild in the breeze, cheek glowing with cold. The applause continues, some people facing me rather than my mother as they smile and clap.

"Holy crap." Noah's words echo what is screaming through my mind.

I remember my mother asking me to take a photographer for a hike, something about photos for a marketing campaign. I hadn't even blinked when he'd asked to borrow my beanie, my scarf, didn't even question when he even asked for my gloves. *What photographer uses gloves?* I never saw him take a photo of me, which is why most of the shots are from the side or behind.

And now the connection that Alexis never acknowledged, let alone valued, is immortalized in undeniable full-color HD. How many people have seen this? Hundreds? Thousands?

I don't hear Alexis's acceptance speech. All I register is the buzzing in my ears and the bile in my mouth.

I know I'm angry at my mother. But I'm mostly angry at myself.

Because I don't know how I can feel betrayed by Alexis after all these years.

But I do.

11

NOAH

I don't think I've ever seen Eden angry before. But the feeling, stretching all hot and tight in my gut, isn't mine. I'm fairly certain it belongs to the pale girl next to me, who has taken on a very statue-like stillness.

Eden takes a very measured, very controlled breath.

Yep, definitely hers.

The ad that captured Eden's beauty and her link to nature so artfully has finished. It was a flippin' darn good ad. There's something primal and fundamental in connecting to our roots, and Eden on that screen epitomized that feeling. I'm surprised I didn't see a few hands pick up cell phones and book right there and then. If I didn't already have one foot in that wild, wild world, I'd have booked in myself.

But it's the ultimate betrayal. To use Eden like that, to exploit her for profit and publicity, then blatantly project it larger than life right before her, is not what this reclusive girl would ever want.

Alexis would have known that. And she did it anyway.

The tight anger beside me is justified. I touch her back, and tilted eyes, dark and turbulent, turn to me. 'How could she?' is screaming from those green depths.

I wrap my arm around her waist, trying to absorb some of the pain. "She shouldn't have done that."

Eden looks back to her mother, and she's so still. So angry. "I don't know why I'm so surprised."

And here I was trying to tell her she cared.

Alexis returns, gliding through congratulatory kisses and handshakes, all smiles and grace. Eden's jaw is tense, her back excessively straight. She doesn't turn to congratulate her mother as Alexis slides back into her seat. Eden doesn't even move.

With the awards completed, the desserts start descending on the tables. Big square plates hold little creations that could be mistaken for one of Tara's artworks. I'm deciding whether I should speak up, whether the angry protectiveness I would like to unleash on this excuse-for-a-mother would be more about me than Eden, when a tall dude in a dark suit approaches our table. It's Charles, the runner-up with his environmentally sound, morally conceptualized campaign.

One arm behind his back, Charles practically bows. "Congratulations, Alexis."

Alexis flicks her shiny hair. "Thank you, Mr. Everett."

Charles looks from Alexis to Eden. "It was a very effective campaign. I never stood a chance." Fair point—Eden has the beauty, whilst Alexis has the non-existent ethics. "I've heard about the new proposal."

Alexis waves a bejeweled hand in dismissal. "I don't know if I'm committing to it at this stage."

Charles's lips angle up just a notch. "We should collaborate —our skills are quite complementary." With that English accent, the offer sounds nothing but proper, but it has Alexis shifting a little nonetheless.

"This is not an industry that collaborates, Mr. Everett."

Translation—I'm not a woman that collaborates, Mr. Everett.

"Exactly, Alexis." And this time he does bend at the waist. "They'll never see us coming."

And with a very British incline of his head, Charles spins on the heel of his shiny black shoes and melds back into the crowd. What is most noticeable, proven by the fact that even I see it, is Alexis's response. Alexis doesn't flick her hair, jut out her chin, and take a little sip of wine. Instead, she watches that tailored pinstriped back disappear then glances at the people around the table as she straightens her shoulders, fixes her perfect hair. Only then does she jut out her chin then take a sip of wine, and a hefty sip at that.

Eden never sees the exchange. I don't think the shaft of anger spearing down her spine allows her to move. I use the hand she's holding so tight and hard to tell her I'm here if she needs me.

Alexis is back to beaming as the congratulations flow around the table. Just as many are aimed at Eden. But Eden doesn't pick up a fork, doesn't look up.

Alexis notices, as do our dinner companions. She leans to the side, speaking through a great big smile. "Don't make this bigger than it is...darling."

Really? We're minimizing our actions?

Eden doesn't look at Alexis, doesn't acknowledge her statement.

Alexis places her fork on her overgrown plate. "You never would have agreed."

Now she's trying the how-else-was-I-supposed-to-do-it defense? I don't know if I should shake my head or shake hers.

Eden's only movement is a long, slow blink.

"I thought you'd be happy, five minutes of fame and all that." This one Alexis says through gritted teeth, eyes looking from left to right.

I'm guessing 'sorry' passes Alexis's lips as often as Eden's name.

The chin jut and hair flicks are back, along with the glass of wine. "This silent treatment is unacceptable and juvenile. We will finish this at home."

And in desperation and frustration, Alexis goes on the attack. It makes me angry. It makes me sick.

"No, we won't, Alexis." Eden bites off each word as she rises. I'm right there with her. "It will never be on your terms. Ever again."

And with that, we leave. We leave slowly and stiffly. With hands held, a beautiful, silent, straight-backed girl and a guy that is doing all the hurting for her.

Eden walks out and takes with her the façade of their happy family, leaving behind the knowledge that a mother chose her career over her daughter. Leaving Alexis's actions as an indisputable exhibition for her valued associates.

I take note of what Alexis created by ignoring Eden's right to choose, by putting her in the limelight. And I feel how the dark betrayal and anger is briefly lost in a burst of satisfaction Eden creates by making her own decisions.

I realize, with a sinking heart and diminishing hope, that Alexis is doing what, for a brief moment, I considered.

I promise to myself that's something I will never do to the girl I love.

12

EDEN

"Y ou sure you'll be okay?"

Standing in our driveway, the limo's tail lights fading to black, Noah's concerned eyes scan mine.

"Definitely. She won't be back for hours."

Noah steps in closer, his hand cupping my face. He's probably checking for confirmation, but I lean in, happy for the warmth. Little black numbers aren't so good at trapping body heat. I slip my arms up his shoulders, sliding in and slotting myself against him.

"You really sure? I don't mind staying."

"Really, really. We've got school tomorrow." I try for a smile. "Plus, you're kinda angry."

As we'd driven off, my anger had cooled as the shock and surprise had worn off. It was the last lesson I'd learn from Alexis, one that's left me wiser and better prepared. I will never make myself vulnerable again when it comes to my mother.

Ironically, as my anger had calmed, Noah's had grown. The whole trip home I'd felt it bubble and heat. His statements like 'who does that?' or 'she needs to know that—' had continued to puncture the silence. I'd leaned in and kissed those kissable lips to stop the final thought before it spawned an intention to act.

Noah frowns. "What she did wasn't okay."

"No, it wasn't."

"What are you going to do?"

I rest my forehead on his shoulder, suddenly tired. "Go to bed. Get some sleep. Pretend I'm an orphan."

Noah's arms slip around me, and I revel in the sensation of being cherished. I feel him take a breath, hold it, and I wonder if he's going to say something. But it puffs back out, ruffling my hair. "Okay."

With a sweet kiss and a tender brush of my cheek, he's gone. Inside, Caesar greets me, and sensing my somber mood, attaches himself to my side. It makes changing into my sweats a little tricky, but I'm glad for the company.

I'm brushing my teeth when I hear a car. Inexplicably happy that Noah decided to come back even though I told him I wanted to be alone, I skip out to the lounge room.

But it's not Noah that stands in the entry, hard and still, grey eyes flaring when I enter the room.

"Don't you ever do anything like that. Ever. Again."

I look at Alexis, composure lost, possibly left behind at the hotel. If she's ever been upset with me before, there's always been the icy rule of control. But it seems tonight is different.

My fists clench, and I feel Caesar lean his warm weight into my leg. This is where I would walk out, not quite backing down, but never facing my mother's aloof disapproval.

It looks like tonight is going to be different. "My thoughts exactly."

Her steel grey eyes widen as her breath sucks in. "Your reaction, the way you walked out, was humiliating. At one of the most significant nights of my career."

"Let me tell you about some of my important nights, Alexis.

The night I was five and was scared to be alone in my room. The night I was eight and asked you to braid my hair for school. The night I was twelve and asked if I'd ever meet my father." With each statement, I take a step forward. I don't remember when I've been close enough to my mother to smell her perfume. That spicy, musky scent whips away the tiredness, sparks the desire to finally tell her. "And you walked out on every one of them."

Anger flares across Alexis's face, her cheeks flush as her eyes narrow. "I was trying to teach you to be smart. To depend on yourself."

I think of my surprise at Alexis using me in her marketing campaign. I'd been defenseless. "Well, it didn't work."

"I know. It was wasted." Alexis steps forward herself, and we're only feet apart. Possibly the closest we've stood in a very long time. "Look at how you cling to him, to their family."

And then I realize I was never defenseless. Noah was with me. And as weird as it is in this moment, my heart smiles. "He's taught me more than you ever have."

Alexis's face transforms again, and a war of emotions seem to battle for domination. If I'd spent more time with my mother, I may have been able to decipher them. But I haven't, so instead, I watch the clouds storm and clash in her grey eyes.

Then she straightens and steps back. "All he will teach you is pain."

I stand and watch, anger disappearing but unsure what to replace it with, as for the first time in my almost eighteen years, Alexis leaves first. She spins on her spiked heel and jabs her stilettos into the timber floor as she stalks to her room.

In the new silence, I do a scan. The fight finished, my anger is gone, and for some reason, I don't mourn its loss. I've cut myself free. It's not a happy sense of freedom, nor is there any sense of victory. But I've cut loose a huge chunk of the anger and resentment. My mother's actions, her reactions, finally slammed the door I hadn't realized I'd kept open.

I lean down to my silent companion, Caesar telling me that on so many levels, I've never been alone. As I head to my room, I realize now I'm looking for another door to open.

GLANCING up from the numbers I'm struggling to focus on, I see an opportunity to do what's really on my mind. Mr. Rosenberg scrawls furiously on the board like he could do this all day. *Maybe we should study tonight?*

My phone vibrates almost instantly. *I do like studying...*

I smile, the movement catching Tara's eye in the seat beside me. She glances at my cell phone held beneath the desk, shakes her head like she's an adult, and then gives up on the grownup persona as she tries to peer a little closer.

I tilt the phone, cutting off her line of sight. *Should we invite Tara and Mitch?*

No

I almost giggle and quickly glance up at Mr. Rosenberg, but he's helping someone else with their differential equations.

When the minutes draw out a little longer, I hope Noah hasn't been caught texting in class. My phone vibrates just as I consider biting my lip. *At yours?*

I smile, knowing Noah's probably thinking of the endless supply of gourmet pizzas available at my place. My phone vibrates before I get a chance to respond, but my screen lights up with a different name. *We can't come anyway*

I glance in surprise at Tara, and she gives me a cheeky grin. "Multiple younger siblings remember? I'm pretty sure I can see around corners."

I flush, feeling like I've been caught out. "You're welcome to join us."

Tara rolls her eyes. "You're a good friend, Edes. I doubt I would have invited you to a study sesh with Mitch back in the beginning."

Now I'm all-out blushing. "I was going to work on my English assignment."

Tara's eyes practically do a revolution of her head this time round. "Sure you were—it's not like you've already been accepted into Wyoming State. It's all cool. We've got to go out, do some Alpha schmoozing with the pack."

My smile loses some of its happy power. Surely Noah knows that Tara and Mitch won't be home. And didn't he say he wanted to talk last night? Specifically under Grandfather Douglas.

"It's a good idea though, doing it at yours. Don't you need a bodyguard if Alexis is there?"

I stare at my phone, wondering if Tara's right and that's why Noah is wanting to go to my place. "I haven't seen her since last night."

I told Noah earlier that I doubt we'll be talking anytime soon. But what other reason could there be?

"I'd say it's the pizza rather than Beth's vegetarian creations then."

I tell myself to get my insecurities under control. Noah's protective streak could slice the mountain range beyond our window in half. With a quick glance at Mr. Rosenberg, I type in the shadows beneath my desk. *It's a date.*

AT HOME, it doesn't look like Alexis is in. I enter our overgrown timber cottage to find that it is, indeed, empty. I smile. Just Noah and me.

A quick call to the Inn's chef and Tony has our pizzas under-way. A quick scan through the fridge and sodas are sitting on the coffee table. A quick brush of my hair and I remind myself to stop being vain.

I'm revising the evolutionary theories of humans, each agreeing that we are mammals and descendants of apes, but disagreeing on the road that got us here, wondering which branch would hold Weres in this centuries-old family tree, when the doorbell rings.

Caesar gives an excited bark, and we both skip over to the door. I fling it back to find Noah's broad shoulders filling the doorway, happy eyes trapping my own, his lean legs stepping in, those delicious lips finding mine.

I throw my arms around his neck, pulling him down, as his arms tighten around my waist, pulling me closer. It's a happy kiss, one that reaffirms how glad we are to be here.

I don't know why this is so special or exciting. Noah and I get time alone when we're here, when we're hiking, when we're at his house. But this unexpected gift is significant for some reason. I know why I'm grasping every moment I have with Noah.

I wonder where Noah's enthusiasm stems from.

We separate in time for Caesar to jump up on Noah, broad paws hitting him in the abdomen.

"Hey, boy. You get a playdate, too."

Stash, the Phelan Labrador, bowls past Noah, leaping up to meet Caesar. Tails wag madly, threatening to take out anything at knee height.

"Come on, you two; you can take that enthusiasm out the back."

When I return, Noah's sitting on the lounge, open laptop on the coffee table, one arm stretched across the back, like there's a special spot just waiting for me.

I climb in, legs tucking up, facing that sculpted face I could watch all day. All week.

For the rest of my life.

Noah brushes a strand of hair over my shoulder. "No Alexis?"

I shake my head. "Like I said, I doubt we'll be making eye contact, let alone exchanging words, anytime soon, which suits me." I go for a change of subject, one where the outcome isn't already decided. "So, Tara and Mitch are out wheeling and Wereing?"

Noah blinks, the hand that was playing with the ends of my hair stilling. Was it the sudden change in topic? "Yeah, most of the Channons are happy with their new leaders, but they're just making sure."

I wonder if they'll be seeing Seth, but I don't get a chance to ask. Noah leans in and gifts me with a quick kiss. "So, why don't we start on our English stuff then finish up with the biology assignment?"

It's my turn to blink. "Sounds like a plan."

Noah brings his arm over and leans forward to retrieve our computers. He passes me mine, and settles his own on his lap. "What's your topic?"

I fire up my laptop, pretending this is what I wanted to talk about. "I have to do the book review on *The Outsiders* and its relevance to today."

I turn a little, leaning back on the muscled arm he tucks into his side, taking up our study position.

Noah snorts. "At least yours is in English from this century."

With my back to him, my eyes pretending they're absorbed in my laptop, I click open the document. "Wasn't there something you wanted to talk about?"

Noah clicks something then clicks it again. "Nah, I figured it out."

My assignment flashes open on the screen; the title of the book, black on glowing white, looks at me. The irony of our allocated reading is not lost on me. I'm pretty sure I can't write an essay on a human girl wanting to fit in with shapeshifting Weres. On all the reasons she can relate to Ponyboy and the obstacles that he has to face, although it's not wealth this time around, just supernatural laws.

I don't turn around to check Noah's expression; I don't sigh. Instead, I focus on growing the words on my screen and losing myself in arguing that Ponyboy's patience and perseverance pay off in the end.

A tingle on my scalp brings me back from the East Side. My curious mind stills then realizes Noah's fingers are tangling in the ends of my hair again. Little shivers of warmth ignite where his fingers brush, and I have to hold myself still, reminding myself we are here to study, that Noah is still trying to translate Hamlet.

Noah's shoulders move a little as he readjusts the laptop, and that hot upper arm massages the middle of my back. That banked fire flares a little more. My fingers have stopped, hovering over the keyboard, and I know the heat has flushed my skin. From the corner of my eye, I see Noah smile.

He knows exactly what he's doing!

I remember the look, those wide eyes burning a little hotter when we were on the dance floor. With a hidden smile I raise one arm, brushing my hair out of my face and over my shoulder. Till the ends brush his thigh.

The movement behind me stops.

My secret smile grows a little.

Then I sit forward, like I need to stretch. I roll my shoulders, ever so slightly arching my back before leaning backward again. The back that is not nearly as relaxed as I just made out to be reconnect with the statue of muscle behind me.

Now I can't even hear breathing.

But Noah doesn't move, which is not really where I saw this going. I type a few more words, and as gibberish scrolls across my screen, I realize my little plan has backfired. I'm hot and bothered but still supposedly studying.

One glance over my shoulder tells me I'm not the only one with the elevated pulse. One glance over my shoulder and it ignites.

Laptops are carelessly dumped on the coffee table, and I'm on top of Noah like I'm about to devour him. Lips touch then mesh, breaths hitch then exhale in an excited new rhythm.

Noah's hands are on my waist, gripping then moving, making me arch. My hands find the strip of bare waist, fingers molding to the heated skin. I love the feel of the hot silk, and my hands want more. Searching hands creep across over the ridges, to the valley of his spine.

Trembling hands, overwhelmed with sensation, move up. I feel the muscles shift beneath the smooth heat, bunching, releasing. Just like my heart is. Leaving his waist, I discover the hills and valleys of this new world. Noah's t-shirt rides up as my hands reach for his shoulders, wanting to see if they are just as smooth and sculpted and scorching.

With a gasp Noah pulls back, wide eyes looking almost... scared. My hands slide down, and Noah's shirt tumbles after them, until all three rest at his waist. Did I do something wrong?

Then I hear the almost silent whirr of the garage door. Oh, Alexis is home. Noah's sensitive Were hearing would have picked up the sound. We scramble back to our upright positions, returning computers to our laps, trying to get our breathing under control.

I glance at Noah to find his eyes full of nothing but laughter. I grin back, glad my overactive insecurities aren't getting any more fuel.

"Am I allowed to mention mother of the year is coming up, just in case she wants to start collecting awards?"

I throw him a don't-you-dare look. "My guess is she'll go to the office."

I watch Noah's face and see my prediction is correct. His face widens with surprise as his sensitive ears hear Alexis's heels stride down the path and away from our house.

I nudge him with my shoulder. "Told you."

He shakes his head, and I'm reminded of the relief I now feel that she no longer surprises me. It means I don't get to experience the disappointment and disbelief that I know underscores Noah's quiet statement. "Unbelievable."

I'm about to suggest we look at biology, deep down hoping that the passion we had to bank so suddenly might find an opportunity to flare again, when Noah's phone dings. He looks down, rolling his eyes when he mumbles Mitch's name.

His thumb swipes the screen, and his brows come down. Blue eyes come up to meet mine, no longer light with laughter. "Mitch needs me to check something out."

"Now?"

"Yeah, sorry."

Like straight away? I wait for an explanation for the urgency, but Noah is collecting his computer, stuffing it and his books into his bag.

"Okay."

Was that as pathetic as it sounds?

Noah stops, and I think his shoulders drop an inch. "He didn't say why. I don't think it's anything major, but I'll head home and check it out anyway."

"Sure." I smile, because isn't that what an understanding-girlfriend-who-desperately-wants-to-be-an-insider does?

"We'll talk biology tomorrow. If we're in public, I might actually write something that makes sense."

My smile becomes a little more genuine. I don't doubt Noah's feelings for me.

Once Noah is gone, I pick up the worn, rumpled copy of *The Outsiders*. Ponyboy learns that some things connect us beyond our wealth or class. I live that every day with Noah.

I flick it back onto the coffee table. I've read the whole thing. I know that Ponyboy looks for doors to open. And I know that although he finds some that open to whole new worlds, I also know that some not only stay shut, but firmly locked.

13

NOAH

You need to see this PRONTO

This had better not be Forgotten Fire's latest video clip. As I tap impatient fingers on the steering wheel, fed by the frustration that I'm creating more secrets with Eden, I admit why I left in such a rush. Mitch wouldn't call me home unless this was significant.

Whatever prompted that single line has me edging the speed limit the whole way home.

"You're home early." Mom is sitting in the dining area, photos spread out over the table. Scrapbooking night has grown to scrapbooking year.

"Yeah, we finished early."

"I'm pretty sure you don't just go there to study."

My eyes bug out to twice their size. Did she just imply what I think she's implying? "What?"

"Well, you guys walk the dogs, eat pizza, solve world peace. All the usual stuff teens do."

That's what I thought she meant. "We were both a bit done, so we decided to have an early one."

Mom gives my lame explanation the look it deserves. Chin

pulled in, one brow arched. "Right. Well, I made some lamb hotpot if you want some."

My stomach simultaneously sinks and clenches as I realize I haven't eaten, and lamb hotpot is going to have to go in there.

"Thanks, I'll get some later. I've got to check something with Mitch."

"Sure, honey. I'll warm it up when you're ready."

I head up the stairs as my stomach drops another few feet. I wonder what I've 'got to see.'

Mitch is in his room, correction, his and Tara's room. A double bed takes up most of the space, the rest sucked up by the extra wardrobe we managed to cram in. Tara's paintings are on the wall, Mitch's woodwork creations covered beneath various feminine shirts and jeans.

They're both on the bed, his laptop balanced over each one of their legs. Neither looks up when I enter; they heard me coming minutes ago.

"Well?"

Mitch has his serious pants on. What's more worrying, so does Tara. They shuffle on the bed, and I climb over, propping my back against the wall alongside them.

"Here."

Mitch passes the laptop, and I see it's on YouTube. They'd better not have dragged me away from Eden, alone time with Eden no less, for the latest cat video. The title that catches my attention and my own serious pants hitch up.

WEREWOLF SIGHTING — WE TOLD U THEY R REAL!

I press Play, knowing we see these all the time. Usually, amateur jobs that get so few hits they're barely worth acknowledging. But the two Weres beside me are quiet. It's an unsettling absence of light-hearted humor kind of quiet, one that doesn't usually accompany watching these things.

The square screen shows what's probably a camera phone

held by a person running through the forest. He's panting, but it sounds like the huff and puff of an exerted panting, not a scared kind of panting. The picture jerks and jiggles through a forest, the multi-trunked, umbrella-canopied forest you would find in more temperate climates.

The phone is bumped, for a moment angling up to show a twilight sky, then zips back down, leaving you reeling. I don't know how the amateur documentary maker kept hold of it, because it's a big animal that thunders past, a huge furry animal that almost knocked the phone out of his hand.

A huge animal, much too big for its species. A fast animal, far quicker than you would have thought possible.

A wolf.

It runs ahead, not glancing back, unconcerned by the human and the hand videoing it. It powers ahead, all greys and browns, heading for the trees. The camera tilts down, showing a massive paw print in the soil.

Okay, a mutant-sized wolf doesn't prove the presence of Weres.

The camera focuses on the trees then zooms in on the disappearing wolf. The focus readjusts, blurring the tree line, then sharpens. Just in time to see the wolf straighten and shrink, lighten and straighten, just in time to see a human disappear between the grey trunks.

The camera blacks out, like the battery died or its motherboard couldn't handle that much supernatural information. I consider doing the same.

My hands come up to massage throbbing temples. Four eyes are watching me very, very closely.

Now I understand the seriousness, the quietness. The urgency.

There is a stream of comments below. A lot are critiquing the CGI graphics. The odd one claims they refuse to reveal their true identity. One woman claims the guy is her boyfriend and she's pregnant. I look to see how many hits it's had. If this video falls into the obscurity of the World Wide Web then we don't have a situation on our hands.

The numbers, clocking into six digits, do the math for me.

We have a situation on our hands.

"Have you found anything out?"

Mitch shrugs. "It was uploaded two days ago. The vegetation is not from around here. It could be anywhere. And it looks pretty real."

Even if it's not real, it's a little too close to the truth to sit comfortably.

"Well, we know Weres have expanded beyond the natural distribution of the wolf."

It was a contentious decision. It's easier to explain a wolf sighting in Wyoming than somewhere like Australia. But Weres didn't want to be limited. And we were all committed to the Precepts, our secret.

Until now.

"Anything else?"

"It's all over social networking."

I'm struggling to find a word that won't offend any delicate sensibilities. My mouth opens, an 'F' precariously hanging, puckering up my lips.

"Flunky fudge fish?" Tara contributes helpfully.

I look at her. Then look at her again. *Really?*

I suck in a deep breath. "Flunky fudge fish!" That wasn't nearly as satisfying. I take another deep breath. "Who would do something like this?"

"Someone who wants to make some waves."

I want to growl. "Where is this guy's Alpha? It's their responsibility to ensure this doesn't happen."

Mitch rubs his lower lip. "And do what? I don't know if we

have enough power to enforce them. Banishment doesn't carry the same weight it used to."

The growl leaves my body in a rush. Valid point. In our over-populated, uber-connected world, probably not. Technically, I've broken Precepts for Eden. And I don't regret it. Banishment would never have stopped me.

Mitch hasn't finished. "And what if it was an Alpha?"

Silence hangs heavily in the room.

Tara leans forward. "It seems the appearance of the last Precept was timely."

Two hands jam into my hair, staying well away from my mark. "It was the last Precept that started all this."

Tara shakes her head. "I think it addresses what was inevitable."

Mitch stands. "Although the 'who' and 'where' are pretty important, what we need to be asking is 'why?'"

Why would someone deliberately, and publicly, break a Precept?

Tara's voice is small, but it doesn't need to be big for us to hear. "It seems Dad wasn't the only one with ambitions for more."

I think of Seth and his speech. *The Channon pack is destined for more...*

Mitch's eyes widen then turn to me. "By breaking the Precepts, they can claim Prime Alpha."

Flunky fudge fish.

The Smurfs jingle vibrates through the room, and Tara's glances at her phone. The moment she presses the green button, Dana's voice hits every Were ear. "Have you seen it?"

Dana's voice is high pitched, fast. Like she's worried or excited.

Tara climbs off the bed, heading for the door. "Yeah, we're

just deciding what to do now." Tara disappears down the hall, taking the high-pitched response with her.

Mitch crosses his arms. "Well?"

"We need to tell Dad...about the video." And nothing else.

Mitch sighs in a way that says he really doesn't agree. "About the video. Then what?"

"We do nothing."

"What?"

"Everything has a shelf-life on the Internet. We just need to wait for the Kardashians to lose their bikini, and this will go away."

"I don't think this is going away."

"Of course it will. Human attention span is the equivalent of a squirrel on steroids."

The joke hits Mitch's unsmiling face and falls flat. "You know what I mean."

I won't touch my chest. I won't protect my mark. "It's too soon."

"It looks like Weres need a leader."

I've barely been a Were, let alone a leader. "Eden needs more time." I think of her growing spontaneity, how much she's shed that shell. What would something like this do to her? To us?

"She needs to know."

"No." The word is low, final.

"Noah, you're the—"

"Every pack has their Alpha. Weres don't need a leader." My hands clench because every muscle in my body is tangled with tension.

"Apparently, we do."

"I won't choose." I spin on my heel and head for the door. There's nothing more to say.

But apparently, there is. Because a soft breath follows me, carrying three words. Three words that fall, slide across the silent floor, then gain momentum as they follow me out the room. Three words that grow, snowballing until they are indisputable. Snowballing until they have the power to slam between my shoulder blades, spear through my chest, pierce my heart.

"You just did."

14

EDEN

"Mitch seems quiet."

The school is as empty as its parking lot after we stayed back and worked in the library. The whole time we sat at that table with generations of initials scratched in black and blue ink Mitch had been lost in his text. Tara and Noah talked like nothing is amiss. But something is different with Mitch.

When Tara wanted to stop by the art room on our way out, Mitch had grabbed her hand, changed direction down the hall, and walked off without another word. I wonder if I've done anything wrong.

Noah stares straight ahead, like he's paying attention to where we have to go. The same car park in the same school he's been going to his entire high school career. "I think he has a bit on his plate."

I step closer so our arms are brushing, like the contact of our hands isn't enough. "I suppose he's coming to terms with becoming a leader," I muse, "especially when it was something he never considered as a possibility."

Those blue eyes flicker to me but then find the forward-facing position again. "Yeah, it takes some getting used to."

"And we have grad coming up."

"True. He still needs to keep his GPA up."

I nod, although Noah can't see it because the school grounds seem so fascinating. "That carpentry apprenticeship is pretty important to him. At least he has Tara."

Noah's body seems to sink in a way I don't understand. "Yeah, at least he has his mate."

When Noah continues to stare ahead, saying nothing, the unease grows. I don't need to see his face to know he's worried. The emotion carries loud and clear through our proximity, our clasped hands.

And I don't know why. He hasn't explained why he rushed home, why he's worried now. It's the unknown that makes me uneasy. It opens a space, no matter how small. And those niggling doubts, those undermining uncertainties, only need a little crack. A little gap to slip their insidious claws in and latch on.

Is he worried about Mitch?

Has something come between them?

Or someone...

I try to shake off those embryonic fears. "Why don't we go to the Glade? It's been ages."

A run in the Glade is just what we need.

We've reached the Phelan truck, and Noah finally turns toward me, those chiseled lips tipping up on one side, eyebrows quirking up. "Like five days?"

"That's what I said—ages. There was the extended siesta over winter, you know."

"Making up for lost time, huh?"

I take in the spring sun touching that tousled hair, picking up the blond highlights, creating darker depths. Those eyes regard me with love and gentleness. And I feel my own love grow and expand. Almost, almost crowding out the uncertainty.

The physical contact, the sheer emotional intensity of our runs with Noah as a wolf affirms our connection.

I could use some affirmation right about now.

"I think that's a great idea." We turn to see Mitch and Tara approach. Mitch grins, but there's a seriousness in his dark eyes that doesn't match the broad smile.

Tara skips on the spot, barely keeping hold of Mitch's hand. "Oooh, I'm putting money on the black and red wolves!"

Noah snorts, his arm coming around my shoulders. "Eden hasn't eaten that much cheesecake."

It's Tara's turn to snort. "Who are you kidding? That girl's moved on from consuming to dealing, just to supply her habit."

I cross my arms. "Hey, I don't think it can be called dealing if it's free."

Tara grins her mischievous grin. "That's how they all start, get you hooked, then..." She punches her fist into her palm.

I tap my nose with a finger. "I do have a salted caramel number in my fridge."

We giggle as Tara looks like she's contemplating my offer. She puckers up her mouth in determination. "You've got to have gained a pound. It'll be enough to give us a fighting edge."

We turn to our respective guys. They're both looking at each other; Mitch has his arms crossed, eyes narrowed, looking like he's challenging Noah to something a bit more serious than a race at the Glade. "Scared?"

I realize Noah's taking far longer to decide than I thought he would. Since when did he have to think twice? "If you don't want to, that's fine."

"Of course we do," Tara says, already opening the truck door.

I look to Noah, needing to know if he wants this. It feels like he does, but something is holding him back.

"Let's do it." Noah smiles, but it sounds more like an ultimatum.

The trip to the Glade mostly involves Tara and me talking about the upcoming Wyoming State Open Day. Noah turns to me once, mouth open like he's going to say something. But those sculpted lips snap shut again. I pretend it doesn't make me nervous.

We pull into the dirt carpark to find four other cars already lined up beneath the trees. Disappointment has me frowning. We've always had the Glade to ourselves.

Noah's breath escapes in a huff. "Great."

I hope we can still go for a run. "Why are they here?"

Noah looks at me with those serious eyes again, the ones that make me nervous. "I'll show you."

Tara pauses in opening her door. "You haven't told her?"

Hasn't told me what?

Noah frowns at Tara. "I was waiting for the right time."

She smiles sweetly, a little artificially. "Well, it looks like you've been given the gift of the present."

Noah doesn't answer, just climbs out and waits for me to join him. Mitch still hasn't said a word. He's certainly epitomizing the strong, silent type.

We walk through the green tunnel to the Glade. Noah is quiet as he holds my hand, and Mitch is quieter as he holds Tara's. Without the usual I'm-going-to-whoop-your-hairy-butt banter, the silence leaves an uninterrupted rein to my anxious imagination. I bite my lip, knowing the questions multiplying in my mind will probably be answered soon. The discomfort distracting me from the knowledge that I might not like the answers.

As we enter the Glade, we see a group of people at the head of the green circle; they're all clustered around the Precept rock. Noah slows, one foot taking a split second longer to overtake its pair before picking up the pace again. If I didn't spend every spare second watching, admiring...memorizing this guy then I would have missed it. The fact that I don't recognize any of the Weres multiplies those questions until their overcrowded presence starts to hurt. My lip hasn't left the grip of my teeth.

There is one person, one voice, which seems to stand at the head of the largely male group. I look to the three Weres with me to see what they think, looking for some clues of how to process this. Noah's eyes have narrowed, his chest expanded. Tara straightens while, Mitch visibly hardens, lips thinning and muscles tensing.

I'm not sure why, but we just went on high alert.

The group has already sensed our approach, and they fall silent as they turn to watch us cross the grass.

Tara walks a little faster, coming to the front of our group. She releases Mitch's hand, and he steps beside her. "Hello, Seth."

Seth turns, the barest slip of a smile angling his lips. He scans us all slowly, tilting his head in what could only be described as arrogance.

"Hi, guys." Tara addresses the rest of the group. They all nod, deference apparent in the way their eyes tilt down, their shoulders drop. There's a round of rumbled 'Tara' or 'Alpha' as they return the greeting. So, these are all Channons.

"Great minds think alike, huh? We were discussing the game changer."

Game changer?

Tara shakes her head. "We came here to run."

I look to Noah, whose eyes flicker to me, and I feel something move and shift, but I don't know what. It feels scratchy, prickly. My eyes scan the group, about five Weres, all young and strong, are all staring at me. At the only human.

And all of a sudden, instead of being part of the group, I instantly feel like the outsider I am.

What's worse, I've figured out the emotions shifting within

the tense body beside me. Noah is uncomfortable with me being here.

My eyes fall to the ground, instantly regretting that I suggested this outing. But wounded eyes never reach the grass. They're caught by the Precept rock. Trapped by an extra line that now sits below the original four. Fixed on the *game changer*.

HE WHO IS ABOVE THE LAW IS THE LAW

Eyes wide with shock fly back to the tense bodies around me. Seth is the only one watching my reaction, his little posse are all watching the three Weres they face. Mitch and Tara are just as preoccupied with them. Noah doesn't need to look; I know he can feel my shock and confusion. I wonder if he can sense the hurt that he didn't tell me. At being excluded.

Seth crosses his arms, his head giving a single nod to the side. "It seems the food web just got a new top tier."

"That's not what the Prime Alpha is about, Seth." Tara's voice remains low, tight.

The Prime Alpha. The term sounds intimidating. All-encompassing and prescriptive at the same time. Final. Fated. Prophetic.

Seth doesn't say a word. He just looks at Tara, never verbally disagreeing, but quite obviously disagreeing. I don't know much about Were etiquette, but he looks quietly defiant.

Mitch shifts subtly, coming a little closer to Tara, skillfully creating a united front.

Seth's posse starts to drift apart, some Weres moving to the right, others stepping back and heading to the tree line. They want this conversation to end.

"Who?" The word slips out before I can call it back. Those questions have finally gained substance and are demanding some answers.

Tara turns to look at me. "No one knows."

Mitch speaks straight ahead. "No one's stepped up."

Noah takes a step forward, bringing me with him. "We don't need some super-leader. Weres have their Alphas, their packs. They don't need a dictator to tell them what to do."

"You're wrong." Seth never raises his voice. He doesn't need to. We are in nature's auditorium with a bunch of super-hearing Weres. Each one would be registering every word. "Weres have no direction, no purpose. They're a loaded gun without a target."

"We don't need a Prime Alpha," Noah growls, his hand clenching around mine.

Seth smirks a little and continues like Noah's angry words were never said. "It just needs the right Were."

"Seth." It's Tara's voice that cuts in, carrying the authority of an Alpha. "You should go home now."

Seth's head tilts down and a single brow arches up, giving the compliant gesture a sarcastic slant. "See you at the Council." He takes two steps back and starts to turn. But as his body twists, he starts to change. There's a flash of skin, the wolf tattoo with its Channon mark blazing across his chest, and four paws hit the ground. It is a brown wolf that powers toward the trees. He never looks back at the Alpha he just disobeyed.

The moment he changes, I feel it. His anger. But not the hot, wild anger you'd expect. No, it's a hard anger. An anger contained by steely determination.

It looks like this gun has been loaded.

And it has a target.

"What's a Council?"

Noah shifts, and I can feel his discomfort. Tara's hands are on her hips, "You didn't tell her that, either?"

"It was only decided yesterday."

The excuse sounds lame, even to me.

Mitch is the one that answers. "A Council is like a court of law."

I turn to Noah. So far, all I'm getting is half-answers. "A Were was filmed changing, and it got onto YouTube."

"Actually, it went off the Richter Scale on YouTube," Tara cuts in.

"And he's been identified. Some guy from the far end of the state."

"When was this?"

Noah's mouth tightens. "Last week."

There is so much to process. Mitch is watching me with his serious blue eyes. Tara is looking at Noah with her ticked-off hazel gaze. Noah is looking at me like he's trying to tell me something with those compelling summer eyes. Is he trying to answer the question that is probably undeniable in mine?

Why didn't you tell me?

But I look away. Because I already know the answer.

So instead, I smile as I grab Noah's hand, heading for the trees. "So, I'm putting a chocolate cheesecake down on us. You ready, Tara?"

Y*ep, it's him all right.*
The strapping piece of stupidity standing all proud in the center of the Glade is the Were from the YouTube clip. All around him are the Alphas and pack representatives from the North West. Phelans, Channons, Lyals, Tates. In front of Daniel —every Were now knows this guys name—stands his own Alpha, John Tate. Daniel looks straight ahead, no one but John in his vision. Certainly not the Precept rock right beside John, the one spelling out the law he disregarded. Despite the number of bodies, the Glade is a whole lot quieter than it usually is. A silence full of judgement.

This is my fist Council. Actually, it's the first real Council in generations. Weres are generally Precept-abiding people. The last Alpha to banish a Were was me, and that was pretty extreme circumstances. Dad said they are short and sweet. The Alpha speaks, the Were responds, the Alpha makes the ruling. Bing, bang, absolute-irreversible-boom.

John Tate, Mr. Judge and Jury, steps up. Big and brawny like an Alpha, although a little more potbellied than most.

"We are here to discuss Daniel's actions. We ha   ll seen the evidence. It is irrefutable. This Council does not have the burden of proof, but the weight of his sentence. Daniel, what do you say about your actions?"

The audience turns to Daniel. Even I know remorse earns leniency in any court of law. But Daniel isn't a poster boy for hunched shoulders, downcast eyes. He turns slowly, tall and straight, looking at those around him with an open, challenging gaze. Like this was the audience he was waiting for rather than dreading.

"I did what needed to be done."

What?

Daniel is still turning, addressing each and every Were. "The time for Weres is changing." He stops, his arm shooting straight out like an arrow, his finger pointing at the Precepts. "That proves it."

The Tate Alpha doesn't move to look at the rock, but quite a few heads do. I resist the urge to shuffle. This is not how a Council goes.

John crosses his arms. "You broke a Precept, undermining the trust, and risking the lives of all Weres."

With his arm still pointing at the blasted rock with the blasted extra Precept, Daniel shouts, "Why do we hide?"

A collective breath is sucked in around the Glade. It practically draws the trees in as all the air is dragged into shocked lungs.

Daniel stops, his back to the Precept rock, his Alpha. "How many of you have asked yourself this question?"

Although no one answers, there's a low hum of noise. A few feet are shuffling, that collective breath held, some Weres' eyes searching others, some sliding and looking away.

"I have." Stunned faces turn and all that air is expelled in Seth's direction. *What did he just say?*

Tara turns to face her pack member behind her. Seth steps

forward, until he is almost flush with Tara. Almost. "Daniel gives voice to a question many Weres have been asking themselves."

Tara pulls herself up, going all Alpha on Seth. No one speaks up at Council, certainly not a non-Alpha. "That's enough, Seth."

"It's a valid question...Alpha." Seth finishes the statement, the one that just defied his Alpha's command, with a submissive incline of his head, the deferent use of Tara's title. My teeth clench at the blatant pseudo-compliance.

Mitch steps behind Tara, angry and dark. Seth practically curls his lip at the Phelan behind his Alpha.

Tara has a decision on her hands. Command Seth step back and shut up, and risk him defying her in front of dozens of Weres. Or respond to his question...essentially backing down.

It's a lose-lose situation.

Tara's chin has just jutted up when Daniel's voice booms through the Glade. "There is no reason."

Everyone swings their focus back to Daniel, who has again fanned the winds of discontent, and neatly taken the spotlight off Tara and Seth. Everyone focuses on him but me. I watch Seth cross his arms as he watches Daniel along with everyone else. Why do I get the sense that even without a resolution to his little mutiny, Seth is satisfied with the outcome?

"What could we be if we didn't hide?" My attention joins the other Weres. Daniel seems intent on digging himself deeper. He does another slow pirouette. "Our strength, our presence on every continent, our unique skills are wasted if we act as if they don't exist." His fist thumps his chest, a low thud that carries in the silent Glade. "That we don't exist." He's almost finished the complete circle. "You can't say you don't feel it."

Everyone's eyes are scanning everyone else's. I'm not sure what they're looking for. Looking to see who thinks that's a load of crap?

Who agrees?

Daniel's mouth opens again, and I really don't want to hear what he has to say next.

"Silence!" John roars.

It appears obeying his Alpha is not totally forgotten because Daniel complies.

"Your words do nothing but incite discontent through generations of peace. Our children deserve better than the world you propose. For breaking our law, for treason against all Weres hold true, Daniel Tate, you are banished."

Daniel doesn't react, doesn't even blink. He was either expecting this...or he doesn't care. He squares his shoulders and schools his face. I can't tell if he's hiding a scowl or a smile. Daniel exits stage left, past his Alpha and his pack, never looking back at the kind that have now exiled him.

No one moves, shocked at what just happened. Banishment is unheard of. And this is the second in the space of a few months. That feeling is moving inside me again, and there's little I can do to calm it.

From the corner of my eye, I see one person move. Seth's arms drop to his sides as his chest expands, like there's something inside feeding and growing.

Shoulders that want to drop a few feet stay still and tense. I wish Eden were here, so I knew whether I was reading this right.

The deed done, the Weres begin to disperse. Some have a long drive home. One family will have one less member in their car, which is something none of us wanted to see. Tara would have found this Council particularly difficult. I've seen what the loss of a member can do to a family, but she's had to live it.

I look at the Tate Alpha, knowing it's a tough choice to live with. I look at the rest of the Weres disappearing down the path. A choice that needs to be made for the safety of all.

Seth is the last to leave, following the procession across the green grass. As he walks past me, he sees me watching. His hazel gaze grabs mine and doesn't back down, not that I expected it to. He leans in as he approaches me. "The Tate Alpha is right." Surprise has my eyebrows wanting to head for the canopy. "Our children do deserve better."

A few of the Weres in front of him stiffen, a couple look down. One or two look at each other. They all heard what he said.

I tilt my chin up, looking at him hard, making sure my voice is just as sure. "Yes, they do."

I don't break my gaze from Seth's retreating back. Letting anyone who may still be watching know how solid my belief is.

But it's all a show. Because here, inside the wide-open world of the Glade, the place where magic hangs and time stands still, I feel the trees move in. My eyes move around the closely packed sentries, the dozens of Weres flowing past me, feeling the weight of something sinking through my chest, settling in my gut. I purposely don't look at the Precept rock.

A handful of Alphas are left behind. Mom and Dad, Mitch and Tara, John and his Alpha mate, and me.

John scratches his chin. "It's not a good day when a choice like that has to be made."

I sigh. "You did what needed to be done, John."

John's green eyes catch mine. We now have something in common. Living with the decision of banishment.

Dad's eyes squint a little, looking very chief-of-police. "What I'm wondering is who was holding the camera."

Mom's eyes widen. "Daniel wasn't alone."

Tara's eyes are just as large. "How many others are there?"

We all quieten as we digest it all.

Daniel's words. Seth's actions. Rules and law are slowly being eroded.

Dad is stroking his lip. "There was some truth to Daniel's words."

I spin around. "You're kidding, right?"

John has crossed his arms. "He's right. Things are changing." He turns to Dad. "There's more unrest than we thought."

I cross my arms, too, but I doubt John has the same feeling slithering in his belly. "The last Precept has started something."

Tara shakes her head. "I think it may have fanned the flames of something that was already there."

I rub my own lip, not entirely convinced. It's inevitable that she would think of Kurt here, today.

With my head tilted down, I get to see Tara's shoes shift in the grass. "Maybe we do need a Prime Alpha."

I don't scowl, although I really want to. I'm getting tired of the Prime Alpha talk. "He's not the answer to our problems. What is he going to do?"

Tara looks at me squarely. "Well, I could sure use some backup."

I deflate, because that wretched feeling isn't in my gut any longer. It simultaneously sinks and expands like a black balloon. Heading to my feet and anchoring me in the too-small Glade, compressing my chest from the inside out.

The way Mitch is looking at me doesn't help. His eyes are screaming so loud I want to cover my ears. I can translate every single word that is being hurled in my direction.

I turn away, lifting heavy feet and dragging my pounding brain, heading for the car.

I will not choose.

16

EDEN

I've had to wait long, anxious hours to get some answers. We can't email or even text about it, seeing as Weres keep everything off record. And we certainly can't talk about it at school. All through Biology, Math, Chem, English, I did little but fiddle with my pen, jiggle my leg. And just to draw out time, I had two frees. Noah was all smiles and grins like everything was normal. Mitch was even more serious, if that was possible. Tara got to be the buffer between her two best friends.

Then we had to drop off Dana like we always do. Today the bright, substance-less chatter had my teeth on edge. I had to tell myself it's not Dana's fault. She already knows everything that happened.

Then we had afternoon tea with Adam and Beth. Beth, bright and welcoming, like I'm part of the family. Adam, reserved and polite, like you would expect with a visitor. The warring halves of my heart represented in Noah's dark-haired mother and carbon-copy father.

It's well into the afternoon when we finally sit under Grandfather Douglas. Noah rests against his grooved bark, my back against his front, his arms and legs circling me. Mitch leans back, long legs stretched before him as Tara curls into his side, one leg slung over his. The spring winds rustle through the porcupine branches above us, blowing my hair in my face. Before I get a chance, Noah's fingers brush it away. Like he knows I wear it down for him, even though it drives me nuts.

I grab his hand, brushing his fingers with my lips in thanks. His hand squeezes my own. "How did it go?"

I feel Noah's chest expand and deflate. "Daniel wasn't very apologetic. He's been banished."

"Oh." I know what Daniel did was serious. I've seen the clip. But I know what it's like to be someone who's not quite the same as everyone else. To try and fit in somewhere you don't. That's about to become Daniel's life.

I pick up a pine needle, all dry and brown, twirling it in my fingers. Its motion mimics the sensation I can feel churning behind me. "He did it on purpose?"

Mitch grabs a handful of needles, crushing them in his palm. "He said it's time we stop hiding."

"You're not serious!"

Mitch looks up. His eyes have never been more serious.

Noah lets out a breath, fanning my hair. "Yeah, this darned Prophecy is getting everyone edgy."

That's not edgy. That's Precept-breaking talk. "Well, what does the Prime Alpha do?"

I feel Noah shake his head behind me. "There's no job description."

"What does it have the potential to do?"

"Nothing new from what I can tell. Every pack already has an Alpha."

I see Mitch move, leaning a little to the side, his head dropping down to brush Tara's. All I can see is his scrunched brow, the tense mouth. His face says he doesn't agree, but I'm not sure with which bit. His blue eyes look up. "What do you think it all means, Eden?"

I stop mid-twirl. Why would he ask me? "Ah, I'm not sure."

Tara turns a little in Mitch's arms. "C'mon Edes, you've seen the rock, you've seen the clip. What's your opinion?"

"Doesn't everything happen for a reason with you guys?"

Noah grunts behind me, and I'm not exactly sure what that means.

"Well, what does the Prophecy predict?"

"Again, no-one knows." For some reason, I know Noah is staring at Mitch.

Mitch doesn't drop his gaze. "He's the Were to rule all Weres."

Noah snorts like he's heard that one before. "And then what?"

Mitch points a pine-needle in our direction. "Well, I'm not sure Daniel is reconsidering his actions. And a lot of people saw his lack of remorse, heard his sentiments."

Tara flops a little, her rounded back folding into Mitch. "And Seth agreed with him."

I think of Seth's passive-aggressive defiance. "So, he's some kind of law enforcer?"

Noah is shaking his head again. "The last thing we need is some super-dude running around being the firm paw of the law."

I smile a little at Noah's joke and feel his arms tighten around me. Then the smile fades when I remember Kurt. I don't look at Tara as the words he said, so chilling and angry, rise in my mind...*I had plans, a destiny to be something more than just an Alpha.*

I think of the stilted explanation Noah had given me in the car home from the Glade. His denial that the Prime Alpha was needed. "What would you want him, or her, to do?"

Tara gives me a fist to the air in feminist solidarity.

But Mitch isn't in the mood for social statements. "Stand up and lead, for starters," he growls.

"And then what?"

Tara stares off into space. "He would give us something to stand for."

I think about that. Weres seemed so peaceful, content with living their lives, secret but connected to their kin. Now that seems to be changing, and with the door of possibility being forcibly opened, a world of opportunities awaits.

"How do you decide who's going to do it?"

At this question, Tara leans forward. "I think he's already been chosen."

"Why do you say that?"

"It makes sense. The final Precept wouldn't appear without him"—Tara winks at me—"or her, being chosen. Otherwise, the challenge of who is going to be Prime Alpha would be an almighty fight."

By people like Kurt. Or Seth. Or maybe even Daniel.

"Then why hasn't he stepped up?"

Tara shrugs. "Maybe she doesn't know."

Mitch has another handful of pine needles being pulverized to dust in his hand. "Maybe he doesn't care."

Noah stiffens. "Maybe he's waiting for something."

Like what?

Mitch arches a brow, blue eyes on me again. "What would you do?"

My own brows hike up. "Me?"

"Sure, you've asked the most intelligent, unbiased questions so far. What would you do?"

I bite my lip. Noah has gone very still behind me.

Weres are a powerful species. But is their strength in their raw power? I think of the big heart I can practically feel beating against my back, of Noah's patience and protectiveness. Of Mitch's steadiness and passion, of Tara's bubbly, nurturing spirit. Telling me there is more to Weres than their animal strength.

And is their power better off in the open? Exposing themselves is a dangerous sentiment. The consequences unimaginable. Wouldn't it be more useful behind the scenes?

I suppose it depends on what they're working toward.

I shrug; I know what I would do if I was a leader. "Make a difference."

Noah's arms tighten around me. "How?"

I shrug again. "That, I don't know. But give people, or Weres, a purpose they believe in, and they will follow."

Silence descends again. No one speaks. Noah is quiet behind me, and I can feel a kaleidoscope of emotions churning back there. They're difficult to distinguish, but they feel faintly hopeful, maybe a confusing sense of pride. Mitch is looking at me like he's rearranging some stuff in his head.

I don't mind. This is the most open conversation I've had with them. The most inclusive one. Warmth spreads through my chest, matching the heat behind me.

I look to Tara to see what she's thinking, just as she springs to her feet. "Why don't we go for a swim?"

I arch a brow. It seems Tara has moved on.

Hang on a sec, a swim? The water will be freezing! I turn to look over my shoulder, to see what Noah thinks of the idea. But Noah is looking at Mitch, who is watching him right back.

Noah shakes his head. "Nah, it's not warm enough."

"What? We always go swimming this time of the year."

"Yeah, but Eden would turn into a Popsicle."

"Swimming is a great spectator sport." I wouldn't mind watching Noah swimming, tracts of body exposed, especially that chest that I never get to see, water running down his smooth skin...

Another glance passes between Noah and Mitch. "Yeah, I don't feel like it either."

Tara's hands are on her hips. "No twin talk, you two. Share it with the group."

"Twin talk?"

"Yeah, those two communicating between themselves. It used to drive me nuts." Those hazel eyes narrow. "It still does."

I suppose Tara is entitled to demand open and honest communication.

Mitch flushes, looking down to pick up his own pine needle. "I just don't feel like swimming."

Those hazel eyes narrow another smidgen. "Mitch Phelan, you're half wolf, half dolphin."

Noah jumps in, almost like he's rescuing his brother. "We could go for a walk, see how they're doing with the foundations for the house."

Mitch stands up, eyes alive with enthusiasm. "Hey, yeah. Another couple of weeks and the frame will be up."

Tara's lips turn down for a moment, and I wonder if she's going to call them out. "Fine, but we go next week."

Another look passes between the two brothers. Mitch shrugs, "Sure, although finals are coming up."

I stand, and Noah follows. He seems intent on brushing off the pine needles that stick like Velcro. Then he grabs my hand without quite looking me in the eye.

Tara is already moving away from Grandfather Douglas. "So, should I be worried I could get lost in one of these foundation holes?"

Noah finds another pine needle and flicks it at Tara. "Probably, I'd say they're deeper than three feet."

"Zip it, Alpha heir."

We head to the clearing, the banter lighter than I've seen it in a while. Even Mitch is joking about his rise to Alphadom.

I manage to laugh but can't quite bring myself to contribute. That look that passed between Noah and Mitch, their 'twin talk' moment, hangs on, refusing to leave.

And now it's here; I can't deny its implication.

Because despite the deep connection I have with Noah, maybe because so much passes between us, another revelation lines up beside the others.

Noah is keeping secrets.

17

NOAH

Why are all universities pale and square? Big cream buildings with rows of big square windows overlooking big rectangles of uniform grass.

I think it's to make them look scholarly and intimidating.

Well, architects seem to have a good understanding of the human psyche, because Wyoming State manages to do a little of both.

The main building, bigger and more cream than the others, sits in the center of a square, all formidable and I'm-so-important. Green and white banners, you never get away from pine trees in Wyoming, hang from the second floor for the open day. At least it doesn't have columns.

There are eager soon-to-be-graduates wandering everywhere, some wide-eyed, others keeping their cool like they don't really care if they're accepted. Eden's head is in the map we were given by a preppy-looking student at the front entrance. I look at that dark hair falling over creamy cheeks, eyes scanning the page.

My arm comes to rest on her hip as I look over her shoulder. "Isn't it the same as their web page?"

Eden's lips twitch at the reference to the amount of time spent in front of her laptop, but she doesn't look up. "This one fits in my pocket better."

I did have to convince her not to bring it. I lean in to kiss her cheek. This is what we need, time together, being normal, keeping it light.

Eden's hand comes up to stroke my cheek. As she looks up, something catches her eye. "Here they are."

Tara and Mitch walk toward us, holding hands. Looking normal and even light themselves. Tara skips a little, and even Mitch's serious smile is a little less serious today. The little shock wave, okay fine, the tsunami from the YouTube clip, has done what all waves do. They build, peak, dissolve, and you never know they were there. It had taken a few days, but a laughing goat compilation had eventually taken the coveted trending slot. With Daniel banished, talk of the Prime Alpha should die down.

My brows dip a little when I see Dana jog up beside them.

"Hi, guys"—she smiles brightly—"thought I'd check out my options for next year."

"Good thinking." Eden's shoulder presses a little more into my side, the heat noticeable even on this spring day. "Nice jacket."

Dana glances down, like she's not sure how she's ended up wearing a Wyoming State blazer. "I totally forgot I had this on." She spins on the spot. "A friend lent it to me. But I think it kinda suits me."

Eden smiles. "Is there any area you are particularly interested in?"

Dana waves a hand through the air. "I'm not pinning myself down to anything specific, yet."

"The place is packed and kinda big." Tara turns to look from one side to the other. "I'm thinking we divide and conquer."

"Great idea," Dana gushes. She turns to look at Eden and me. "What are you two checking out first?"

Tara rolls her eyes. "It doesn't really matter, we're finding the arts faculty first, you need to start 'pinning down' your options."

Did Dana's smile just tense a little? She turns to Tara. "Sure, which way?"

Tara shrugs. "I have no idea, but the helpful peeps standing at every corner can point us in the right direction."

Mitch gives us a wave as Tara turns toward a blonde girl standing not far from us.

I look at Eden, whose happy smile at the prospect of investigating this educational maze together matches mine. "Where should we start?"

Eden grabs my hand, already knowing where to go. The map she tucks into her pocket is redundant after all the time she's spent memorizing it online.

We walk past Mitch, Tara, and Dana, their three heads tilted over a map held by the blonde. "We'll see you guys in an hour?"

Tara waves a hand without looking up. Mitch nods and almost smiles. We head down the path dividing two rectangles of lawn, off to who-knows-where but I don't care. It's me and Eden and a future I want to believe in. I squeeze the hand holding mine, in reply Eden nudges my shoulder with her own.

Dana's voice, carrying on a sigh, follows us. "They're so cute together."

Judging by the way Eden shakes her head, a little smile on those rose lips, you didn't need to be a Were to hear that.

Eden heads west, and seeing as I don't need my head in a map, I check out more of the buildings. There are old buildings and new buildings, big ones and little ones, popular and less popular destinations. To add to the eclectic mix are old people and young people, trendy kids and alternate types, Eden and me, all with one thing in common. All excited and hopeful about what this place could mean for their future.

We come to one of the newer buildings, the ones with lots of grey and glass. Across the front is stamped DEPARTMENT OF POLICING AND JUSTICE STUDIES in old, very important looking letters. Eden's brought me to my faculty first?

Her excited eyes are scanning the building. I've moved on to scanning the people entering and exiting. There are lots of guys, but a good representation of girls, too. One dude, built like a chiseled piece of steak, walks past us, but his head stays trained on Eden. Even once he's down the steps and on the path, I narrow my eyes at him, my arm coming around her shoulder, the movement expanding my chest. Eden, still taking in the architecture, slips her arm around my waist and snuggles a little closer. It's all I need to forget the ogling dufus, and I turn back to the front.

"Come on, we don't have much time."

Time for what? I'm about to ask when a guy, a mop of black curly hair falling onto his glasses, steps forward, several bags hanging over his shoulder. "Welcome, thanks for taking the time to find out about our Diploma of Policing."

"Thanks." I take the calico show bag, glancing at the papers and pamphlets inside. Dad's already had these sitting on the coffee table at home for weeks. I doubt there's anything in there I haven't read.

"The Head of Faculty will be saying a few words in the auditorium in ten minutes."

Eden throws a quick 'thanks' before tugging me through the door.

"You knew about the speech, didn't you?"

"Yep. So did anyone else who read this." She holds up the opening day booklet. "Let's see if there's anything you don't know."

The way to the auditorium is clearly posted, so I don't get to find out if Eden also memorized the floor plan. Inside, we walk a few steps up to a middle row and sit. The room is full enough to create a low hum, but not jam packed so that you have to sit adjacent to a stranger.

Eden grabs my hand, and I love the excitement that buzzes through her palm. It's not even her faculty, and she's loving it. This is how I saw my future. At Wyoming State with Eden. Responsibility on the horizon, but not in my present.

A young woman in a suit steps up to the lectern. "I would like to welcome Patrick Sheldon, our Head of Faculty here at Wyoming State. Patrick spent forty years in the police force, retiring as a police commissioner, and is now involved in several of our research projects. We are extremely lucky to have someone of his experience and distinction. Patrick." The woman steps back as we all dutifully clap.

And Humpty steps up. Not literally, but the round, short, shiny bald man may have been one of his offspring. It's a little hard to imagine this guy instilling fear in Little Miss Muffet, let alone a criminal.

Patrick cum Humpty smiles as he places his hands on the lectern. "Welcome to your first step to the greatest profession in the world. This is your opportunity to begin a career that will truly make a difference in the lives of others. To be the next generation that will serve and protect."

For someone so round, Patrick's voice sure is hard. It slates through the room, full of authority and power. He's certainly got my attention.

"But if you're considering this career, consider this. You will need the commitment and dedication to achieve the appropriate GPA. You will need a clear criminal history."

So far so good.

"You need to know that you will always be under public

scrutiny, on or off the job, for every action you take, or don't take. You need to learn to be focused, guarded, and tough. You need to understand that that action based on emotion can have life-long consequences for others."

I shift a little in the lecture seat, bumping those fold down desks beside my thigh. Eden notices my movement, but Patrick keeps speaking, reclaiming her attention.

"Because as a police officer, you are not only the first line of defense for your family and your community, but society as a whole. You are also their future leaders." He smiles a proud smile, shoulders dropping back, chest popping out. "There is no greater honor and privilege"—he scans the crowd, eyes narrowing just a touch—"or duty and responsibility."

I want to sink down under the weight of those words. But Patrick hasn't finished.

"So, if you want to take the path of truth, make a choice. Wyoming State University will be the one to get you there."

We all clap again, Eden far more enthusiastically than I would like. She turns to me. "That was a great speech."

That speech hit a little too close to home. I'm talking words that went straight past the front lawn and invaded my too-full head.

"It was like listening to my dad." In one form or another. Were or human.

"Do you want to ask some questions?"

"Nah. I've got all the pamphlets and info, and they look pretty busy."

Eden squeezes my hand, no doubt picking up on the turmoil that's churning in my gut. "Second thoughts?"

"Humpty certainly didn't sell police work as a fairy tale."

"You already knew that, and it never bothered you before."

"Yeah, I suppose it just hit home. It's going to mean making

some pretty tough calls that will affect a whole lot of people."
And Weres.

"That's a no-brainer. You were born to do this, Noah."

That's what makes it worse. "Yeah."

"We'll do it together."

That's what I'm hoping. I just don't know how to make that happen. "Yep, you're right." I stand and grab her hand. "Now, let's check out your neck of the campus."

Eden looks at me a little longer, obviously not entirely convinced. A barely perceptible sigh escapes, so minuscule I wonder if I imagined it. Particularly when she gives me a bright smile, turns, and heads for the door. Like Caesar on a leash, I'm right behind her.

As we head to the south end of the campus, I know exactly where we're going. There's only one place here that Eden would know as well as the recipe to a New York cheesecake.

The veterinary science building is one of the more ancient ones, a senior citizen of Wyoming State. It actually has columns. There are fewer people here, not surprising considering the GPA you need to consider placing a toe on these yellowed steps.

Eden just stands there. We don't need to be touching for me to feel her excitement. Any stranger could see it in eyes that look like they just saw Santa and feet that look like they belong to the Easter Bunny.

"Where to first?" I ask.

"I still haven't decided between the labs or the wildlife welfare display."

"We've got time to do both…"

Eden bites her lip, like this is a significant decision. "Wildlife welfare."

I wait, knowing we'll be going there directly, no passing go to collect a calico bag. Eden doesn't disappoint, and we're in a room with tables holding skulls and bones and weird shiny metal things within a few short minutes. Almost like she did, indeed, memorize the floor plan.

There are quite a few people wandering around, mostly nerdy-looking types with their parents. We wander down the tables, Eden looking at the wares, picking up the odd medical-looking instrument, peering at more than the odd skull, totally absorbed. We've reached the head of the room when I see a man, academic enough to be wearing plaid, but too young looking for the Dr. Neil Olsen printed on his name badge.

Eden is looking at yet another skull when he approaches us. "That's an *Ursus Americanus*."

"Only a young black bear, though."

Dr. Olsen's brown eyebrows rise into his brown hair. "That's true. This was a young female, injured by a hunter, but we couldn't save her."

Eden's fingers brush over the smooth bone surface. "That's sad."

She looks up. "It's too bad your wildlife welfare subjects aren't a major here, Dr. Olsen," she says without glancing at his badge, like she already knew his name.

Dr. Olsen smiles as his eyebrows rise. "Are you considering veterinary science at Wyoming State, ah...?"

"Eden St. James, sir. Yes, you offer some unique opportunities here."

"Well, the wildlife welfare section is my baby. We have a wonderful program that is involved in both rehabilitation of injured wildlife and lobbying state and federal governments about policy change."

"That sounds really interesting. I work regularly at Shoshoni, and the wildlife side particularly interests me."

I continue to smile politely although my jaw wouldn't mind dropping an inch. Lobbying politicians? That would involve more than three people in the room.

"Wonderful." An assessing glint sparks in Dr. Olsen's brown eyes. "The president will be graduating this year. Meaning we'll be electing a new one..."

I almost want to pat the guy on his plaid arm. Eden's more of a behind-the-scenes kind of gal.

"Sure, let me know what's involved."

I manage to catch my jaw as it drops, but my lips still make a small sucking sound as they open in surprise.

"Here's my card, Eden. Come and see me next year."

"I look forward to it, Dr. Olsen."

A guy whose acne has yet to clear up captures Dr. Olsen's attention. He bids us goodbye before turning and walking away.

We're barely out of the room when Eden grabs my arm, turning me to face her. "Did you see that?"

She's bouncing, holding the card like it's the recipe for some new cheesecake.

I'm still a bit stupefied. "I didn't think you'd want a role in the limelight."

Eden shrugs one shoulder. "It's not my ideal place to be. But sometimes we have to step up if it's something important."

"Right."

"What?"

"Nothing. I'm just a bit surprised, that's all."

Eden narrows her eyes, playfully jabbing a finger into my chest, right above my mark. "Underestimating the introvert with a mission again, huh?"

My hands go up as I grin. "It would appear so."

Her eyes narrow a smidgen more, making sure I've got the point, and she steps back. "Good. Now we check out the labs."

A tour of the labs involves three laps of benches sporting microscopes with slides of moving blobs and more shiny metal thingies. Eden reads everything, even writes some things down, and generally has more fun than Mitch in a tool shop.

We're back outside the building when a tall mother-hen fussing over her chick which is about to leave the nest, walk past us. As they follow the path around the corner, their conversation floats over to my Were-sensitive ears.

"Everyone has been so welcoming, and it seems like a lovely campus. What do you think, dear?"

"I don't know, Mom. The bigger universities have more electives."

The bigger universities...The ones that Eden could walk into. The ones that her mother doesn't know she's no longer applying for.

I stop in the middle of the grey path, cultured lawn on either side, waiting for those green eyes to turn to me. "Are you sure you want to do this...here?"

Eden looks around at the buildings then back at me. She gives me a half-smile. "You mean because I almost turned into an ice-sculpture over winter?"

"Well, I was actually thinking—"

"Oh, you mean because I've always dreamed of escaping my mother by running away to college?"

"That's more what I—"

"And by choosing Wyoming State I would have to stay?"

I duck my head. "Uh, yeah."

When she doesn't answer, I cautiously look up, breath lodged in my chest. Tilted green eyes, open and honest, look straight into mine. "Yes, I want this."

Eden leans in, those wide eyes not closing until the moment our lips touch. And gifts me with a kiss so full of love, so jam-packed with tenderness, that it steals my breath. And in that moment, I don't care whether I get it back. Because I don't need it.

I just found heaven.

We pull back, eyes locked, her lips smiling just a little, mine slightly parted. I think she made her point.

She quirks a brow, tilted green eyes sparkling. "Okay?"

"Okay."

I step back, hope has that uncomfortable feeling that is always with me shrinking, taking a back seat.

I take Eden's hand again, cocking my head to the side. "We need to meet Tara and Mitch in about twenty minutes. Anything else we need to check out?"

"Well, I wanted to see the memorial gardens..."

And she would know exactly where they are. "Lead the way."

There are more student volunteers waiting beside the wrought iron gates hanging from more of the pale square brick. Two stand on one side, a girl and a guy who look like they're flirting, whilst the person on the other side is on their own, leaning down to look at a flower.

The tall, lean physique tells you it's a guy. It's the pale blond hair tied in a knot between his shoulder blades that confuses you for a second. A knot that is vaguely familiar...

He stands and turns. Green tilted eyes light up when he sees us.

"Hello, Eden."

18

EDEN

There's only been one time in my life that I've looked into eyes the same as mine.

And just like last time, all I can think is *he looks like me!*

Unlike the last one, the guy in front of me is blond. He still has flawless skin that is hard to age, but he's certainly younger than the other man, although I would say a little older than me.

This time, I'm much quicker on the uptake. "Who are you?"

He inclines his head, gentle eyes looking down then back at me. "My name is Orin."

I sense rather than see Noah pull his phone out of his pocket; this time I'm not taking my eyes off the guy in front of me. "I'm just going to text Tara and let her know we'll catch them at home." His voice is soft and serious.

Orin raises his hand, palm up. "I thought we might talk."

He wants to talk? I'm torn between looking at Noah, getting a sense of what he thinks of this situation, and not tearing my gaze from the one *who looks like me*. Like he understands, Noah moves in a little closer.

"I'd like that."

"Let us go somewhere private."

I nod, thinking I should probably reduce the size of my elephant eyes.

Orin enters the memorial gardens through the gate and walks, more like glides, as if he knows exactly where he's going. Paths branch and meander through rounded beds full of butterfly colors and springtime buzzing. Narrower paths, little gravel offshoots, sprout sporadically, inviting you to investigate their seasonal secrets. But Orin stays on the curved main path, every now and again reaching out to brush a branch or a weeping head of flowers. The further we go, the fewer visitors I see.

I finally tear my eyes from the blond knot that's like the one *I used to wear* and turn to Noah. His eyes are full of questions, theories, suspicions, and more questions. Just like the ones that fill my head. He leans in, whispering in my ear, "Wow."

Wow, all right.

At the back of the gardens, we reach a stone arch, words embedded in its curved bow—The Reflection Garden. Noah cocks a wry brow, one that almost has me smiling. It's cordoned off, a sign saying Under Construction hanging from a chain strung across the entry. Orin steps over the chain and floats under the arch, a smiling glance indicating we should follow.

The Reflection Garden is simple and beautiful and certainly not under construction. A pond, clear and glassy, sits in the middle. It reflects the blue sky, the green trees, and the three people that just entered. Emerald lawn surrounds it, stone benches dotted between trees and shrubs and flower beds. The heady scent of spring gives the place life, whilst the absence of sound tells you it's a place of contemplation.

Orin waves a hand at a nearby bench. "You may want to sit."

My hands are torn between wanting to cross my arms and wanting to grab onto Noah with everything I have. Noah knows, and he entwines his fingers with mine. "I'm fine, thanks."

Orin gives a small nod and threads his hands together. He smiles a little, those tilted eyes shining. "How did you react when you discovered Noah was Were?"

Noah stiffens, and I feel energy surge through him. "What did you say?"

Orin's green eyes turn to Noah. "There is nothing to fear. We have known of your kind for a very long time."

We?

Orin turns those tilted eyes, so much like mine, back to me. They are full of calm and something else...acceptance? He waits, pale brows slightly raised.

I think of the time a massive white wolf came to my rescue, then a short while and a painful change later, watched it shrink and transform into Noah. "Ah, well, I had to change some of the assumptions I held about the world, but I managed."

Noah's other hand is as clenched as the one around mine, that energy has settled but not dissipated. "She's been amazing."

Orin smiles again. "That doesn't surprise me. And now you know there is more to this world than meets the eye."

"I've certainly seen that for myself."

"Are you sure you don't want to sit?"

It's Noah that answers. "I think you should get to the point."

Orin does that incline of his head again. "Very well. Our father, Avery, is the—"

"Our father?"

Orin nods, smiling a little. "Yes, the man you met is our father, but you already knew that."

I've never admitted it though. I freeze, my hand in Noah's, my mind in overdrive. *Holy crap, that makes Orin—*

"You are my half-sister, Eden."

Orin was right; I should have sat. I take two shaky steps back and drop onto the stone bench, pulling Noah close beside me.

I have a brother?

I look to Noah, those elephant eyes back again. His blue gaze matches my own.

I have a brother!

Shock has me forgetting to breathe, forgetting to blink. Doing nothing but repeating that one statement over and over.

I have a brother.

"Our father, Avery, is King of the Fae."

19

NOAH

E den is stunned into silence. Her mouth open, like it's looking for words. But empty, because it hasn't found any.

I have to say, I'm glad we're sitting down. I realize I'm getting a taste of how Eden must have felt when she discovered there was more to the world than is supposed to exist. That the supernatural beings you thought belonged in books are guides at your chosen university. Are blood-related to your girlfriend. That the one you already knew was special is special in a whole new way.

Mind. Blown.

I want to take Eden in my arms and shield her as she tries to process this. The girl I love was just served up more secrets, more complications. And a family.

"What are you talking about?" I ask, giving Eden's shock a voice.

"I feel I should explain."

Ah, yeah.

"Fae have always lived amongst humans, as Weres do."

I frown. "Then how come we don't know about you?"

"It was more important to keep our identity as secret."

More important than Weres? "What is it exactly that Fae do?"

"We are protectors of the animal world. Our connection with animals allows us to be their advocates and their champions."

I look at Eden, quirking a brow. "Well, that explains a few things."

Eden closes her mouth then opens it again.

"When humans began degrading the Earth and impacting the lives that depend upon it, we were concerned. But when it not only continued but escalated, we decided to expand our reach."

Eden glances at me again. We are both thinking the same thing. This time she speaks. "What does that mean?"

"Fae can mate with humans, and pass on our gifts to our children."

A few more pieces click into place.

Now Eden frowns. "And then you leave them."

Orin smiles, a gentle smile, maybe a sad smile. "The children must grow up human, understanding them, working with them, bringing change from within."

I frown myself. I think of Eden's life with her single mother. "That seems a little harsh."

Those green tilted eyes look straight at me. "Shielding others from pain is admirable...but not necessarily beneficial."

What is that supposed to mean? Protectiveness has me straightening, moving closer to Eden. *Who runs around impregnating women then leaving them?*

Orin seems to read my thoughts. "It is how we will ensure the survival of Earth."

I don't point out that it doesn't seem to be working.

If I wasn't holding Eden's hand, and she wasn't holding onto mine like a sinking half-Fae, I'd cross my arms. "Does the medieval talk ever raise eyebrows?"

Orin smiles again, only his lips moving in that calm face. "It is very popular with the women."

I snort, shaking my head.

"But wasted. I do not seek relationships with humans."

"So, you talk this Fae policy of yours, but don't subscribe to it."

Orin inclines his head, the most movement we've seen in a while. "Something like that."

Orin turns back to Eden, "Where is your mark?"

Is there anything this guy doesn't know?

Eden's hand comes up to rub behind her ear, in the way she always used to before...I quickly stamp on that little thought, just in case Orin does have some kind of mind-reading abilities.

"Behind my ear."

Orin looks surprised, and for once more than just one set of muscles move. Both blond brows shoot up as his mouth parts. "On your head?"

As opposed to ears being elsewhere?

Eden pulls her hair to the side, leaning a little toward me. Her wildflower scent stirs up the next wave of protectiveness. Orin steps forward and looks at the five-pointed star resting within its circle. Then just stands there, stiller than still.

Eden picks up on the too-still weirdness. "Why?"

"It is usually on the chest."

I wonder what would happen if I mentioned it was on my chest. Orin would probably never move again. Then I'd be the guy that froze my girlfriend's long lost half-brother. Just another reason to keep my mouth shut.

"Great, I'm not even a normal Fae-Human."

"Changeling."

"Changeling." Eden repeats the word quietly, testing it, exploring it.

Sitting so close, I feel Eden's feelings change as under-standing sinks in. As more questions form.

"Why did he appear then leave?"

Orin knows exactly who Eden is talking about. It's a flipping valid question, too.

"We do not inform Changelings of their heritage. Our secret is too important. We seek to reconnect humans with their roots in nature, nothing more."

Confusion tangles Eden's face. "But he showed up."

It's a look I probably share. "And you just told her. And me."

Orin shrugs, a small, smooth movement. "Maybe it is because you are of royal blood; our father does not have any other Changeling children." His green eyes flick to Eden's ear, where her mark rests. "Your Fae heritage is...more powerful than we predicted." That was almost a 'the Force is strong within this one' comment. "The rules do not seem to apply."

Orin looks at me again, serious and still. I shift, straighten, and look away. Eden straightens, too, matching emerald eyes connect and lock. "So, what do you want from me?"

Orin takes a step forward, a soft, gentle smile is gracing his face.

"We want you to learn about your heritage. Fae have such a wonderful, incredible part in this world. We want to help you reach your potential."

"Okay." That one word says so much.

For some reason, those cryptic words and Eden's response has me putting an arm around her shoulder.

Orin ignores the movement, taking another small step. "And Eden, I want to get to know the sister I was never allowed to meet."

"Oh." The quiet word almost whispers out of Eden's surprised lips. "I think I'd like that."

There and then it starts to sink in. Eden is half supernatural, which really explains a lot. Pretty much everything. It also makes her more like us than we ever considered. I can't wait to tell Dad, and Mum, and Mitch and Tara.

"You cannot tell anyone that you have a brother."

Eden nods. "I know. I figured that."

I grimace a little. I don't even want to imagine how Alexis would react if she found out Eden has a half-brother. Actually, I have no idea how she would react, but I doubt it would involve smiles and hugs.

"I mean, neither of you can tell anyone about the Fae."

What?

"Oh. I'd like to tell Tara, she's my closest friend."

That would mean Mitch, too. Tara and Mitch aren't an open book, they're volume one and volume two of the same book. I'm pretty sure Eden knows this.

"And her mate, he's Noah's twin, Mitch. I would trust them with my life."

"You are trusting them will all Fae lives." Orin frowns. "They cannot tell other Weres."

Eden looks at me as she realizes she's going to have to ask me to keep this a secret from my parents. And my pack.

Orin steps forward. "Our power is in our invisibility. Reconnecting is not something that can be taught. It must be discovered and experienced." His green eyes come up to connect with mine. "Nor do we have strength to protect ourselves if we are discovered."

Unlike Weres.

I look at Eden, eyes steady. It's a no-brainer; she never questioned the need for secrecy with Weres. "You carry mine, I carry yours."

Eden smiles a sweet smile, one of the ones that make my heart clench and swell at the same time. "Okay."

Although Orin barely moves, I can sense he's excited. It

could be the brightness in his eyes, or maybe because they quadruple in size. All of a sudden, I wonder how he's felt knowing he has a sister but never being able to meet her. I think this may have been something he wanted. "Shall we meet soon? Perhaps tomorrow afternoon?"

Whoa, for a guy that doesn't move he sure acts quick.

Eden bites her lip for a moment, contemplating the grass at her feet.

That all-of-a-sudden moment keeps going. In less than an hour, everything has changed again. But this time, THE feeling isn't there. I notice what happens in its absence. Because there were some things I already knew long before Orin's bombshell, the ones I never doubted. I knew Eden's differences made her special, that she is more than she ever thought possible. And it turns out I was right. Which means all the things I wish for could turn out to be true, too. It leaves a space for a new feeling to take root. It feels like light in the dark, like a present with a future.

Eden looks from me to Orin, and says the words, even though we all know what her answer is going to be. "Yes, tomorrow sounds good."

20

EDEN

I'm more nervous than I was for my entry interview at Wyoming State. That nerve-wracking scenario had three people in suits, a big room with an even bigger desk, and me, all twitchy and uncomfortable in my own power outfit.

But I'd been prepared for that. There were rules, clear expectations, and known outcomes.

I stand at the edge of the trees, looking right, looking left. This is where he said to meet. The middle of nowhere. A one-hour hike from the visitor's center, into the reserve, without the guidance of a trail. I check the instructions again, scrawled in script that looks like it was written by Grandfather Douglas. Old and curvy and penned deep into the paper. I'm sure I've got it right, but nervousness has me second guessing, double checking the map.

"Hello, Eden."

I jump, turning to see Orin a step behind me. *Talk about a walking ghost!* He's wearing a smile, and his eyes hold a warmth and acceptance I'm not used to seeing in family.

"Ah, hi."

"You needed a map?"

This was actually the first time I pulled it out. The terrain of this reserve has slowly become part of my anatomy. Navigation points created by animals I've encountered, magnificent vistas I've memorized, overwhelming moments I've experienced—like Were sightings, human threats...meeting up with your newly discovered half-brother. My internal compass means I can navigate the atlas in my mind largely without the man-made map. I fold it and shove it into my bag. "Just checking something."

Orin smiles, and I wonder how much of the churning in my mind he senses. "Shall we begin?"

"Sure." *Whatever it is we're starting.*

Orin enters the shadowy protection of the pines, and I follow. Only a few steps in and he stops, sucks in a deep breath, holds it then releases it. I can't see his face, but I practically feel the wave of peace and contentment that washes through his body. Without conscious thought, I find myself doing the same. As pine and earth fill my lungs, I feel something light and expansive enter alongside them. It's a peaceful feeling, so serene and effortless. It's one of those feelings that's so earthy you want to sit beneath a tree and grow roots beside it, but so light and free you want to dance over the pine-needled ground, arms thrown to the sky, face kissing the sun right back.

I look over to see Orin watching me, that acceptance still glowing in those green tilted eyes, now smiling. "You feel it."

I nod. "I love it. It's always stronger in the forest." *And when I'm with Noah.* "I'm just not sure what 'it' is."

Orin nods, like it was the question he expected, or I was supposed to ask. "Come."

He walks further into the forest, hands reaching out to brush grooved bark, whorls of pine-needles. "It is you, your soul, your spirit, connecting with the elemental dimension of yourself. It is remembering, remembering and returning home."

Orin's words swirl in my head. "Home?"

"Yes, Eden, home. All sentient beings are embedded in the natural world."

"Is that what makes you, ah me, Fae?"

"In part. But this deep affiliation with the natural world is universal. Yes, it is deeply rooted in Fae, but it is also just as much a part of human biology. Or Were."

I nod, eyes scanning the world around us, sensing the rightness of his words.

We keep walking, no clear direction apart from heading deeper into the body of the forest. I glance at Orin and find him equally lost in thought. "Where does the melody come in?"

"You hear the music?"

"Yeah," I say the one word uncertainly.

Orin beams. "That is wonderful."

"But not normal."

"There is no normal in nature. Diversity is a beautiful, wonderful thing."

It's the first time my differences have been seen in that light. It's liberating. Unsettling. Quite a few beliefs would have to be rearranged, maybe a couple moved out, to accommodate this new perspective.

Orin stops, and I pull up beside him. Around us the pines are still, silent. "Hold my hand."

I look down at the outstretched palm and tentatively slide mine into it. Straight away I feel it. Orin's feelings, so tranquil and peaceful and blissful, I look down at our joined palms. It's the first time I've felt the connection with someone other than Noah.

Orin smiles at me; I can feel his happiness, and it lifts me, lightens me. "Close your eyes."

My eyes drift closed, and in the darkness the melody starts but stronger than before, amplified, intensified by my brother beside me. It brings with it the peace I have always felt, but this time there is more. The harmony holds a timelessness, balance, harmony, somehow so complex but achingly simple.

I open my eyes to find they keep going, widening until they hurt. Animals, so many animals are scattered through the trees. Butterflies flutter around us, a halo of color. Furred bodies leap and dance and play, some so close you could touch. Beetles and bugs crawl over the leaf litter, surrounding our shoes. Birds are everywhere, some big, some small, some still, some flickering with infinite energy.

The scientist in me tries to name them, find their place in this amazing ecosystem. But the other part, probably the Fae part, just watches in wonder. Predators, prey, competitors, loners. They all come and wait.

I wish Noah could see this. The space around us is a kaleidoscope of life.

Slowly the animals start shifting, moving in closer. Wings touch, fur brushes. All the animals surrounding Orin and me, like they are welcoming me to the place I have always felt is home. My smile is the only thing moving, growing wide with wonder. As each animal touches, it leaves and slowly our clearing empties.

When a Canadian lynx arrives, I lose the ability to breathe. Their status has never been formally documented in the reserve, and yet the pale grey feline, his black pointed ears erect, is most definitely a lynx.

"He's unsure," I whisper to Orin. The lynx's stubby, black tipped-tail is twitching, pale eyes wide and watchful.

"Reassure him."

I reach out to the lynx with my mind, finding the edgy distrust that his body communicates. I call up the melody, finding the hint of curiosity flickering in the feline before me.

Long legs carry those wide paws closer, toward a species he instinctively avoids. A few feet in front of me he stops.

"What now?"

"He came to see you. It is your decision."

Somehow, I know I could have the lynx closer, maybe even touch it if I wanted. And that thick, pale grey fur has me curious. But for what end? The lynx doesn't gain from my human contact. So, I give him all that I can.

Thank you.

I kneel, knees sinking into the soft ground, and smile. A sighting of this threatened, reclusive species can be the beginning of conservation efforts. A blink of those canine-like eyes and the lynx turns. With a graceful leap, his stumpy-tailed body disappears between the pines.

The blond head beside me is moving, and I turn to find Orin shaking his head. The nervousness that felt so far away suddenly creeps back. "Was I supposed to pat him or something?"

"No."

I wait, bracing myself because I realize I've done it wrong. Again.

"Well done."

"What?"

"You know the influence you can have, but you did not use it for your own gain. Our gift is powerful, but you did not abuse it."

"I didn't want to do anything that would hurt it."

Orin has gone from shaking to nodding. "Yes, we feel it because we are connected. It is not the same for so many others, those that have distanced themselves from their roots. The tear in the human-nature relationship means they no longer feel the pain of the natural world."

I glance at the timeless beauty around us, feeling sad that others don't get to experience this.

Orin nods, no doubt sensing my thoughts. "But when they

cut themselves off from painful feelings they stay numb. They stay stuck."

I suck in a breath as his truth hits me. Orin just described Alexis.

"That's what you do, isn't it? Help people reconnect with nature, to heal it."

"And to heal humans. One does not stay healthy without the other. That is what we do."

We. "How?"

"That answer is as infinite as snowflakes, as endless as time, as evolving as nature itself."

"I don't think that's an answer."

Orin smiles. "You will figure it out."

"That's even less of an answer." I glance at the trunks and branches that just swallowed all our visitors. "I'm going to be a vet. That will make a difference."

Orin inclines his head in agreement. *Why does it feel like he just said, 'if you say so?'*

My arms have crossed before I've realized. "What do you do?"

"I will be a counsellor. I hope to heal people's internal ecosystems by reconnecting them with their wider ecosystems."

"So, you're focusing on the human side."

"This is not a coin; there are no sides. The two are so interrelated they are indistinguishable. They are the same whole."

I always felt my focus is the animals. Orin's saying I am missing half the equation.

More reshuffling is going to have to happen. What Orin's suggesting is that the one person who just betrayed me, who has hurt me the most, who has hurt me all my life, is the type of person we are trying to reach.

To heal.

That little concept hits a wall. A wall composed of distrust, skepticism, and a big fat 'not in my lifetime.' As I mentally turn from one parent that has abandoned me all my life I look at Orin, the one I share a father with.

"Will I see him again?"

Orin's eyes are a deep, troubled green. "I do not know. We are already overlooking the rules by meeting you, teaching you. It would be best if he did not meet you again."

Once again rules laid down long before my birth, so far beyond my control, are keeping me from being with those that my heart yearns for. Were laws keeping me from Noah. Fae laws stopping me from meeting my father.

Orin's arm slips around my shoulder so naturally, it's like we've being doing this all my life. "I am glad to be with my sister."

I've just become more again. A year ago, I was just Eden. Freaky, awkward Eden. Now I'm a Changeling. A girlfriend. A bestie.

A sister.

"I never once considered I had a brother, Orin. But I'm glad I do."

Orin turns, and we start retracing our steps. "A brother that you cannot tell anyone about."

"I know, and it's fine." *How would Alexis react if she found out I had a half-brother?*

"So, little sister, tell me about this Were of yours."

My feet falter, scuffing the pine-needle ground. Getting used to being a sister is going to take time. Trusting family with your deepest emotions is probably going to take a little longer. "I've spent a long time not letting myself wish for much, Orin, but even if I did, I never could have dreamed up Noah. He's amazing, he's everything I never let myself hope for."

When I look at Orin, I find him smiling, his eyes full of questions, but he says nothing as we leave the edge of the forest.

Out in the open, I look up at the calm, blue sky. "It's the most inexplicable feeling I've ever felt."

"That's something for a Changeling."

"Yes, it is."

"You two have something very unique."

I can't tell from Orin's tone whether that's a good thing. "It's certainly not your usual relationship."

"Diversity is wonderful, remember? It creates strengths we never knew were possible."

Goodness, I hope so.

21

NOAH

"Sorry sis, can't. The four of us are heading out to the movies." Tara skips as she climbs into the back seat of the truck. "Yeah, it does sound like fun, but is there anyone hotter than Captain America?"

I start the engine and Tara smiles, her gaze unfocused out the window as I reverse onto the driveway. "That's true, Thor does spend more time without a shirt, but I spend enough time around hammers as it is. Sure, seeya Dana."

Tara hangs up and quicker than seems Werely possible pokes her head between the two front seats. "So Edes, how was the walk in the woods?"

Eden smiles a big, beautiful smile as she turns to Tara. My heart skips like it always does, like it wants to capture that happy look, but I stay quiet, even more curious than Tara.

"I need one of your words to describe it, Tara. It was..."

"Amazeballs?"

"Remarkeaballs?" I volunteer.

Tara gives my shoulder a shove. "That's not a real word y'know. Incrediballs would have been better."

Eden smiles. "All of those and more."

"What did big bro say?" This one's from Mitch. He leans forward and pulls Tara back so she can put her seat belt on.

"We walked, we talked. Fae have an amazing connection with animals."

At the intersection to the highway, I throw her a glance. That's not news.

Eden smiles a little wider. "Fine, we walked in the woods, we played with the animals."

I thought as much. "Which animals?"

Her hand comes to rest on my thigh, a gesture of affection that has the wrong effect. That warm palm has my pulse and body temp spiking. "Mostly little ones. But we did see a lynx."

"Wow, people weren't even sure they're in the reserve."

"I know. I can't wait to tell Emily."

I can feel her happiness. A warm, settled glow.

"That's really great, Edes."

From the corner of my eye, I see her lip slip beneath her teeth. "The Fae, me being a Changeling, has to be a secret."

In the rearview mirror, I see Tara roll her eyes. "We're used to keeping secrets."

Eden turns in her seat, her head scanning the three of us. "No, I mean you can't tell anyone."

Three pennies drop at once, but it's Mitch that says it. "Like our packs."

"Yeah."

Her tilted eyes, the legacy of her heritage—look at me, apologetic and unsure. I don't need to turn to know Mitch is also watching me. "How come?"

"The Fae's work depends on them being unknown. Weres don't know they exist. It's better if it stays that way."

Carrying secrets is not a new concept for me. And I'd do anything for Eden. "You keep mine, I keep yours."

Eden leans over; a brief kiss on my cheek tells me her thanks. "I appreciate it."

Eden's heritage will be a secret amongst the Weres. I know from experience some secrets get lighter with time, easier to carry. You hardly notice they're there. But I've also found out that some get heavier, like the blasted things are growing, and you get tired of carrying them.

Tyrrell's Cinema parking lot looks a whole lot like our school carpark. It seems most of our year group has turned out to see the latest Marvel movie. I pull into one of the back spaces. They might actually have to use the rear car park they flattened last year in anticipation of expanding the cinema, only to find out they were being overly optimistic.

I don't really pay attention. All my senses are full of forest green and warm wildflowers.

Inside Tyrrell's I wonder whether they should have put all the money spent on the carpark into updating the décor. The burgundy carpet covers not just the floor but also the walls. The glass behind the front counter just reflects the sea of stained red.

Dale, breaking the vista of beetroot with his faded black, grins at us as we approach. "Hey, dudes, double date, huh?"

I pull out my wallet. "Yeah, four tickets to—"

"The dreamboat-bod of hotness!" Tara squeals.

Mitch rolls his eyes, possibly because she almost ruptured a Were eardrum but probably because he's watched this obsession with Captain America since we were young teens.

"Right on, guys." Dale passes us the four tickets, two big buckets of popcorn, and the associated oversized drinks. "You're in cinema two."

As we enter the second of Tyrrell's two cinemas, I can't help but grin. Eden's excitement is contagious. A normal double date—well, as normal as we get anyway. Either way, it's kinda cool.

The cinema darkens as the curtains open the last few inches. My hand finds hers in the dark. Beside me, Mitch is munching his way through his bucket. Tara hasn't taken her eyes off the screen.

I lean over, sucking in her scent, finding her happy eyes in the dark. "What did he say?"

"I'm betrothed to a Fae prince."

"What?"

"Shhh!" Tara's voice in an angry hiss.

Eden giggles, bringing up a piece of popcorn to my lips. "He said he likes having a sister."

I munch on the salted Styrofoam, feeling how much this means to Eden. I swallow, wondering which part has been the most significant. "Anything else?"

"I'm completely normal by some standards, but I still manage to break a few golden rules."

I look at her closely in the dim light. It's the first time I've heard her talk about being different in such a positive light. "In what ways?" I'm not sure if I'm asking about the normal or not-so-normal aspects.

Eden opens her mouth, but her eyes widen as she looks over my shoulder. I turn to see the obsessive focus that Tara had directed at the screen lasered on the two of us. Even Mitch is leaning back, holding the popcorn well away from the explosive that leans across him. "If you two don't zip it, I'm gonna ask Beth to cook asparagus risotto again when we get home."

The threat is enough to silence the two of us. I didn't think it was possible for Mom's cooking to reach a new level, but the vegetarian meals she's been experimenting with have sunk way below palatable.

It looks like finding out the details is going to have to wait. I tuck that hand in a little tighter, grab my own handful of popcorn, and sink into my seat. I've put money down that Ironman will cameo in this one.

The credits roll, and the moment our blond-haired, broad-shouldered hero appears on the screen Tara becomes the quietest, most focused I've seen in a long time. Well, since the last Captain America movie, anyway. After two hours of explosions, shooting whilst leaping from tall buildings, and a few more really big explosions for dramatic effect we're done. Tara has that weird dreamy look in her eyes that tells me we are about to analyze the plot, which is really analyzing Steve's superior jawline, the whole way home.

"So, pizza at mine or dinner at yours?"

Mitch, Tara, and I all adopt grave faces. I shove my free hand into my pocket. "Mom's made ratatouille."

Even graceful Eden misses a step at that one. "She does know it's not rodent-based, doesn't she?"

"I double checked." Mom had laughed, waving me out with her wooden spoon. I took my unconvinced butt out of the kitchen, reminding myself that rodent-colored didn't mean rodent-tasting.

Dale is no longer at the ticket booth when we leave. We wave to Jordan as he walks past with a couple of friends. We're out the front, two couples looking happy and normal, happy and human, when a voice has us all turning.

"Wow, what a coincidence."

Seth swaggers toward us, a superficial smile planted on his face. *Great.* The one guy that has me on high alert with a single twitch of that smug smile had to turn up tonight. Although my shoulders want to drop, they tense.

Seth leans against an overgrown flower pot, resting an arrogant hip against it as he crosses his arms. "Hello, Eden."

"Hi, Seth." Eden is still, the strange storm of emotions I can feel only apparent in the hand that tenses around mine.

"We should chat—"

"Zip it, Seth." I growl, stepping forward.

"You should go home, Seth." Tara's tone is flat, an Alpha command.

Something flares in Seth's hazel eyes; it looks like pain but I know it's anger. Just like I knew he would, and Tara probably did, too, Seth stands there. Mutinous.

It's a jovial voice that springs through the tension. "Get your dose of hotness, Tara?"

Tara smiles, turning to Dale, but not quite turning her back on Seth. "We're going to have to redefine hot, Dale."

"That good, huh?"

"Un-flipping-defineable."

Mitch steps up to slip a casual arm around Tara, effectively slipping between Seth and me. "Spontaneous combustion was a concern for some of us."

Tara slaps his arm, her smile practically believable. "Don't be silly. I wouldn't miss a second!"

Dale grins, telling us the act has worked. "I'd love to hear the details, but I only get a five-minute break. See y'all at school."

Unlikely. "Sure, see you then, Dale."

I fist bump him as he ambles past and heads to the laneway at the end of the building. I look back at Seth to find him watching Dale as he rounds the corner of Tyrell's, heading to the rear of the building.

"You're right, Tara, I will get going."

No one is fooled by Seth's sudden compliance. He grins at us, and my back stiffens another notch when he winks at Eden.

Then Seth casually, without ever looking back, follows Dale around the corner.

"Gob dash it!" Tara quickly heads in the same direction, Mitch by her side.

I turn to Eden, fishing the car key out of my pocket. "Go home. I'll pick you up on the way, through."

"Noah—"

"I promise, this won't take long." Seth probably parked his car around the back because he refuses to be a sheep and is making a show just to get us all riled.

"Maybe I should come."

That grabs my attention. I actually look at Eden, rather than the laneway that just swallowed an angry Were and unsuspecting human, or the backs of my twin and friend that just followed them.

Two wide eyes, all green and serious, lock me there. "I think I could help."

For a moment I'm torn, between the earnest emerald eyes holding me still and the implications such a choice holds. I look to the corner, down at Eden, then back to the corner. A yo-yo of emotions following the motion. The need to protect Eden wins.

I think it always will.

My hand comes up to cup her cheek. "You can't." *I can't.* "We don't know what he's capable of."

Those still eyes look at me another second before dark lashes come down. "Okay."

There's no time to analyze the single soft word carried on a sigh because Eden takes the keys and turns away. Instead I run toward the corner, round it.

And stop.

An asphalt clearing, one that has never had a car use it as a resting place, opens out. A small storage shed sits in the back corner, its door open, sounds of movement coming from inside. Seth is halfway across, Tara and Mitch not far behind.

"Your car's parked out front, Seth."

"I know where I parked my car." Seth doesn't bother to turn around, but continues his long-legged stride toward the shed.

"I've ordered you to go home."

"I will," Seth calls over his shoulder, not bothering to be quiet despite its redundancy amongst three Weres.

"Now."

That has Seth spinning around, big chested and angry-eyed. Tara doesn't stop; she keeps stalking forward until she's almost toe to toe with her defiant pack member. Seth leans over, breath sucked in and held, clearly using his height and size to try and intimidate her.

But Seth obviously doesn't know that Tara grew up as a part-time mother to six wild younger siblings, or that she was best friends with twin boys who sometimes acted like they shared a brain between them. Only two of us know that she was the first person to stand up to Kurt.

Tara is an Alpha, from her red hair to her dancing toes.

Her hands don't come to her hips. Her fingers don't clench. She's simply still and hard, staring right back. One word repeats through the twilight. "Now."

"Or what?"

"The Precepts are pretty straightforward. You don't need a preservice teacher to spell it out for you."

More banging rises from the shed, this time followed by a few muffled curses that would raise a brow in most bars.

Seth leans back, his head tilting toward the sound. The eyes that return to Tara are smiling. Hard but smiling. "And I'm about to break three of them in one move."

"Don't do it, Seth."

"That's one."

Seth shifts, disobeying his Alpha, ignoring the last Precept. In a flash, a brown wolf dwarfs Tara as he stands only a few feet in front of her.

Just as Dale exits the shed.

Two sets of human eyes and one set of wolf eyes turn to

watch him stumble out, drop a rolled piece of paper, and stamp it into the black asphalt with a black boot. Smoke that distinctly doesn't smell of nicotine curls from the doorway.

"Hold that thought dude, I just gotta find the gents."

Black-clad, now beanie-headed Dale, takes two, three steps from the shed, his head down, focused on the hands fumbling at his zipper. He staggers another three steps before he looks up.

Then stops.

Glazed eyes widen, pushing up his brows as his mouth drops, plunging his chin into his black-pilled chest. His hazy mind is trying to absorb and decipher the scene before him.

Tara then Mitch, me not far behind. All facing a hulk-sized wolf.

Seth growls, no doubt an intimidating, terrifying noise for the human not far away. But we can see the smile in those brown eyes. Seth doesn't need to be human to voice the two words that are heavy in all our heads.

That's two.

'You shall not reveal the bloodline' just got blown.

Dale's eyes haven't gotten any smaller, nor has his mouth. He just stands there, the ability to think wiped by drugs and shock.

Seth shifts, his center of gravity moving back. I realize in a split second there's a three. Words that every Were knows shift in my mind.

'You shall not attack a blood member.'

Seth lunges forward, and I start running. He's like an arrow, straight and fast. Mitch grabs Tara by the shoulders and yanks her to the side. Brown fur brushes her shoulder as they crash to the tarred gravel. Mitch twists and Tara lands on him, a grunt wretched from beneath her.

But Seth doesn't stop, dark brown eyes staring dead straight. He doesn't stop because Tara was never his target.

Anger, full of anticipation and satisfaction, flares in my veins.

I can't change, not with Dale, not with my mark, so it's human legs that propel me forward. A human body that is small compared to the feral strength that is only paces away.

But one fueled by anger. I've had enough...

That brown-furred face grows larger; the sound of his harsh breaths gets louder. I have no plan about what I'm going to do when we collide, only that this has got to stop. Seth has got to stop.

At the last second, as the final sliver of air between us disappears, Seth twists. One slash, a razor claw on a mammoth paw, strikes my upper arm. A sting of pain and three red lines open from one side to the other. The massive body sails past, taking my breath with him.

I spin in time to see Seth change then stop a few paces away. As a human he stands, his back to us.

The horizontal lines across my arm have me clenching my teeth, gravity drawing crimson vertical lines to my elbow, creating a gruesome noughts and crosses board on my upper arm, I resist the urge to follow Seth. To run, cover those few feet, and repay the favor.

"Seth Channon." Tara's voice is panting but clear. "You will face Council on the full moon."

Seth's shoulders sag as his chin raises to the sky. He speaks to the nothing before him. "I didn't think you had it in you...Alpha."

And with that, he walks away. Stiffed backed and straight legged, he rounds the corner of Tyrell's and leaves behind the mess he just created.

"Dudes?" Dale's voice is small and confused.

"Dale." I turn to the guy who never should have seen what he just did, keeping my bleeding arm from view. "I want you to head back into the shed, get your friends to roll you another one, and stay there."

Eyes that may never shut again scan the three of us standing there, cool, calm, and collected. "Ah, sure man."

With steady, measured steps Dale follows my instructions, this time pulling the metal door shut behind him.

Muffled voices once again waft out. "Jeez, what did you do, water half of Wyoming?"

"Shut up, dude. Just give me one of those."

Silence descends on the asphalt, as the teens inside the shed fill their lungs with oblivion and the teens outside the shed wish they could join them.

I sigh. "That was three."

Tara and Mitch are heading over, Tara's hands reaching out to my forearm streaked in red. "Are you okay?"

"Yeah. We'd better get home."

"Here." Tara passes me her cardigan, and I wrap it around my arm. The blood has already stopped.

We follow the path Seth took to leave and round the corner. The hustle and bustle of teens and movies and soda hits me like a reality slap. As two worlds that are never supposed to meet collided behind a cinema, everyone else had been getting on with Marvel and rom coms.

Our truck is parked out the front, in a new space just outside the cinema. Mitch raises his brows when he bends and finds the keys resting above the wheel. How did Eden get home?

Eden. Thank heavens she didn't come.

I pull my phone out of my pocket, knowing she'd be worried. *All okay. Heading back now*

The reply is almost instantaneous. Like worried fingers were waiting and hovering. *Good. See you soon.*

Not that soon. We're going to have to go home and tell Dad. And we're going to have to call another Council.

It's a given that Mitch is driving, so I climb into the back seat, wincing as I pretend my arm isn't stinging because an animal just clawed it open.

The quiet continues in the truck as we head home. The moment Seth changed then slashed open my arm, Tara got served up a whopper of a test. A newly appointed Alpha is about to run a Council. A young female Alpha. With a Were who openly defies her.

Although it's possible hers looks like a side plate compared to mine. But only one person knows I'm carrying that platter.

"I've had enough." Mitch's angry voice fills the cab.

Tara's head falls back against the headrest. "Tell me about it."

But it's my gaze that Mitch holds in the rearview mirror.

I look away. I don't want to face what's on that plate. "He'll go to Council. It will be dealt with as our law says it will."

A hand thumps the steering wheel. Mitch's angry movement makes Tara jump, the rattley thud has me hiding my surprise. "How many will we hold?"

I open my mouth with a reply I don't have.

"No, Noah. How many more people will see?" Blue eyes flicker right; he can't see my arm but I know that's what has his face tightening. "Who else has to get hurt?"

I shut my jaw, closing off the pretense that I have an answer.

Eden. The feeling is moving, growing, taking up more space than I have to give.

"What's going on, guys?" Tara's voice isn't her usual demanding teen, it's a very grown up Alpha voice.

At the corner of our dirt road, Mitch pulls over. As the dust settles on the hood he turns to face me. "Tell her."

All I can do is stare back. I can't. Those words are too big.

"Show her." This time his voice is softer, with just a little less edge.

"Show me what?"

With a sigh of resignation, I pull down the collar of my shirt, stretching the seam. Exposing my mark.

"Holy shi...itake mushrooms."

I'm not sure who's more stunned, Tara at my mark, or Mitch and me that Tara almost cursed. I try for a grin, but I don't think I make it. "Yeah, that holy."

Mitch is looking at Tara. "You realize what it means?"

Tara arches a brow at her mate. "My art extends to hair, remember? I know exactly where that little star and circle comes from." She turns to me. "Correction. Whom it comes from."

"He hasn't told her, has he?"

"Nope. I think he thinks he's protecting her."

I open my mouth, this time I definitely have something to say.

"Hang on—" But it seems I'm not part of this conversation, because Tara snorts then keeps talking like I just disappeared. "Eden doesn't need protecting. That girl is one of the toughest people I know."

Mitch looks thoughtful, and I wonder how long before he strokes his lip. "No one's ever considered that a human, or half-human, would lead Weres."

I don't point out that we're half human.

My backseat view sees Tara roll her eyes. "I didn't say it would be easy. But it happened for a reason."

Yep, there's the lip rub.

Tara shoots up in her seat, her head almost reaching the top of the headrest. "It totally makes sense. She's the best person for it."

"What do you mean?"

"Eden has it all. She's part Fae, the link between animal and human. Weres have always struggled to connect. But she's also human, one that knows about us, and is now bonded to one of us.

Mitch's eyes widen. "She's the intersection of us all."

They both turn to me. The desire to add to this conversation has disintegrated along with the air in my lungs.

Tara arches a brow at my twin. "If only there was an opportunity coming up for them to talk..."

Mitch's eyes twinkle. "Like a camping trip or something?"

Tara's face lights up, like she hadn't considered that. "You're a genius bonded-mate-of-mine."

Like they've been bonded for years, Mitch and Tara speak in unison. "You need to tell her."

22

EDEN

"This is all you're bringing?" Trev's ventriloquist lips barely move, meaning I have to differentiate the this-all-you-bringing?

I'd quickly figured out Trev is a mutterer. He muttered a hello when I entered the little building at the back of the airport tarmac. He'd muttered all through the pre-flight safety checks. Whilst flicking through pages on his clipboard he'd muttered through the argument he had with his wife about buying another dress. For their Chihuahua.

His eyebrows had hitched up when I'd brought over a daypack to stash in the rear of the helicopter.

"Ah, yeah."

"And there's two of you." Trev looks doubtfully at the lone bag strapped into the small cargo hold. I'd managed to jam a tent, two sleeping bags, and as much food as possible into its confines.

"Um, we're, ah, survivalists." I really hope that's a term.

"You know they're forecasting a cold snap." The words are said slowly; I'm not sure if he's making sure his words are understandable or assessing my IQ.

A sinking stomach had registered the weather map two days ago. A cold front was steadily dragging rain toward the mountains. With luck, we'd be back before those swirling masses of white and grey drop their load.

I smile brightly, trying for a Tara-like optimism. "I don't really feel the cold."

Trev opens his mouth to respond but a door opening cuts him off.

Noah, Mitch, and Tara tumble through the door. Tara looks far too excited for a person who isn't going, whilst Mitch heads straight for the window that overlooks our little-chartered helicopter. Noah looks wind-blown and delicious.

Trev scans Noah. "You got a bag?"

Noah looks to me; I told him not to pack anything. I shake my head.

He smiles at Trev. "Nope. You ever seen Bear Grylls?"

Trev shakes his grizzled head as he walks to the door, muttering something that sounds suspiciously like 'kids these days.'

I turn to Noah, nervous and excited. "Ready?"

He grabs my hand and heads for the door. "Am I ever!"

Oh, we need to say goodbye. It seems anticipation shrinks my world to just a set of sparkling summer eyes and the body attached to them.

Mitch and Tara have followed us to the door; I think I see an eye-roll pass between them. Mitch slaps Noah on the shoulder. He gives him a long stare. Noah nods, and I know more twin-talk just happened.

Tara has me in one of her hugs, all giggles and bounces. She doesn't see, or purposely ignores, her mate and her friend. "You two kids have a good time, you hear me?"

I arch a wry brow; she just went all bonded-Were on me. "Thanks."

Noah and I head to the bubble with blades sitting in the middle of the tarmac ocean. We climb into the back seat; anticipation feels like soda in my belly. We wave to Mitch and Tara, hands flapping madly.

Noah takes in the million little switches and lights, watching Trev flick one, adjust another. We do up our harnesses, and Trev turns to make sure they are tight. My smile is about to touch my ears as I watch Trev double check Noah's. He probably thinks it's necessary for the ping pong ball beside me.

As we lift into the sky Noah mouths one word, "Wow."

Something about Noah looks younger, lighter. Like a whole lot of weight just got left behind. He pulls my hand to rest on his leg, the warmth of his palm pulses in mine, the heat of his thigh warms the back. The love in his gaze warms my heart.

I know this is going to be an amazing flight, a wonderful couple of days.

A memorable, incredible, unforgettable trip.

I want to lean over and kiss him, but the harness has me pinned to the seat. Instead, I squeeze his hand. Noah makes my soul fly.

The black tarmac shrinks as clear blue becomes our world. A muffled roar pulses around my ears. The anticipation can't be contained by the two people sitting side by side fills the cockpit. It has us both smiling giant smiles, holding hands like we're about to embark on something special.

Once we're in the sky, Trev steadily moves the joystick forward. My stomach ever so gently rocks back to my spine as the helicopter propels forward. Noah's eyes don't know where to look first. They dart back at Jacksonville disappearing behind us; they roam over the sea of alpine we're slicing toward; they swallow me whole with their excitement.

Miles are compressed into seconds as the helicopter speeds through space. Below us is a puffed quilt of greens, the mountain up ahead jutting through it. We head north, circling the slumbering giant, white winter at its peak, waking spring below.

The reserve from this eagle view is breathtaking. It's almost too much to take in. The blazing wealth of earthy browns, tranquil blues, infinite greens. The throbbing noise, sucked in breaths, and a surprising sense of peace. Two held hands, my right, his left, communicate our sense of wonder and astonishment.

Periodically this patchwork of nature opens out to grassy plains in shades of blond and sun-drenched yellow. A herd of elk, spooked at the roaring machine overhead, gallop erratically through one area of open terrain. My hand touches the glass in sympathy as I watch their frenzied run; my eyes barely blink as I marvel at the mass of animals that move with the coordination of a single organism.

I look to Noah, and I'm pretty sure his face mirrors mine. Open and happy and smiling and totally bowled over. We both say that one word simultaneously. "Wow."

It's over before either of us is ready. I think we could circle this wonderland for hours. A clearing, stubbly green surrounded by tall pines, opens out then starts to grow closer. Trees whip and bend as the helicopter straightens and begins descending. The grass whips and flattens as we touch the ground. That roaring finally dulls then stops. The silence is a sharp contrast as we all sit in shock.

The trees recover from their beating. The grass regains its upright posture. Noah and I reel from the dazzling sights we just shared.

Trev, astounded at the stupidity of the generation that will inherit his world. "You got enough for three days?"

Trev's right, a human would need three days to trek out of here. "Sure."

That just earns me another kids-today shake of the head. "You guys got a PLB?"

I climb out, taking the backpack with me. I pull the emergency GPS beacon from the side pocket. "Yep. Safety first, Trev."

Trev takes a good look at us, probably thinking he'll be part of the search and rescue. Or this is the last time we'll be seen alive. He climbs back into the helicopter, muttering some more; I think I hear something about drugs being the ill of all society.

With the backpack slung over my shoulder, I take Noah's hand and head for the trees. I plotted this hike carefully, finding the clearing deep in the reserve, measuring the distance, calculating the time it would take a Were to get back. One that runs as fast as Noah. Then charted our way out, knowing we don't need roads or tracks. Knowing we don't want roads or tracks. That dense forest and craggy mountain sides were ideal.

At the edge of the trees, we turn to see the chopper lift, the rotors whipping the trees that had just breathed a sigh of relief. I can practically hear them groan as the man-made hurricane pummels them all over again. The rotors pick up every pebble, twig, and piece of forest floor, sucking them in and flinging them out. I put my hand up to shield my face, only to find it pulled into Noah's chest. He turns us around, curling around me.

We straighten in time to watch Trev disappear into the sky, the sound disappearing before the sight. All that's left is silence. Any animal or bird long gone, thanks to our landing.

Just me and Noah and the wilderness.

Noah looks at me, the engineer of this adventure. I shrug. "We just head south."

He smiles, summer sky eyes alight with anticipation. "Ready?"

"Yes." *Yes, yes, yes!*

Noah grins like he heard me, or gets it. He walks toward a nearby tree, always putting space between us when he shifts. He changes so fast now. I watch every time, practically salivating at the flash of smooth broad shoulders, the flat planes of his shoulder blades, the width of those muscles narrowing down to...I blush but don't look away.

It's amazing how much detail you can memorize in a split second.

He turns, and the same blue eyes look at me from a very different face. Why does it feel so long since we've run?

The massive snow-white body approaches me, all untamed grace and breathtaking stealth. Wild blue eyes lock with mine, telling me everything I need to know.

I take two long strides until we're face to face. Happy eyes meet, wolf to human, wide smiles matching. I lean in to kiss his velvety nose. In return, I get a cheerful tongue across my cheek.

"Ew." I giggle, not bothering to wipe it away. I press my forehead to his, breathing in sandalwood and wolf and pine.

Let's do this.

"Let's do this," I reply out loud.

I vault onto his back; warm white fur hugs my thighs, and I can't help but sink my fingers into its lush thickness. Noah angles south, and with a powerful push, he powers forward. There's no gentle walk, easy lope; we're stationary to speeding in a second, flying through the shadowy forest.

This deep in the reserve, the forest is thick and untamed. But the tightly packed trunks are a welcome challenge for Noah's reflexes. Left, right, slower, faster. He navigates the obstacles with agility and enthusiasm.

The sound of my excited breath fills my ears; the scent of sandalwood and pine fills my senses. The feeling of love and life overflows from my rapidly expanding chest. It's exhilarating. It's amazing.

We run for hours. The trees open out sporadically to meadows filled with spring color then close in again to create an army of pines. We duck under branches as old as Grandfather Douglas. We follow the rise and fall of Mother Nature's hills and valleys.

In the open, craggy areas there are giant-sized hurdles that we line up and fly over. Chasing the wind, leaving it behind to find that place where time stands still and it's just a girl and a Were.

We don't talk; there's no silent communication. All we do is see and feel.

We stop for lunch beside a stream, the sun flashing diamonds on its sapphire surface. I rest in Noah's arms as we eat squashed cheese sandwiches. Neither of us talks, the silence and connection too sacred to breach.

I spend a lot of time looking at the age-old pines, outstretched branches getting smaller and smaller as their pyramid shapes reach for the sky. Taking in the fragile flowers, the grey, mossy rocks. Gazing at summer eyes that reflect everything I feel.

Another flash of naked shoulders, arrow-shaped back, and lean legs etched into my memory and we're off again. This time we go slower, a rhythmic lope through the changing pattern of nature.

Some p.eople think pines are all the same. Rows upon rows of identical soldiers, indistinguishable from one another, lacking identity or uniqueness. But the forest around us is alive in individuality. Each tree a unique constellation of branches and needles, each one hosting its own colony of mosses, insects, birds and mammals. Everywhere microcosms can be found within microcosms.

When you look at it that way, all of a sudden the forest becomes an irreplaceable, limitless place of wonder. I point out warblers and flycatchers, the squirrels and even a badger, Noah slowing down so we can watch them for a few precious moments. The redundant need to speak means we barely disturb them.

Until they see the enormous white wolf, for all intents and purposes an intimidating predator, walking with a human sitting on his back. It confuses some animals, and they freeze, staring. It frightens others, and they disappear into the never-ending trees in a flash.

As the sun approaches the tips of the trees, I know we need to find somewhere to camp. Noah's ears prick back, telling me he heard. His head tips up, eyes scanning as we both keep a look out for somewhere to stop for the night.

We see it at the same time. The trees open out as we reach another stream. This one slow moving, the clear water curving over pebbles in cool greys of clouds and mist, dawn and dusk. It's a small clearing, riparian grass thick and lush, just waiting for a tent to be pitched, lichen-covered rocks waiting to oversee a campfire.

I slide off, feet hitting the soft ground. A cool breeze tangles with my hair, whispering 'tonight will be a cold one.' I look up; the sky is mottled with the forecasted bearers of rain. I rub my arms; the temps will drop quickly once the sun disappears behind the pines.

Noah changes before I get a chance to ogle. He slips his arms around me, smelling of sandalwood warmed by the sun and a faint metallic scent, the scent that always lingers after a change. I sink into the welcome warmth, slipping my arms around his waist, tipping my head up to look at that beautiful face.

Warm palms cup my face as Noah leans down. Wind-kissed lips touch mine, so softly, so gently. I suck in a breath, Noah filling my lungs, love filling my heart, and I can't tell if it's his or mine. My hands come up to mirror his, my mouth opens beneath his. The kiss is long and deep, touching me somewhere profound and beautiful.

Noah pulls back, and I'm lost in blue. "I love you more than I ever thought possible."

I touch those warm lips. "I love you more than I ever dreamed possible."

They're the first words we've spoken since we left the helicopter. I make a concerted effort to memorize those glowing summer eyes, soft just-kissed lips, warm palms framing my face, the sincerity and adoration that enfolds me.

Maybe we could just stay like this for the rest of the night... week...our lifetime.

That breeze, the one that won't let winter go, gusts again, grabbing at my pullover. We're going to have to stay like this, because the minute I leave Noah's embrace, goose bumps are inevitable.

"I'll go find some firewood?"

I smile. "I'll set up the tent."

Noah heads for the trees, where an abundance of branches and twigs litter the forest floor. I pull out the tent from the backpack, the one I bought especially for this trip. State of the art, the two-person tent packs into a bag smaller than a sleeping bag, unfolding into a yellow, dome-shaped home in a few short minutes.

I pull out the sleeping bags, two micro-fiber pellets that spring out to thick, warm duvets. I look in the tent, for the first time today biting my lip. I know how much Noah eats, which meant there was no room for sleeping mats in the single backpack. But the ground still holds the cold bite of winter. Plus, Noah and I, two separate caterpillars, is not how I saw this.

With a shaky breath, I unzip the two blue, puffy bags, not sure what I'm communicating. Not sure what I want to communicate. I spread one out, creating a soft, thin mattress. I spread the second one out, creating a warm, intimate double bed.

I zip up the tent, keeping out unwanted insects, concealing

our sleeping arrangements, just as Noah enters the clearing, an armful of wood stacked up to his chin. I look up at the tree line; the sun just hugs the jagged, green edge, meaning we have a little while before dinner.

The happy, light feeling that has me filled with helium gives me an idea. It's time to have some fun. I give him a very Phelan grin and get a puzzled one in response. "I've never played hide and seek."

And then I run. A few strides and I'm in the trees, ducking and weaving further into the shadowy depths. I quickly spot a large, old spruce, and I slip around it and stand still, forcing slow breath, ears pricked for sound.

I wonder how long it will take Noah to find—

"You know my dad works in search and rescue." Two hands hit the bark on either side of my head, Noah's smiling face fills my vision.

He leans a little closer, and a metallic scent fills my nose. "You cheated!"

"Love and war, baby. Apparently, anything goes."

I narrow my eyes on his dark blond hair and blue-eyed, grinning face. "Is that so?"

"Ya ha."

I duck beneath the arms that I want to hold me forever, sprinting to the trees, heading deeper into the forest. "Count to ten. And no shifting!" I see a thick patch of pines ahead. "Make that twenty."

Noah's voice follows me. "Whatever head start you need, babes."

Babes? Cocky Noah is kinda sexy.

This time I keep my run light-footed, disturbing as little as possible, calling through my mind as I go. It appears Orin's talk was timely.

At the stand of trees, I duck behind one, not the largest, but wide enough to hide me. There I close my eyes and let the music flow.

It's only a couple of minutes before I hear heavy steps crunching through the forest. I smile; I figured it wouldn't take long for him to find me.

I peek around the tree to see Noah standing amongst the pines, his back to me, turning slowly. I duck back around as his face comes around, in time to see his eyes closed, lips smiling, and a confident step about to happen.

"Ouch."

I have to stifle a giggle, peeking again, to see Noah rubbing his head and looking up at the canopy. I bite my top lip this time, having to work at keeping the laughter in. I move around slightly to the left, keeping the tree at my back.

I glance up at the trees myself, nodding, the smile growing even wider.

More crunching footsteps heading my way. "Ow!"

This time I hear the pinecone connect with Noah. I glance around the trunk again to see Noah rubbing his shoulder. He looks left then right, eyes narrowed. He's starting to figure it out. "Love and war, hey?"

You said it...babes.

Striding steps start moving toward me, telling me he knows exactly where I am.

Now!

I step around the tree, ready to run, to see Noah under a deluge of nuts and cones, a family of squirrels in the branches above him, chattering and leaping. They throw then jump, throw then jump. One brave little cherub leaps, and Noah ducks reflexively as the little ball of fur lands on his shoulder, in a split second leaping again into a nearby tree.

I can't contain my laughter as it spills out, the sight of big, blond Noah under siege from a squadron of cheeky fur balls is something I wish I could film. I use the opportunity to run again, lining up another hiding tree.

"Hey! Talk about not fair."

Those fast footsteps are behind me again, and I know I won't make it, particularly when laughter makes my knees weak and eyes wet. I duck left, imitating the elk we saw earlier in the day, then suddenly right.

But my maneuvering is no match for the predatory intent behind me, and a few frenzied steps later I feel strong arms band around me. I let out a Tara-like squeal and twist, inadvertently losing balance.

My eyes widen as our trajectory changes from forward to down, then my breath hitches as Noah spins us with split-second timing, and instead of landing on the pine-littered ground, I land on a solid warm body. There's no time to absorb the delicious sensation because Noah twists, and in the blink of an eye I'm on the ground, a laughing, blue-eyed, leaf-littered face above me.

I grin up at him. "You said it, anything goes."

Happy eyes narrow down at me. "I wonder what else you haven't tried."

My heart stutters, considering stopping altogether. My lips part, but I can't think of a retort. *What?*

His grin widens until I can see those pearly teeth come out to chew his bottom lip in thought. I'm captured and mesmerized. He angles his head. "Like...are you ticklish?"

I blink. "I don't think so."

Strong fingers are on my ribs in an instant, wriggling up and down, playing them like a frenzied piano. All of a sudden I'm squirming, twisting, squealing, and doing everything I can to escape them. But I'm trapped beneath the mass of muscle above me, helpless and choking on laughter.

All of a sudden Noah stops. "Is that a yes?"

"Yes." I'm all breathless and giggles, happy and laughing.

"Thought so." Those delicious summer eyes narrow again. "Does that make me the winner?"

I huff. "I don't think so."

And he starts again. Unrelenting fingers dancing over my ribs, wrenching more helpless laughter from my trapped body. My hands try to push his away, but every time they find them those nimble fingers fly to the other side, keeping up the merciless torture.

"Stop, stop. Okay, you win. You win!"

Noah sits back, his own breathing a little puffed, like that was more work than our run. He's smiling as he pulls me upright. "I hope you learned your lesson, young lady. Cheaters never prosper."

I skip away. "I wouldn't call that a loss."

Noah comes up beside me, and I don't have to look at him to know how he's feeling. I can't miss the joy and light that is practically glowing from him.

His arm comes around my shoulder, and I snuggle in for the walk back to the campsite. "Best birthday present ever."

"And it's not even my birthday."

Noah chuckles, squeezing me for a moment. I hold him tight right back.

We start walking back, the sky holding the indigo of almost-twilight, the breeze gone, leaving behind tranquility and coolness.

Back at the campsite, I watch as Noah efficiently creates a stack from the wood he collected, small twigs at the bottom, thicker sticks at the top. He strikes a match; a few gentle breaths later and the first flames of a fire come to life.

I collect our dinner from the bag, canned soup, beef hotpot for Noah, chunky vegetable for me, and the solid loaf of rye bread that I banked wouldn't get demolished by our run through the forest. Two spoons and I've set the table.

When I return, Noah sits back, a merry fire crackling a few feet away. I stop, soup, bread, and spoons clutched to my chest, taking another memorizing moment.

One leg bent, an arm resting across it as he leans on a rock, Noah is breathtaking in the twilight. Light dances across his body, so rounded and casual, but one I know is hard and sculpted. Red and orange flames caress his features, finding the blond highlights in his hair, sharpening the contrast of his angles and planes. My fingers tighten around the silver cans, wanting to touch everywhere the light touches. Wanting to explore everywhere it doesn't.

I walk away from the tent behind me, toward the one I'll be sharing it with.

23

NOAH

What an amazing way to spend a day with my girl. There's something magical about Eden and me together. It's always there, the feeling that this is so right, but it's intensified, strengthened when we run. We're far more connected, in tune, when I'm a wolf and she's carving the wind with me. I can feel everything between us, so pure, so true, and it settles my soul in a way nothing else can. Or ever will.

Like it's fated.

Or prophesized...

The thought startles me, and I still. Then it makes me shift a little, the rock behind me digging into my back. Tara and Mitch's words, the ones that haven't really left my mind, swim the forefront. Is it possible?

Eden heads over, hair loose and wild from our run, body caressed by the fire, and passes me dinner. I open the two cans then sit them at the edge of the fire. She sits beside me then shuffles over until her side is flush with mine. I wrap my arm around her shoulder, pulling her even closer. With a sigh that calls to my masculine pride, she rests her head on my shoulder.

"Thank you."

She's thanking me? "This was your present, remember?"

She smiles, her eyes staring into the fire. "It may have been a little self-serving."

"You can be self-serving whenever you like." I look around at our little slice of heaven. "How did you find this place?"

She shrugs. "I didn't. I figured we'd find somewhere"—then snuggles in another micro-inch—"and we certainly did that."

"I'm getting used to that."

"To what?"

"You taking my expectations and throwing them to the wolves."

Like when she found out Werewolves exist—*Oh, you're part mega-wolf you say? Sure, I'm cool with that.* Then willing to go all public face and political for something she's passionate about at Wyoming State. Not to mention the hostess with the mostess alter-ego when we were at the awards dinner. Eden's not as shy or retiring as I'd prematurely concluded.

Maybe...

Eden blushes, a rosy glow I haven't seen for a while. "If we aim a bit bigger next time, we could end up solving the global environmental crisis."

I chuckle and she smiles. Right now, anything feels possible with Eden. I wonder if she feels it, too.

Maybe...

Pulling down her sleeve to cover her hand, Eden pulls the cans from the coals. She passes me a spoon and a chunk of bread. As silence descends with the twilight I wonder if it's time to take a chance. I take a breath and decide to start from the beginning.

"Things seemed straightforward when I was growing up. Turn sixteen, change, train to be Alpha." Find a mate, become the Alpha.

I pause, but Eden doesn't say a word. Her breathing is so shallow, it's almost non-existent.

My eyes return to the fire. "But I didn't change, and I went from normal to freak. All of a sudden, I discovered what it was like to be different, to not fit it."

To feel how Eden has felt all her life. I'm not sure if I pull her in closer, or if she snuggles closer, but we are melded side to side.

"But now I'm a Were, only because you made it possible, Eden, and I'm not sure what to do with it." Or the Prophecy.

"Noah." She stops, and I turn to her. The firelight is dancing in those tilted forest eyes, sureness radiates from their depths. "You were born to do this. It's all in there." She places a hand over my chest, my heart. The two parts of me she has changed forever. "I'm glad I got to be part of it."

Her use of the past tense makes me pause. It's the future I'm talking about.

I need to know. I want to tell her.

"Eden, I'm guessing this a cliché somewhere, someplace, but I'm nothing without you. My life started with you, and a future worth dreaming isn't possible without you in it."

Those eyes light up with a flame far brighter than the blazing fire beside us. "Noah."

Hope flares hot and hard. I need so little encouragement right now. "Eden, will you...you..." I falter, but the intensity in her eyes keeps me going. "I want you to be mine, to stay with me Eden, Were, Alpha heir, and..." My breath suspends for a second, the fire flickers, her eyes never waver. That feeling that I thought was gone rises, tightens around my throat. I swallow, "...all?"

Eden's mouth practically pops open, and I wonder if I've gone too quick, all of a sudden glad I haven't said the rest. Her hand, the one that trembles ever so slightly, comes up to cup my face. "Noah, a life without you is a life without light."

Hope explodes, happiness blazes, until nothing else has room to breathe. I'm gonna take that as a yes.

We kiss, and although we've kissed so many times before, this time is special. This is the first time I've started to believe I can do this. We can do this.

That the Prime Prophecy might be possible.

I haul her in close, until you couldn't fit an electron between us, so much emotion swirling through and around. *She said yes.* Mitch's face takes that moment to intrude, all stern and serious. I push it away, no one wants their twin in on their special moment, the moment their future is mapped out in the direction they desperately want. There'll be time to go over the logistics...tomorrow.

The fire has died down in the time I've laid my heart out, and a little shiver runs down Eden's body. I glance at the tent, knowing we should go to bed, where we'll be warm in our sleeping bags. In that little yellow bubble of enclosed space. Where it'll be dark and intimate. After a magical day of running, right after she's said she'd commit to an Alpha heir.

Uh oh.

She shivers then snuggles again. You know what? I can do this. Eden has given me so much more than I hoped for today. She's given me...hope. A hug, a sweet kiss, maybe three of four more; I'm only Were for Pete's sake, then I get to sleep with Eden in my arms. Two microfiber caterpillars in love.

With that image, I look at her fire-kissed face. "Why don't we go to bed? It'll be warmer in the sleeping bags."

"Yes, it will."

Something in Eden's tone warms my blood. *Cool it, big guy.*

Hand in hand we cover the few steps to the tent. Eden unzips it and as the yellow curtain falls away, I see what caused that husky note.

The soft, solitary bed has my mind stalling and my pulse rocketing.

"There was no room for sleeping mats, and I figured we'd be warmer..."

She's right. Eden would turn into a caterpillar icicle sleeping on the ground without something keeping her warm. And that something should be me.

"Seems logical." My voice stays completely calm and composed, right until the last syllable. Then it wobbles and wavers. I swallow, knowing my willpower is going to do the same thing. I climb in like that didn't just happen.

Inside the tent, we sit side by side, the gentle glow of a lamp highlighting how little room there is in this little yellow dome. When they labelled this a two-person tent, they obviously didn't mean one Were and one Changeling. Eden sits forward, dark hair waterfalling down her back, all quiet grace as she closes the tent. Is the sound of a zipper closing meant to be sexy? Wildflower scent is everywhere. Hormones, heart rate, everything spikes at the thought of sharing this bed with Eden.

We pull our shoes off then I take my socks off. Eden takes her jacket off as I peel down to a t-shirt. I'm going to have trouble maintaining an even body temperature without extra layers of warmth. I don't turn to see where Eden is looking as I climb into our bed.

Eden's teeth are already chattering by the time she climbs under the sleeping bag. I'm pretty sure she wasn't a polar bear in a past life.

"Come here." I pull her in, her shoulder to my chest, and she burrows far closer than I had hoped, then sighs as the tremors disappear. I wonder if I should be sainted for this as I smother the urge to pull her in closer. "I think you only love me for my ability to be a human heater."

She tilts her head up, those green eyes so close to mine. Those rose lips even closer. "Of course not."

"Oh?"

Eden frowns in thought. "You can move heavy furniture."

This is good. Mundane, safe conversation. "Keep me in mind if you're ever moving."

"You can sniff out a cheesecake for miles."

I cock an eyebrow. "So can you."

I get a great big smile for that one. "You are the fastest Were ever seen."

"Good to know if they ever have Were Olympics."

She flutters her eyelashes at me, those green eyes flickering like a movie screen of old, and I suddenly notice her hand on my arm. Is she getting flirty? "And for your hunky good looks."

Deep inside my chest, my ego does a puffer fish impersonation. I give an exaggerated sigh, letting my shoulders drop on the exhale. "It's a burden."

Her sympathetic look is equally as exaggerated. "You poor thing."

"Do you know what's an even a bigger burden?"

"What?"

"When your girlfriend's a stunner."

"Oh."

"Yeah, she turns heads everywhere she goes."

She gives me an unimpressed eyebrow raise. I decide to deliberately misinterpret her disbelief. "Okay, maybe that's a bonus. She is with me."

"I think we're done now."

"And she makes your heart skip a beat each time she looks at you." Eden's eyes fall to my chest. I tip her chin up with my finger, my voice dropping. "Okay, that's definitely a bonus."

A shy smile curves across her rose-colored lips.

"Although it is pretty doggone hard to keep your hands off her."

Her breath hitches, stalling my own. "Who made that rule up?"

Her voice has dropped a few decibels, too, a husky whisper that flutters over me. The butterfly effect whipping straight through me. I take a deep breath, trying to steady the instant reaction. And get a lungful of warm wildflowers, fanning the flames, whipping up a storm.

I give in to the longing that I never wanted to resist.

My mouth comes down on hers, to find her not only waiting, but well past the halfway mark. Mouths lock, open and hungry. Eden falls back, pulling me with her, so that we're face to face, chest to chest. I kiss her like I'm starving, like I've been holding back for too long. She kisses me like some barrier I hadn't know was there has just been exorcised.

Her hands are everywhere. My hands want to be everywhere. They spear into the thick mass of her hair, trying to hold her still. But my two palms are nothing against this tidal wave of passion. She's moving; her hands roam. They start in my hair, down my arms, fluttering across my shoulders, exploring my upper arms. And then they're on my chest, leaving trails of fire across and through my shirt. They move further down to where it's hiked up in our restless movements. Oh man, I want to feel her hands on my skin. Goosebumps ripple down my back.

My breath hitches, holds, as I wait. Want.

Her fingers edge across the hem, and in the dusky dark my shirt comes off, hers rides up until it might as well be off. We've started something that can't be stopped.

When skin meets skin it's like an explosive has detonated. Sparks, flashes, a multitude of small and too big eruptions. If this were a movie, it would be a flashing montage of desire.

You'd see silhouetted hands roaming, fumbling one moment then so doggone sure the next. Lips touching again and again, tasting over and over and over. Bodies moving then freezing, then moving once more. You'd hear sounds of gasping, groaning, whispered words of love and wonder, punctuated by the silent pauses of stuttering hearts and faltering breaths.

But you wouldn't get to experience how it *feels*. All scorching and hard, wondrous and soft, fast then slow, new but timeless, sexy and fragile, hot then hotter.

Eden's soft, hot hand has found its home on my chest, like she knows that's where I've ached for it to be. It stills and strokes over my wolf tattoo.

My mark!

Our bonded mark!

And I know I have to stop this before we reach critical mass.

I pull back, sucking air into my gasping lungs. I don't want her to regret anything. She still doesn't know... I grasp at something light. "We need a handbrake or something."

Something flashes in her green eyes, something that cools those glowing emerald orbs. They tell me exactly what she's wondering.

"No, Eden. You didn't do anything wrong. I don't think this could be any more right."

A small smile tips up swollen red lips. Lips that almost, almost make me forget why I'm having this conversation. "Okay."

Tell her... Jeez, what a great time for my Mitch-conscience to pop up. I pull back a little more, away from the voice, away from temptation. "You gotta know I want this."

"I do."

"I just...want to take it slow." *I need you to be sure.*

"It's okay."

But her quiet answers, downcast eyes, and the dense feeling that has congealed in my gut tells me it isn't.

"Eden, you're the one I want to spend my forever with." Tilted green comes up to meet my gaze. "Today topped amazing and headed off the charts, and there's going to be so many more. Why don't we save some our firsts for the others?"

For when you know everything.

"Okay." This time those two syllables are different. A little breathy, a lot lighter.

My hand comes up to curl around her cheek. I kiss her, slowly and meaningfully, trying to put everything I'm feeling into the contact between our lips. My heart touching hers. Our souls connecting.

I pull back to see a soft smile tilting just-kissed lips. "Just as long as you know I love you."

I breathe a sigh of relief. "I'm stopping because I love you, not because I don't want to."

That one gives me a puzzled twist to her brows. "Okay."

"Because I really, really want to." Man it feels good to be honest, for one sentence to hold the whole truth.

That warm glow heats up to an all-out blush as her eyes dip once again. "Sheesh, I said okay."

And I got a blush out of my girl.

I lie on my back, pulling her in close to my side. "Now, young lady, it's time for sleep. You have another big day of running ahead of you."

With a giggle and a sigh, Eden's head drops to my chest. "You know it's only a few weeks and I'm eighteen, too."

"And I'm going to squeeze every drop of advantage I can."

Eden stifles a yawn, like she doesn't want to admit I'm right. But I feel her relax, melting into me as the day finally catches up with her. The tent is warm and black, full of contentment, happiness, a slight undertone of unrequited passion. Her breathing slows, and I match mine to the steady, soft sound. Once she's asleep I can stop gritting my teeth.

Then her hand on my chest starts to move, a drowsy, lazy sweep back and forth. It's probably supposed to be calming and relaxing. But that affectionate, loving movement is anything but. I suck in a deep breath, trying to slow my heart, stop my hand from holding hers. From pulling her over me and picking up where I foolishly left off.

This is a whole lot harder than I thought it would be.

It's gonna be a long night.

But the truth is, there's nowhere else I'd choose to be.

24

EDEN

Noah asleep is a sight to behold...for as long as you possibly can. I can't decide if I want to touch those tousled, dark blond strands first? Or taste those sleep-softened lips?

Or do I want to lie here and watch the gentle rise and fall of his chest as his words from last night sing through my heart?

I could do all three...

I shift, the sleeping bag rustling. Could it be possible?

Noah spoke of a future, of a forever. There were no specifics, like is a bonding even possible? And how to tell his family. But it's all I need. Any shred of evidence that dreams can come true.

Noah moves a little, and sleepy, blue eyes open to find me watching him. A slow smile, relaxed and enchanting, climbs up his face. "Good morning."

"Yes, it is."

Noah's smile hikes a few more inches as I echo his words. Said so long ago, in a school parking lot, the day after I discovered he was a Were. The day after I said I would give us a chance.

I sink into the arms that open, resting my head on his chest. I hear his drowsy heartbeat, regular and soothing. "Sleep well?"

"I want to sleep like that always."

The song in my heart turns into a symphony. A rhapsody of sunrise and sound and blushing and sandalwood and heaven. "Me, too."

Although maybe with a little less stopping and a whole lot more touching.

I look up to find humor lurking in those blue pools, telling me he read between the lines. "We should get up."

"Yeah, we should."

Neither of us moves.

Today we head home, back to reality. Where we'll have to face the implications of everything we've committed to. What a scary, exhilarating prospect. I want to stay here forever, but also rush out and face our new life. Together.

A gust of wind rattles the yellow polyester around us. Mother Nature appears to be hurrying us up, making the decision for us. We both climb out of the tent to find dawn shadowed by clouds. It seems the storm front has crept in during the night.

"I don't think we'll beat it," Noah says, pointing at the growing blanket of clouds.

I shrug, grabbing the first sleeping bag and jamming it into its cover. "You're fast."

Noah does the same with the second. "I don't think I'm that fast."

I grab a tent pole and pull it out. I smile at the guy who has promised me forever. "Only one way to find out."

In short time, we've packed up the very first bed Noah and I have ever shared. It's a cold wind that whips the crumbs from our fingers as we eat our muesli bar breakfast.

The whole time I'm smiling; Noah and I touch. Is this where Tara's eternal well of optimism stems from? Is it the physical exhilaration of being so close to someone you love, or the wondrous words we exchanged, or the love you know is reciprocated, that has been promised a future?

As I shove the last of the camping gear in the backpack, I sense Noah move, and the metallic scent hits my nostrils telling me he's shifted. The white wolf that approaches me is light-footed and smiling. My own happy feet cover the last few steps, a matching grin across my face. I can feel it all, so much clearer, so much crisper. With words redundant, I leap on his back. We know where we're going.

I turn to look back at the little clearing, scattered ashes and flattened grass proof we spent the night. Physical evidence that we made our commitments. My happy place.

Our happy place.

I just about strain a smile muscle as those words whisper through my mind. I sink forward, burying my face in the snow-white fur. *Our happy place.*

Backpack on my back, we're off again. With the blustering, biting wind, I hunker down, drawn to the warmth of the wolf beneath me. I can feel Noah's tenseness as massive muscles stretch and contract, stretch and contract. They don't slow, never falter. The sky progressively gets darker, starting a patchy blue and grey then condensing to make a bleak, ominous ceiling.

But the cracking pace and determined drive aren't enough, because an hour later the first few drops hit. Icy pelts of cold smack my face. Just one or two, harbingers of what is to come. Droplets of ice promising that winter has managed to cling high in the atmosphere, fat heavy blobs, omens of the amount of water that is being held overhead.

Noah picks up the pace, paws pounding the ground, a steady drum beat that accompanies the growling above. The clouds shift and drop, grumbling and discontent, looking like they're pregnant—heavy and uncomfortable.

We're about to get—

Like Noah just gave the clouds permission, the rain starts. Heavy, cold drops pepper my face and shoulders, big enough to create little pools of water on my clothes. Big enough to land on Noah's fur then gain momentum and slide down.

I look up at the lead sky; the clouds have stretched out, horizon to horizon, like they've made themselves at home and don't intend on leaving anytime soon. It's a cold, unbreakable sight.

Noah runs and runs, like he's fast enough to dodge the pellets of cold. The progressive saturation of my face, hair, and clothes proves he isn't. I hunker down and curl up into the warmth below me. Thankful that at least my front half is warm and dry.

When the incessant heavy drops don't stop, they begin to join, surface tension drawing them together, creating little rivers over my skin. They snake down my arms, over the backpack, down my sides. They saturate my socks and boots, my hair and face, my chest and sides.

I ignore the cold for as long as I can. But when the icy water creeps beneath my clothes, creating a thin, icy sheet between me and Noah, it becomes a battle to disregard the bite of Jack Frost. The shivers start, in waves at first, and then a permanent shudder rolling from my teeth to my toes.

We need to stop and get warm.

Noah's words almost make my numb lips smile. Despite the icy rain, there's only one of us feeling the cold. But I'm relieved when he swerves toward the trees and into the forest, only to discover the branches of pine enclosing us don't stop the determined rain as Noah powers between the trunks. I curl up tighter, hoping he finds some shelter, listening to the heated thrum of his heart deep in his chest.

When Noah stops, I almost don't want to uncurl. I'm cold, a

wet, soggy block of ice, and my only source of heat is the furry body beneath me. When I register there's no more water hitting me from overhead, I look up and around. We're standing on a rocky outcropping, great big boulders a giant dropped in the middle of the forest. A flat slab leaning on one of the rounded rocks has created a small, but dry, shelter.

I slide off, and Noah shifts in a flash, my wet, blinking eyes suddenly finding him before me, my wet, shivering body quickly encased by his.

I wrap my arms around him, his clothes just as wet as mine. "I'm going to have to wring the water out of my bones when we get back."

Noah chuckles, his hands rubbing my upper arms. "We need to make a fire."

It's my turn to half-laugh. Nothing is going to be dry if it's under these clouds.

Noah steps away, and that grin of his sparks warmth deep in my chest. "Dad and I camped out here back when I was Alpha training, remember? Give me ten."

With a hard, wet kiss he disappears into the curtain of water. I shrug off my water-logged backpack, take the three steps to the back wall, and sink to the ground. The thought of a warm fire and an even hotter Were, my Were, has the shudders settling to low tremors. I rustle through the backpack, hoping a spare cracker or muesli bar has been spared from the saturating rain.

When I hear four paws approaching, rocks skidding down, a smile is already on my face before I'm up. When a wolf rounds the tree we both jump back.

The wolf before me is the right size, definitely a Were, but the wrong color. This wolf is slate grey, the color of the angry clouds that frame him.

It's not Noah.

Grey eyes that had widened when he saw me darken to lead

as I stand there, dripping and frozen.

I'm not scared straight away. Startled, yes. But not scared. The wolf watches me, his nose lifting infinitesimally, scenting me out. I can sense his indecision about his next move.

I've never seen a Were in the wild, one I don't know. I don't bother with my tune, this isn't a dangerous wild animal. I'm not a food source; I just need to convince him I'm not a threat.

"Sorry, I didn't mean to scare you."

The wolf's grey head straightens, and I feel his surprise.

"We were just passing through and got caught in the storm."

I look around. Do Weres have territories?

When his eyes narrow, his head sinking lower than his shoulders, that's when I sense it. He's decided what his next move will be.

Then I get scared.

When one paw lifts, moves forward, and drops to the rock floor, bringing the mass of muscles closer to me, it increases to fear. My heart leaps, jarring painfully in my chest, when the wolf takes another step. His body posture, his steely determination tell me everything.

He's not angry.

He's cold and grey and has a target.

Fear thrums through my veins, an electrical charge I can't contain, when I realize Noah will come running. Flashes of his fight with Kurt, of the blood running down his snow-white leg, have trembling hands come up to my mouth, holding in the 'no' that wants to scream past. The one that would make no difference.

This time, I start the melody. It doesn't matter that the thundering rain is a steady drumroll; I know he'll hear it.

Nature's song lilting and rolling through my mind calms me enough that bile is no longer stinging my throat. But will it calm him, too?

The wolf stops, one paw extended in mid-air, grey eyes growing.

He hears it?

I step up the volume, even taking a step forward myself. What do you say to a Were that you aren't supposed to know exists, that doesn't know Changelings exist?

Think about it, the consequences.

His broad head sucks back a little. And then dips again, his muzzle serrating, showing those deadly canines. I stay still, hands relaxed by my side. I can feel it; he's not angry at me. He's frustrated, but it's a frustration born of confusion. Stormy grey eyes look at me, undecided.

Please don't do this.

The decision is made for him when a wall of white muscle spears through the air, slamming into him. Noah's momentum shoves them both toward the trees, rolling over each other, grey, white, grey, white.

When they come to a halt, both wolves jump to their feet, facing each other. They stand, water and mud running down their bodies. You don't need to be a Changeling to see Noah is angry. Fury ripples up and down his back, pulling at his muzzle, shaking his muscles.

The grey wolf copies Noah's stance, but I can feel what Noah can't see. He's scared. The wolf's eyes dart to me, and I start running. But Noah sees the opening for what it is. An opportunity. He powers forward, head down, a white battering ram.

The grey wolf is propelled backward, like his size is insignificant. His grey body rams into a tree, a yelp carrying up to the trees. His body crumples, back arched against the trunk.

Noah, no!

I leap in front of the grey wolf, hands out, arms straight and tense. I reach them just as Noah, mouth open, teeth blazing, aims for the exposed throat.

Noah has to rein in his trajectory, his massive body compresses as he breaks, his paws ploughing into the pine-littered mud as he comes to a stop. Chest heaving, teeth disappearing, he looks at me in shock.

"He wasn't—"

Those teeth reappear as another round of growls rumble deep in his throat.

Okay, maybe initially, but he changed his mind.

I step forward, bringing myself eye to eye with the heaving mass of anger that never got to discharge. It's only when I bring my palm to his jaw, fingers feeling his throat suck in big breaths, thumb stroking his velvet muzzle, that he looks at me.

I'm okay.

A big breath exhales, but Noah's eyes dart behind me when there is a shuffling behind us, and I know the grey wolf is rising.

I turn to see him watching us as he slowly, carefully, creates distance between us. I feel rather than hear the growl deep in Noah's throat.

Let him go.

Noah wavers, anger warring with the need to protect, the desire to pummel fighting with the question of the right thing to do.

I love you.

Blue eyes connect with mine. *Now that's not fair.*

I smile a little. I turn to look into the trees; the grey wolf is gone. Noah let him go.

That's when I sink to my knees. Legs collapsing in the mud, water streaming down my face, I sit there. Shocked. Overwhelmed.

In front of me, Noah changes in an instant. Unblinking eyes get to see that sculpted chest, ripped abs. His mark flashes for a millisecond and is gone.

I blink, once, twice, three times. But my mind is full, overwhelmed with adrenalin, the implications of what could have just happened.

"Eden..."

I look up into concerned azure eyes. "I was so frightened," I whisper.

Noah engulfs me in his arms, my face to his wet t-shirt, even the smell of rain not dampening his sandalwood scent. "I'll always protect you, Eden."

That's what I'm scared of.

Because Noah just attacked another of his kind. For me. And the rapidly beating heart thumping against my cheek sounds out the truth. He would do it again.

"He wasn't expecting to find me."

"But he attacked you."

"No, he changed his mind. I could feel it."

"I wasn't waiting to find out."

Noah pulls me away, intense blue searching, hands roaming as if to confirm that I wasn't hurt. I wait, knowing he needs the reassurance. That done, he stands, pulling me up with him. "We need to get back."

"Yeah."

The Were attack has cut the possibility of waiting out the rain beside a warm fire. Noah turns and shifts, white pelt already wet. I jump on, sinking into the damp warmth, suddenly tired and keen to get home.

As we power forward through the trees, all I can feel beneath me is steely determination. The rhythmic tempo of Noah's run lulls me enough that I can ignore the cold trying to pierce deep into my marrow, that I can disregard the icy water that runs like rivers over and under my clothes.

And allows me to avoid the feelings I can't process right now. Not until I have some distance from Noah.

Then I have a decision to make.

25

NOAH

I 'm trying so flipping hard to get the anger under control. The feeling of Eden so scared, a feeling I haven't experienced in ages, hit me with the force of a sledgehammer. The image of that wolf, that big, hairy, lucky-to-be-alive-Were standing over Eden is a hard one to shake.

Winding back the fury, the burning desire to grab his throat between my jaws, to feel my teeth pressing into his fast-pulsing jugular wasn't easy. All I'd wanted to do was sink them into his rotten, vulnerable throat. It had been so close, so tempting. It would have shown that Were he doesn't mess with my mate.

Whoa.

I check myself before these emotions get out of control. I focus on the rhythmic pumping of my legs, out and in, out and in. I channel that anger into the energy to get Eden home and warm. And safe.

I use the weight of the body clinging to me to remind myself that she wasn't hurt in the end. And once I get past the horror movie in my head of Eden in danger, I start to see the Were hadn't attacked despite the opportunity. That Eden had been the one to make sure I didn't leave him lacking a trachea. I blink the water from my eyes. To be honest, I think Eden is the only one who could have reached me through that red curtain. Tara was right. Eden is the Doolittle of Weres.

I already knew she's everything I ever wanted, but I just realized Eden's everything we need right now. And after our talk, the passion that almost combusted us both, Eden's told me what I needed to know.

I keep my feelings checked. Being happy right now wouldn't make sense. Eden needs care and comfort. Not more revelations. But hope and anticipation lightens my step, until I am practically flying over the wet soil. Eating up the miles. Getting us home.

AT THE GLADE, we find my truck sitting in a puddle in the Glade parking lot.

Eden slides off, and I morph quickly and discreetly, looking forward to the moment I won't have to hide. "Mitch and Tara?"

Eden shrugs shivering shoulders. "You said they owed you."

I snort. "I've been calculating the interest."

In the truck, we're both quiet. Both thinking. I can hardly sense anything from Eden, probably still in shock. I'm glad I can get her home and warm. A good night's sleep, and tomorrow we can talk.

The moment we're out on the highway, my phone rings. I sigh when I see Tara's number; it didn't take long for reality to intrude.

I'm tempted not to answer, but I press the button anyway. "Hey."

"Hey, thought I'd give you a heads up. Your dad wants to talk to you."

As if to provide corroboration, my phone beeps then beeps

again. I glance at the screen, eyebrows raised at the amount of missed calls. Eden glances at me, curious.

My hand tightens around the phone, wondering what this is all about. "We're on our way now. We left early, thanks to the rain."

"That's what we figured. You heading straight here?"

I glance at the shuddering body beside me that looks like it's about to hit seven on the Richter scale. "I've gotta get Eden home and defrosted first. I won't be home till a bit later."

There's a pause, a long enough space of time for a frown to consider tightening my forehead.

"I'll head over; I reckon what that girl needs is a bestie, a hot chocolate, and a warm bed."

I arch a brow even though Tara can't see it. "After you ask for a bedtime story."

Tara giggles and some of the tension that her call has triggered eases. "I gotta get the deets!"

I hang up and know Eden is looking at me. The prospect of no more secrets has my foot pressing on the gas even though we're practically there. I grasp her hand. "FYI, Tara is meeting us at your place."

Eden's eyebrows push up into a 'why' position.

I shrug, determined to end this memory-making weekend on a high. "I gotta duck home for something."

"Oh."

"But I suspect it was all a ploy to start the Tara Inquisition sooner rather than later." Eden's smile is weak, half-hearted. I give her hand a squeeze before releasing it as we turn into her driveway. "As soon as I know, you'll know. I promise."

Eden climbs out of the truck without another word, meaning she doesn't see my smile die. The cold and that dufus-head Were has gotten to her more than I realized.

Under the porch Eden turns to me, and as I step in closer, her slow, glorious smile catches my heart. "Tara's right, a hot shower followed by an even hotter hot chocolate and I'll be fine."

"Were hearing wearing off, huh?"

Eden snorts. "Let's say she could never work in a library."

"Maybe I should stay?"

Eden shakes her head. "Go see what your dad wants. I'll be here getting warm, thanks to Tara's grilling."

I bend at the knees, bringing myself eye to forest green eye, not convinced, and maybe not ready for today to end. Eden pushes up and presses her lips to mine. I feel her love, the other emotions muted by tiredness and probably cold. I smile against the soft red pressing against mine. "Okay, okay, but I can't be held accountable if I'm back here later on."

Eden pulls back, her smile matching mine. "I'll be a whole lot warmer and drier by then."

I brush a strand of wet hair that sticks to her cheek. Eyelashes wet and dark, hair sticky and darker, Eden looks like a soggy waif. A beautiful soggy waif. "That was the most amazing weekend."

"That was an unforgettable weekend."

"I'm not sure how we're gonna top it." I lean closer, whispering over her lips. "But I'm looking forward to trying."

Eden's response is a feather light kiss. I can practically taste the love it holds, but she pulls back before I can respond with my own. "I'll see you later."

I'm gone before I can change my mind, keen to find out what Dad wants so I can get back. The rain stops like Mother Nature hit a switch the moment I turn onto the highway. Typical. I turn down the heat and amp up the music as I have to remind myself the son of a cop shouldn't be caught speeding. It's only a few miles when Tara passes me, Dana waving from the passenger seat beside her. I shake my head; Eden is going to get a double dose of Channon cheer.

As I head home, Eden's brush of love still tingling my lips, the words we shared last night are whispering through my mind.

I think it's time.

26

EDEN

The scalding water rushing over my skin feels like heaven. As the cold washes away, so does the numbness. And with the privacy of isolation the emotions come.

To begin with, there are too many to wrap my defrosting brain around, but like my mind is sorting it all, the highlights start to come to the fore. The day of running. The night of promises. The waking to a future my heart has ached for.

As the scent of soap catches on the steam, I remember the wolf. The grey Were that for terrifyingly long seconds considered attacking me. I watch the suds wash away as I remember Noah, furious and protective.

I bring my hand up to shut off the water, and it freezes. I freeze. The kaleidoscope of memories fade as one plays like a movie thrown onto the glass shower screen.

Noah stepping back, his anger dissipating, my relief turning my legs to jelly. Noah changing there and then, his chest, muscled and beaded with water flashing so much closer than I've ever seen it.

His wolf tattoo a black imprint so close I could touch it.

His mark.

"Hello! I come bearing a curiosity that must be appeased."

Tara's voice slices through the shock. I slam the water off, swallowing whatever thing was creeping up my throat.

"You in there, Edes?"

I clear my throat, trying to rattle loose the lump that's too big to be in there. I have to try again before I can respond. "Just finishing up. I'll be out in a sec."

"Cool cucumbers, we'll get onto the hot chocolate assembly line."

The click of my bedroom door tells me I'm alone. With no time to process what I've seen. What it means.

I wrap my robe around me, knowing I need to face Tara and hot chocolate before any implications can be drawn, decisions made.

As I step into the lounge room, I discover I'll be facing Tara and Dana. Before I've stepped into the kitchen a sweet smelling, steaming mug is pushed into my hands. Tara's eyes are eager, her red hair practically crackling with questions. "So, was it amazeballs?"

I tighten the belt on my robe a bit more, allowing myself to relish the feeling of being dry and warm. The only true emotion I let show is the tiredness, the exhaustion that has crept into my bones along with the cold. "It was amazeballs and then some."

Tara looks at Dana, all big smiles, and Dana smiles back. "I knew it. Tell me everything."

She breaks 'everything' down into each of its syllables, her chin and tone dropping an inch with each.

Don't blush. Don't look at Dana. Don't blush. "We were dropped off in the reserve. The run was amazing. There were so many animals, hares and squirrels and warblers and butterflies, and the first calypso orchids were coming into bloom—"

Tara makes a cutting motion through the air. "I'm not here for a biology lesson, Attenborough. Where did you camp?"

There's that drop of tone on the last word again.

Don't blush.

"We found this pretty little clearing by a stream. Lovely honeysuckle amongst the willows—"

"You're doing it again. Were you cold?"

How can one's eyebrows go so suggestively high?

Dana is quiet, watching us like she's at the movies.

"Ah, yeah. Once the sun went down, the temps dropped quite a bit."

I glance between the two sisters. I have no doubt Tara shares just about everything with Dana. But I'm not sure I can be that open. Tara's eyebrows clearly communicate 'and?'

I think of Noah's words, Noah's hands and lips, Noah in the morning. "It was very...special." The understatement doesn't feel like it captured last night, but it'll have to do. As uncomfortable as it is, this part of the weekend I'm happy to focus on, to relive.

Tara slaps her thigh. "I knew it!"

The blush that's been building up bursts like Krakatoa across my face. I can feel its heat all the way down to my toes. On second thought, maybe I'm not so keen to discuss this. "Nothing happened."

"Nothing?"

"Well, not...you know."

"Not that you have to worry."

Tara and I turn to Dana. They're the first words she's said for a while. She's staring at some watercolor on the wall, mouth pursed a little, fingers twirling her red hair.

"What do you mean?"

Dana startles, hazel eyes shooting to us. "Oh, nothing."

"Yeah, don't worry about it, Edes."

Something tingles down my spine, telling me to ask. Telling me to shut up and let it go. "What?"

Tara stands, all business, flapping her hand at Dana to do

the same. "You need R and R, not something that isn't even rele-vant right now."

I grit my teeth. I don't know why, but for some reason, I clench them hard as I squeeze out that word again. "What?"

Dana looks at Tara. There's a warning in Tara's eyes, but Dana turns away, those identically colored eyes turning to me. They're filled with pity. "Weres can't have children with humans."

I don't move a muscle, an eyelid, a sodden piece of hair. Despite the words hitting me, rocking me, shredding me. Despite the emotion that grows within me. Now is not the time to process this. *Not now.*

Tara shoots an angry glare at her sister, before turning earnest eyes to me. "It doesn't matter, Eden. What you and Noah have is special, we all know it."

Dana steps forward, hazel eyes big and round. "Yeah. Noah chose you."

But instead of making me happy, something big and sharp lances through my chest. I still don't move, pushing the pain away. *Not now.*

I look at the two sets of hazel eyes watching me. Tara's worried, Dana's indecipherable. I really hope only a few seconds have passed. "I suppose that's something Noah and I will have to figure out."

Tara lets out a breath. I don't have the energy to see what Dana thinks. I make a show of stretching taught tangled muscles, hoping they don't snap. "I'm pretty tired."

"How about we watch a movie or something?"

My stomach tightens; I'm not sure how much longer I can hold this together. "I think I might catch up on some lost Zs; you might as well head home."

"You sure? I could hang around, annoy Caesar or something?"

"Nah, you've got better things to do with your time."

"Okay." Tara draws the word out in that slow way that says she's not convinced.

But Dana is my new ally. "Come on Tara, let the girl have some peace and quiet. We'll give you a call later?"

I nod, hoping they think it's tiredness that has me sagging rather than relief. Tara lets Dana tug her toward the door, glancing over her shoulder. I nod, pulling up a smile as I follow them.

"Call me if you need anything. Cheesecake, chocolate, a chat."

Talking is the last thing I feel like doing right now, and I think cheesecake could make me vomit. I stretch that smile a little wider. "Sure."

Dana gives me an I'm-glad-everything-is-fine smile in return. "Bye, Eden."

"I'll catch you later."

I close the door even though Tara is still looking at me over her shoulder, then turn to rest my back against it. All the strength I'd mustered to keep up my happy façade runs out and I sink, not slowly, but quickly, jarring me as I collapse in the hallway.

All the chaos that's been churning in my head slows. The blurry, indistinguishable fears and worries become crystal clear.

It all makes sense.

Noah's turmoil. The secrets. Never telling me that we've impossibly, amazingly bonded.

What should have been the announcement that gave my dreams substance, instead has robbed me of the ability to stand. My greatest fear, the only truth that could steal the possibility of a future, is real.

My fear that he was choosing.

Because he was.

Noah chose me.

But I can't come between him and his pack, his future as an Alpha, the family that is his roots. If he chooses me, he can't have children...he could even be banished. It's the one choice I won't let him make.

I sit there, back against the door, and watch the decision coming toward me. It's big and black and it's going to hurt. There's a possibility I won't be able to find all the pieces after it hits. And I shatter.

So I do the only thing I can.

As that train of pain bears down on me, getting darker than black and bigger than is possible to survive, I step aside. Yes, I leave behind a shell, a ghost, but that barely breathing husk doesn't feel, doesn't endure the impact as she decides.

That shell can do what needs to be done.

27

NOAH

"Did you talk to her?"

"We had a lovely time, thanks for letting me in the door before you asked."

Mitch pushes himself up from the honeyed timber bench beside our front door; it creaks ever so slightly as the folded piece of cereal box beneath the front leg expands. He puts a hand on the door and stops.

"Well?"

I frown, my first in two days. His seriousness, along with the door blocking, is starting to tick me off. "We talked."

"And?"

"What's with the front porch third degree?"

The arm stretching to the door drops a little. "Dad wants to talk to you."

No kidding. My eyes shoot to matching blue. "You told him?"

"What? No!"

Relief washes through me. "Then what?"

"So, you told her."

And he calls me stubborn. "We're doing this."

Mitch lets out a breath, and his hand slips from the door knob. "Good."

"Is that Noah?" Mom's voice carries from the other side.

Mitch opens the door, and I'm folded in warm arms and the faint smell of charcoal. The scent of childhood, the smell of love.

"I only left yesterday."

Mom pulls back, fingers ruffling my fringe like she always has. Those brown eyes seem to know that a lot has passed in the past twenty-four hours.

"Dad's outside."

I head out to the thinking chair, curious, maybe a little nervous. The backyard has been washed clean by the downpour. The lawn Kermit-green, the trees bigger, a deeper shade...Hulk-like. Dad is there on the slightly sideways wooden bench.

His head turns slightly as I approach, although he knew I was coming minutes ago. He faces the trees again as I sit and wait.

And wait.

I'm not sure what for. Am I supposed to say something?

"Noah..."

I realize something unsettling, a feeling like this bench isn't as sturdy as I thought. Dad is at a loss for words.

"There were two attacks in the reserve today."

Now that Dad has found the words, I kinda wish he hadn't. But once he's started, it doesn't stop.

"All lone hikers. No serious injuries, one sprained ankle from running. All claiming it was by a massive wolf."

My hands ball tight, not sure if I should say it. "Three."

"What?"

"There were three." I suck in a steadying breath. "Eden was attacked."

Air gets sucked in beside me, pulled in through closed teeth. Held. It's only once it's back out that I continue. "We were coming back, I was getting firewood. Eden managed to calm him until I got there."

Dad shoots up, all of a sudden his whole body straight. He turns, face tense, eyes tenser. "And?"

I frown, arms bracing beside my legs. "Eden stepped in before it got out of hand."

Dad steps forward, arms coming up like he wants to grab me. But they drop as he takes a step backward. His voice is quiet when he asks, "Did you draw blood?"

I stand, too, confusion deepening the frown. "Why?"

"Did you draw blood?" This time the question is deeper, harder.

"I...I don't think so."

"You have to know, son. Think. Did you draw blood?"

I want to ask why, why so urgent, so intense? But the tense face has me rewinding the tape on those moments in the woods, going through each scene. I'd wanted to, and I probably would have if it wasn't for Eden. But I didn't.

"No."

Dad's eyes close, his head tilting to the sky for a brief second. I decide it's my turn for some answers, so I ask again. "Why?"

Those blue eyes, my Phelan pack heritage, open and come to rest on me. They are steady, serious, and make me more nervous than they should. Dad takes a step forward, his hands coming up to grip my shoulders. With the speed of an Alpha Were, possibly because I never see it coming, his hands grab my shirt and yank.

The cotton tears and opens like a chasm. The vulnerable skin below, and its tattoo, practically glow in the light they hardly ever see.

"Because if the Prime Alpha draws the blood of another Were, he drains them of their power."

I step back. And step back again. *What?*

But Dad hasn't finished. "They become human only."

I want to take another step back. Actually, I want to take a million steps back. My too-full head can't wrap around everything he just said. What question do I ask first? Do I really want to know?

It really comes down to one. "How did you know?"

Dad holds up his hand, ticking each finger off as he reels off a list. "You didn't change at sixteen—that's not a Precept, but it wasn't normal. Overtaking at the full moon run. You weren't flashing your bare chest any minute you could like every other young Were." Those blue eyes sharpen. "Eden."

Involuntarily, my hand comes up to my chest, trying to reunite the tattered material. "You knew!" There's an accusatory note in my voice. I can't help it. "Why didn't you tell me?" The note stays; I'm too worked up to hide it.

"The Prime Alpha is a choice that was made for two people thousands of years ago. It's a big ask, almost too much to ask. You've only just turned eighteen."

Dad takes a step back, like this may be too much for him, too, but his eyes never leave mine. "But we haven't been afforded time. This is getting serious, Noah. Weres are exposing themselves, attacking each other and now humans. There's more than just Seth greedy for power. We need the Prime Alpha."

I swallow, finally acknowledging it. "I think you're right."

Dad's head shoots up. "You've done nothing but fight it."

A sheepish shrug tugs at my shoulders. "Change kinda sucks. Things seemed fine."

"Kurt was the first to show us it wasn't."

"I see that now. I've realized the Prime Alpha is about our laws, but it's more than that."

"Yes, it is."

"Seth's got it all wrong."

"Yes, he does."

"Sure, wolves are powerful predators, but they are about keeping the balance. Humans have the power to actually make that happen. And we're both."

"We need a Prime Alpha, Noah."

The air leaves my tight chest, but I suck it back in along with a little extra. We need Eden. "I know. Eden and I decided last night."

"So she knows?"

I sit back on the thinking chair. "She's willing to have a future." Shrewd blue tells me he's seen evasion too many times. And for some reason, I feel guilty. "Not yet."

Dad's hand on my shoulder feels a lot like the weight of responsibility. "We need the Prime Alpha."

Bloody hell, I heard him the first time. I stand and mirror his gesture; he hasn't seen what I've seen, know what I know about Eden. "I'll talk to Eden this afternoon. This is all going to work out, Dad. I can feel it."

His piercing eyes, wise and watchful, study me for long seconds. He nods as he squeezes my shoulder. It compresses the air from my chest, and I acknowledge the relief I feel that I have his support.

The Phelan grin tickles at the edges of his eyes. "Sorry about the shirt."

I shrug, the ragged edges flapping in the breeze. "It's cool, although Mitch might not be."

Dad shakes his head as he realizes it wasn't my shirt. "You might want to hide it where you put your Mom's carrot cake."

I grin. "Except that's where Mitch put the sunglasses you thought you lost...after he accidentally stepped on them."

Dad shakes his head, rolling his eyes. "Go get changed. Once you've talked to Eden, we'll figure out what to do about the Weres that attacked the hikers."

I nod, keen to find the one that attacked Eden for a whole

host of personal reasons. Figuring out why they did it was going to be the first.

Inside, I head up to my room, grabbing another curtain for my chest, hoping Eden's showered and rested—the talk can't wait until tomorrow. It's time she knew. I smile as I pull my shirt down. Not long now. The attacks, the talk of shedding blood, will be over. Eden and I will be bonded. I can finally show everyone what my heart has been bursting to howl from the highest peak for too long now.

Creaks from the stairway snap me from my thoughts. I know those light-footed steps.

It's only when Eden is in the doorway, her face as pale as death, that I realize I never felt her coming. I must have been really caught up in my thoughts.

"Hi." Her voice sounds hollow. I freeze in a way that would make Orin proud. I hold my chest, my breath, my flipping heart still. Nothing.

I. Don't. Feel. A. Thing. "What's going on?"

"I've figured it out."

I play dumb as the doorknob her white knuckles are gripping. "Eden, I know that Were scared you but—"

"I know, Noah."

My mouth opens a little. My chest opens like a chasm.

"I know about...us, and what it means."

What? "I was going to tell you, Eden."

"I understand why you didn't. And it's okay. I get it."

I step forward, ready to show how amazing we'll be, what this can mean for us and for everyone.

"This isn't going to work."

Everything in my body freezes again, denial streaking through me. "No." I try to move again, but for some reason I can't. "This isn't what I want."

Eden steps back, her eyes a flat, slate green. "I know, me

neither. But what you're asking, I'm not willing to sacrifice. I just can't do it."

The fight leaves my body, actually, I think it suffocates and dies. It chokes under the despair that Eden's words spawn.

"You can't do it," I whisper, a hollow echo of Eden's empty voice.

Eden steps back, not that it matters. The feeling of nothing, the absence of anything, has created more distance between us than I ever thought possible. "It's too much. I'm sorry."

With those words, the only words that would have stopped me from arguing or following, she leaves.

As I look at the empty doorway, the timber framing nothingness, as I feel the hole that was just hacked out of my chest, I still can't find the ability to move. When playing out how this would end, in all the scenarios I ever imagined, this is not one I could have conceived. That Eden would find out then choose out.

That there would be no bonding.

No Prime Alpha.

I didn't see me standing in my room alone, struck dumb with pain, watching her walk out the door.

That there would be no Eden.

28

EDEN

I spend a lot of time watching myself. I feel sorry for the girl who sleeps too much, who eats without tasting, who moves through a world she doesn't look like she belongs in. I feel sorry for her, but there's not a chance I want to be her.

Even though I haven't been at school, Alexis hasn't cottoned on. Possibly because although we were roommates before, we're strangers now. Worse than strangers. We're two people that used to know each other, were supposed to mean something to each other, and now can't stand to look at each other.

Possibly because there's been no tears.

I roll over in bed, looking at my clock. It's after nine. I need to do something about the school situation. I pick up my phone and dial.

"Good morning. Jacksonville High School."

"Hi Mrs. Marple, it's Eden."

"Hello lovely, I haven't seen you all week."

"Ah, yeah, something's come up—"

"Oh dear, anything I can help you with, dear?"

I smile a hollow smile. Nothing I want shared in the staff

room. "No, we've had a family emergency, and I have to go out of state. I won't be back, possibly before exams."

"You do sound...off dear. That's fine; it's only a couple of weeks. Shall I email your work to you?"

"That would be wonderful, Mrs. Marple; I appreciate it." It's amazing how much a well-behaved, regularly attending, high-achieving student can get away with. "Thanks, I'll see you at exams."

I hang up, ignoring how I'm going to get legitimate paper-work to back up my ill-defined excuse.

I dress without care, Caesar watching the slow movement of my ghost town body. He doesn't move forward, just sits and watches, like he knows how fragile I am. I promise myself I'll take him for an extra-long walk when I get back.

I climb into the car and drive, realizing I need a destination. I'm not going to school, and I can't stand to be at home. Even the reserve is riddled with memory land mines. So, I head to the one place that holds the least connection to him, and them.

Wyoming State is much quieter than the open day, which is just what I'm looking for. Avoiding the possibility of eye contact, I head to the memorial gardens. I wonder whether part of me is looking for Orin, but I'm not sure whether even he's safe for my tightly held equilibrium.

If there were anything to soothe, the memorial gardens would do it. Their gently winding paths, the healing colors of nature wrap around me. My disconnected brain appreciates this would be a good place to go to heal, and I'm relieved I don't need it.

I walk the many little gravel tributaries. Each one opens out to a rounded bud of vegetation, flowers, and beauty. Each one holds a small plaque, memorializing someone who managed to make something of their life. Most of the pockets of garden are empty, but despite the gift of solitude each one offers, I keep going.

There's a restless energy buzzing through my limbs, a fortress of numbness that seems to need movement to keep its walls up.

I round the bend of one of the gardens on the east side to find I'm not alone. A lone body in a Wyoming State blazer, tall but somehow stooped, overlooks the garden. I step back, not wanting to intrude and not wanting to be seen.

The shoulders tense, straighten. Shoulders that wrench air into my lungs. Shoulders I recognize and don't want to. Silently I retreat, my fragile stranglehold on numbness knows I can't be here.

But Were hearing has picked up on my intrusive footsteps and he turns, surprise lifting his brows. "Hello, Eden."

I don't respond. I can't. Seth is not someone I can talk to.

Seth doesn't move, but I can see his mind working. He looks at me, takes in my silence. I don't know what he sees; the anesthesia in my mind stops me from going there. But it seems he sees something because his face changes, morphs first to understanding and then to something else.

Pity. I take another step back, almost at the mouth of the walk I shouldn't have taken.

"I would have warned you if it would have made any difference." I step again, so close to returning to blessed ignorance. "But like me, you thought you'd be different, that maybe the rules wouldn't apply to you."

Energy sizzles through my legs, drawn to the exit. Every cell in my body knows I don't want to have this conversation. "Goodbye, Seth, sorry for...interrupting."

I turn, but Seth hasn't finished. "How close do you think you got?"

I pause, stiffening. Too close. Never close enough. "It doesn't matter."

Seth looks back at the garden, down at the silver and black

plaque that sits on its rim. "Actually, it does. It's kind of like an explosion, the closer you are, the deeper the wound, the more pieces there are to find."

All of a sudden I'm not so sure he's talking about Emily. Legs that defy my mind return to the circle. I follow his gaze.

Adelle Channon
Mother and Activist.
Passionate advocate, relentless campaigner.
The silent voices of the park only you could hear say thank you.

Seth's shoulders are curved once again. There's only one emotion that carries that much weight. Grief.

I pause beside him, knowing there's little comfort my shutdown mind can give. "I'm sorry, Seth."

He doesn't look at me, doesn't acknowledge my words, and I wonder if someone else has discovered the self-induced emotional coma. "It's ironic that what she dedicated her life to was what killed her."

I stay silent, knowing I don't want to know. I'm here to escape pain, not find it.

"There were some investors poking around near the Glade, not far from the highway, talking of buying and developing the area. There was lots of talk, but the Channons knew we needed action."

Seth still hasn't looked at me, but all of a sudden I'm rooted to gravel and dirt.

"We went there one evening, just to spook them away. We didn't know they'd brought protection."

Now Seth looks at me, and my reflexes are too slow. I get trapped in agonized hazel. "I saw them lining her up, but I couldn't stop them." His lip curls. "Not without risking our secret."

"It was a tragedy, Seth; she couldn't have stopped it. From the sounds of it, she wouldn't have wanted to stop doing what she loved, what she believed in."

"He's right, you know." There's a breath of time long enough for me to blink, for confusion to join the swirling fog in my head. Wasn't Seth talking about his mother? But there's no time for me to decide whether I want to ask. "My mother was killed by human greed, human selfishness. And we"—he thumps his chest hard, with conviction—"have the power to do something about it."

My mind, hollow and numb, struggles to hold the words, to understand their implication. Seth moves forward, coming closer. I brace my too-tense muscles, but he walks past. His last line, served with regret rather than victory, is the part that hangs long after he's gone. "I wish it had been otherwise, but in the end, you can't bring someone into the fold when they were never part of the fabric."

The walls around my self-control bow in, giving in to the pressure his words exert. I shake my head as breathing becomes a fractured, difficult process. With every shred of my will power, I fortify the fortress. The emotions recede, and I'm left with emotional anesthesia.

Striding to the end of the path, I turn left, deeper into the gardens, figuring Seth would have gone right and out. The gardens no longer look reassuring and relaxing. Nowhere is safe.

I pull out my phone, deciding there's only one person that can offer me sanctuary.

29

NOAH

I lean my head against the rough bark of Grandfather Douglas. I push, ridges and lines digging into my forehead. It stings then hurts, so I push harder, fingers biting into the bark, jamming the ridges into my skin.

I'm a walking wound. I bleed everywhere I go. Pain hemorrhaging out steadily and relentlessly, impossible to contain because it has an infinite source— the knowledge that my choices got us here. It clouds my thoughts, hurts my chest. My whole body hurts.

My whole doggone life hurts.

The car I knew was approaching stops beside the house. The sound of Tara and Mitch's footsteps try to crowd into my head. I step away from the big tree that wasn't able to answer my question.

How do I fix this?

They stop a few feet away, keeping the distance that's become the norm over the past few days. Tara crosses her arms. "Eden's not at school."

What? The whole reason I haven't been going was to give her space. That, and a healthy dose of self-preservation.

"And Seth's gone."

"Gone? Where?"

Tara narrows her eyes. "How the hoopla should I know? I got a text 'places to go, people to see. See you at Council.'"

Mitch adds the obvious, like our twin bond has been severed. "There's no way to find him before Council."

"He'll be back for Council." He has to be.

Tara steps forward, furious red and angry angles. Her little finger punctures the air between us, and I almost wish she were close enough to reach the body she really wants to stab. "You're the only one who can fix this, Noah."

She spins on the pine needle ground and stalks away. Mitch watches his mate create space between us then disappear into the house. He turns to me, blue eyes dark. "I've been watching for weeks, months, as Tara's pack has been slowly disintegrating. Knowing the whole time, you were the one person that could have prevented it."

Veins and arteries step up from oozing to a steady stream. Mitch is the one person who's understood why I kept quiet. "You know why I did it."

Mitch never moves, but I can feel my twin moving away, the distance growing. "I know exactly why you did it." He looks back at the house. "But I thought you'd figure it out."

"She wasn't ready."

With a shake of his head, Mitch turns. "I knew you were stubborn, but I never picked you for a coward, Noah." Shoulders pulled so low you couldn't heap on any more disappointment, my brother walks away.

Leaving me alone.

Well, not completely alone. My choices, fractured shards, crash and glisten around me, slashing through the healthy dose of doubt that now runs alongside the pain.

The next car I don't hear, nor the footsteps, until I find I've once again got company under Grandfather Douglas's canopy.

Dad, still in uniform, looks a bit like someone sucker punched him, too. "I've managed to plant the suggestion that what they saw was nothing but a wolf. We'll probably do some searches through the reserve, make it seem like we're responding, but looks like we might be able to bury the paperwork."

That would have been tough for Dad. Although we live with our secret, manipulating and lying to protect it wouldn't feel a lot like integrity.

"It's just Seth we need to deal with then."

Dad growls, and my chest tightens along with his fists. "Noah, the only way any of this will stop will be with the claiming of the Prime Alpha."

I look away, knowing it's true, but my pain-soaked brain hasn't come up with any answers.

"You need to talk to her."

I blink, hating that I have to say it out loud. "Eden's gone." I haven't felt her since our run. The last run. "She didn't want this." She didn't want me if it meant Prime Alpha.

"You told her, and she ran?"

"She figured it out."

Then she ran. I don't blame her; who would choose this? As in choosing to lead Weres when your life is just about to start, according to a Prophecy people forgot existed. No one would choose that. The knowledge doesn't stop the hemorrhage of pain.

"Then the only way you can claim Prime Alpha is to draw blood."

That suggestion has me flying forward, sick with disgust, full of anger. "And be the ultimate Precept enforcer?" The only one with the power to end a Were.

Dad doesn't move, a mountain that's meeting Muhammad. "You don't have a choice, Noah."

The immutability of his statement, his immovable conviction has me backing down. "I can't do that, Dad."

There has to be another way.

Dad is shaking his head, slowly, propelled by the power of certainty...like there's no other choice. "You're the one who chose, Noah. Chose for us all."

And like everyone else, like all my options, he leaves, too.

I make it back to the massive trunk before I lose the ability to stand. Leaning back against the fir tree, I slide slowly down, welcoming the graze of bark on my back—if it draws blood then at least some part of me can start to echo how the rest is feeling.

There's one way there can be a Prime Alpha without Eden.

But there's no way I can be anything without Eden.

30

EDEN

O rin doesn't live on campus, but I quickly find the small cottage tucked on the far side of Cheyenne, the city home of Wyoming State. The place, perched at the end of a quiet street, is possibly more of a shack. A small, wild garden tumbles around the house, knowing no boundaries, thanks to the absence of a fence. I let out a sigh as I park the car. If I ever start feeling again, I'll be too far away for anyone to find me. Or feel me.

I quickly discover why the place is as isolated as you can get in suburbia. There are animals everywhere. Two dogs rush forward the minute I open the car door, one big and black, the other stocky and brown. No one, single breed is apparent in either. They greet Caesar like best friends of old.

Orin greets me like the prodigal sister returning home.

Inside the cottage is a menagerie of furniture, no one piece from the same culture, and a harem of cats. One feline, one eye permanently closed, the opposite ear torn, limps over on a deformed leg. She hisses, back arched, spitting an unwelcome greeting. I slip my suitcase to the ground, but the melody doesn't come. It seems to have abandoned me along with the ability to feel. For the first time, I realize this barren existence may not be helpful. I heft my suitcase; the alternative is unthinkable.

In the end it's not necessary, because Orin holds out his hand, kneeling in front of the distrustful feline. The cat instantly calms, and with a single-eye glare, leaps to the back of one of the chairs.

"You can command them?"

"Why would we? We do not dominate, we touch their curiosity, their desire to explore, their need to connect. Our relationship is a reciprocal one."

I glance at the tattered, still-wary cat. "What if they're aggressive?"

"How many aggressive animals have you faced?"

"A few." Caesar was the first.

"And?"

I shrug. "Aggression is a means to an end. It's about suggesting to them there's a different way to get there, considering a different outcome."

Orin smiles agreement, leading me past the lounge and adjoining kitchen to a hallway with a handful of doors. He glances over his shoulder. "Your mother is okay with this arrangement?"

The conversation with Alexis had been like a dagger, short and sharp. She'd walked into my room as I'd left the bathroom, heading to my suitcase, glancing from the contents of comfortable denim and bland cotton to the toiletries bag in my hand. "I don't think so."

Ignoring her, I'd stuffed the little bag in, closed the lid, and zipped it up.

"Where are you going?"

I hadn't looked at her as I'd lifted the belongings that would follow me from this house. "I'll let you know how I do in exams."

"You'll have nothing."

I'd continued to the front door, Caesar by my side. "You never gave me anything that counts."

Her heels had followed me to the door. I was through it and at the car when she spoke again. "You don't get to leave and take what you please."

A trickle of emotion had seeped in, little tendrils of anger, hot and piercing. "That would mean I'm using you, wouldn't it?" I'd slammed the trunk, the thud shutting down the feelings I don't need anymore. "How does it feel?"

I hadn't bothered to see what she'd thought of that.

As Orin stops in one of the doorways I shake my head. "Believe me, she'll thank us."

"You are not close with your mother?"

"No."

Orin's eyes seem to track me as I look at the simple room we've stopped at, bed and dresser, blues and greens on the walls and bedspread. "And Noah?"

The walls of my protective shell bow in, like they've been assaulted by his name. For a moment, the world sharpens, there's a ray of pain. I grab the doorway, determined fingers wrapping around the wood.

In a strong, hollow voice I say, "It's over."

Orin nods, green eyes serious. "When you want to talk."

I notice Orin's use of 'when' instead of 'if.' I enter the room of greens and blues, not bothering to tell him neither is an eventuality.

"You'll be sharing with Aria."

There's another cat in the room, curled in the center of the double bed. This one a tabby and much friendlier looking. Orin leaves me to settle in, and I sit next to Aria, brushing her absent-mindedly as I allow myself the feeling of satisfaction. I've found my sanctuary.

It doesn't take long to unpack. Jeans and shirts in the drawers, toiletries in the bathroom. I find Orin reading in the lounge and join him on the mismatched lounge chairs. Orin smiles, the gesture almost feels like a hug, before returning to his book.

I clear my throat. "I, ah, just wanted you to know I have savings, so I'd like to pay board."

Orin's blond head doesn't lift from the book. "Orin?" I'm about to repeat my statement when his hand comes up.

"I heard you. I'm focusing on striking that insult from my memory...sister."

He looks up, a gentle smile gracing his green eyes and familiar lips. My own lips soften, my eyes tilting. It's the closest I've come to smiling. Orin's smile fades, and I almost wish I could have joined him. But I've seen what it could look like if I consider feeling. That's not a place I'm visiting.

"Okay."

I open my book, heading to my favorite chapter on wildlife ecology. I turn a page, and something slips onto my lap. I gasp, leaping to my feet as it flutters to the ground.

"Eden?"

I want to crawl, run, escape, but it's too late, because my traitorous hand picks it up. Faded and brittle, a pressed columbine rests in my palm. Clear and unwanted, the memory it holds plays in my mind.

"Are these, too?"

Noah had stood there, the sun's rays combing through his dark blond hair, making gold the strands it touched. His summer blue eyes so light, sparkling with a touch of humor...and a touch of hope.

I'd taken it, stood there like I didn't care, determined not to let him in. Then tucked the precious little gift into my backpack and pressed it in my favorite textbook the moment I got home.

But he'd gotten in. First slamming through with the force of an angry white wolf. Then knocking down the remaining defenses with feather touches, a hint of a smile, words laden with meaning. Walls that had been so willing to come down.

It's that fragile, pale columbine that becomes the straw, the straw that brings me to my knees.

And breaks me.

It's a shattered body and forgotten text that fall to the floor. A sob, a powerful wail, fill my chest and claw up my throat. By the time they've escaped, they've accumulated all the pain and hurt I've been carrying but avoiding. They escape, gain voice, and don't stop.

The hands over my eyes are wet, their lines and crevices filled with never-ending tears. I pull back to look at them, confused as to why they are glistening clear rather than blood red.

"Eden." Orin's voice, so full of compassion, seeps under the howl I can't seem to contain.

He joins me on the floor, and for the first time in my life, there is someone comforting me as I fall apart. Warm arms slip around my shattered body, holding my shuddering shoulders, stroking the hair that circles me like a shroud.

And it doesn't help.

Every part of me is shaking to pieces. The broken shards of me slip through Orin's arms and fingers. They bleed onto the ground. It's only a matter of time before I'm a fractured, fragmented ruin scattered around my brother.

"Orin, it hurts."

Without the blessed oblivion of ignorance, it hurts.

"I know. I'm here. I'll hold you."

As anguish and heartache, agony and soul-deep grief batter and lash at me like I don't have any defenses left, Orin stays true to his promise.

He holds me as I shatter.

31

NOAH

"I've brought you your favorite."

I peel my eyes from the ceiling and the pointless process of drawing shapes between the faded sticky tape marks. Mom joins me on the bed as I sit up. I don't need to look at the plate in her hand to know what's on there.

Growing up, Mitch and I had a code. The worse Mom's cooking was, the more we complimented it. That way, the other twin could realize and feign a full stomach before they got served, thereby asking for a small portion. The day pigs' trotters had rolled onto my plate, all pale and human-skinned, it was my turn. As the chewy leather had entered my mouth, Mitch had watched closely as I'd chewed. As my taste buds had rebelled, I knew I had to warn him.

"Wow, these are sooo good, so good I think they just became my new favorite!"

Mom had been so delighted she'd made them at every special occasion— my primary graduation, when I got my first high school A, to cheer me up when Tara had given me a haircut. They're a fitting punishment for my latest achievement.

My head sinks into my hands, jamming my fingers in my hair. "I've royally fudged everything, Mom."

Mom places the plate with the pig legs on my bedside table. "Was it harder to believe in yourself, or in Eden?"

What? My eyes shoot to hers. "Eden is one of the most amazing people I know. You don't know what she's had to overcome to be where she is."

Those brown eyes are steady on mine. Waiting.

My shoulders slump. "I just wanted to give her time."

"Noah, do you remember when Grandmother Mae died?"

I nod. "We were ten; she was hit by a drunk driver." Even speedy Were healing couldn't repair the damage the truck had dealt like a wrecking ball.

"I spent a long time keeping you away from Grandpa Ben. It was such a shock, and he was in such a bad way."

I stare at the wall, remembering. "Mitch and I were so confused. We didn't know what was going on."

"Exactly. I realized I was doing it wrong. When I brought you over, Grandpa Ben took you two in his arms and sobbed, and you cried right along with him. It was the most painful thing I've ever seen." Mom's fingers tangle in my fringe, bringing my eyes to hers. "But you grieved together, and eventually you healed together."

"What are you telling me, Mom?"

"By protecting you from pain, I was keeping you separate, even isolated. Sure, grieving was painful, but you didn't do it alone."

My whole face falls. "I've kept her apart; by protecting Eden, she never had a chance to become one of us."

Like the wise woman she is, Mom simply sits there and waits for my slow, pain-riddled brain to process the implications.

"I need to fix this."

Mom slips her arms around my shoulders, leaning her head against mine. "Noah, there was a reason I named you after a great leader. A leader who built something beyond belief, with nothing but faith."

I envelop her with both of my arms, pulling her in tight and close. Words are a little hard to find right now.

She pulls back to smile a little. "Totes awesome, right?"

"Mom, you're that and so much more." I pull back the rest of the way. "I need to talk to her."

Mom stands, retrieving the plate from beside her. "I'll put these in the fridge for when you get back."

Right now, I'd eat those with a grin and a thank you. "Thanks, Mom."

I sprint down the stairs to find Dad leaving the kitchen. He looks at me, registering it's the first time my face isn't twisted and blurred with pain.

He nods. "About time."

I frown. "But you said..."

"I never said I stopped believing in you."

My eyes widen. "You reversed psychologied me?"

"Yep." The 'P' pops like a bubble, showing his utter lack of remorse.

It flipping worked, too. I grab him in a hug. "You've still got a lot to teach me, Dad."

Dad's big bear hands give me three solid pats between the shoulder blades. "Less and less every day."

I head to the door, only to find Mitch there. It seems I have a gauntlet of goodbyes to get through before I can leave the house.

His hand on the doorknob, Mitch smiles a smidgen. "Scared?"

I finally acknowledge that feeling that has been slithering and sliding inside me since the day I found out Eden and I were bonded. "Yep." I'm glad I don't have to tell Mitch scared is an understatement. He can already tell.

With a nod, Mitch opens the door. "That's my big bro."

As I reverse the truck, I lay out my plan. Eden's not at school, so there's no point going there; so I head to the next likely place. At the Inn, Alexis's shiny white sedan is nowhere to be seen. *Please let that mean it's in the garage.* I knock on the door, wrapping false bravado and non-existent plans around me like an armor.

I'm about to knock again, feeling a little tense at the prospect that Eden's not here, when Alexis opens the door. She stands there, unsmiling, as she lifts an arm to grasp the doorway—effectively barring my path. Her perfume hits me hard. Whoa, why would someone wear the entire bottle in one go? Then my Were nose picks up what a human might have missed. The tannin laden, woodsy scent of fermented grapes. I look to the nails wrapped around the door jamb. It seems they serve a stabilizing function.

"I need to talk to Eden."

"She's not here."

My teeth are so tight and hard I have to squeeze my next words through. "Where is she?"

"I don't know."

Frustration, hot and urgent, has me tempted to step further into the wine-laden haze surrounding this woman. "Look, I know I'm not your preferred choice for Eden."—because I have a pulse—"but this is important. Please, tell me where she is."

Alexis goes stonier than her usual granite self. "I don't know where she is. She left over a week ago. She didn't tell me where."

"You don't know where your own daughter is?"

Alexis leans forward, eyes narrowed, as the smell of wine gusts over me. "Don't you judge me."

I turn, a little disgusted, but mostly saddened. What mother doesn't know where her daughter is? "I've got better things to do with my time."

I think Weres in the next county probably hear the door slam behind me as I head back to my car, but Alexis is out of my mind before I'm out of the driveway. Radar or no Eden-radar, I've got to find her.

I decide to drive through town, knowing it's useless, but doing it anyway. I drive past Tyrell's, remembering Eden wanting to help with Seth, and me saying no. I even drive past school, knowing she isn't there, getting to remember all the times Eden's eyes asked for more, and I pretended I didn't see it. When I run out of streets to comb I deflate. I can't face going home yet.

In the end, all roads lead to the Glade. Crossing the big, green and never-changing space, I approach the Precept Rock. I stand before it, reading the four lines I grew up with...the last line that changed everything. I stand like a person at a party where they don't know anyone. Awkwardly, unsure whether to stay or leave.

Eden and I could have made Prime Alpha amazing. Me with the Phelan name, the oldest, most respected of Weres. Carrying everything Dad and Mom have taught me about patience and integrity and the power of responsibility. Man, even the two years spent as a freak weren't wasted. I've spent more time as a human than any Were. I know how precious a gift it is.

But it's Eden who's the link from Were to human to nature and all the infinite connections in between. Eden is living, breathing proof of what's possible by living in two divergent but complementary worlds.

I need Eden. As the Prime Alpha, but far more as a guy who cries for his mate.

Eden. I consider screaming her name, fracturing the oppressive peace, throwing birds up to the sky, frightening away any animal naïve enough to come close.

But I don't.

Instead, I sink to my knees before the Precept Rock. I chant her name like a beacon, over and over and over. Knowing the whole time, that on that radar of ours, she's not there.

I t seems Orin's mismatched cottage is a haven for healing souls.

He tells me the stories of each animal. Amadeus, the stocky brown dog, was found matted and flea infested, probably abandoned most of his life. It had taken three months before he let a human touch him. Treble (possibly named after trouble, because that's what his tail means for anything at knee height) had been nothing but black saggy skin on bones. Diamond, the hissing feline now sitting in my lap, arrived on his own, his tears and scars telling their own story.

And sitting in the overgrown garden, the spring sun trying hard to chase away my goosebumps, I talk, too. Knowing that I'm too far away for Noah to see my tears, to feel how painful this is. Allowing him to move on and take his rightful place. I talk like I've never unloaded before. Orin's silent acceptance hears everything—Alexis's emotional and physical absence, the constant moves to suffocating city after suffocating city, never fitting in, finding solace in animals, knowing that's what set me apart. I tell him about moving to Jacksonville, the last place before I went to college somewhere far, far away. The river of tears dries for a few precious minutes when I tell him about finding Noah...falling for Noah. They don't even start when I tell him about Kurt, Adam being shot, and breaking up. It feels good to tell him about calling the animals, being the one that turned the tide.

But they pool hot and heavy as I know what comes next. I briefly wish for my hollow oblivion to return, because this is going to hurt.

The tears never gain traction because the coughing rumble of a car punctures the quiet then slowly grows. When a faded sedan pulls into the driveway, bursts of rust blooming across the hood, I look to Orin.

He rises from the patchwork lawn that couldn't decide on a uniform height. "What is the purpose of healing, if not to move on?"

In the front sits a dark-haired guy, somehow familiar, but I can't place him. Beside him is an elderly lady. I'm not surprised when he heads to the trunk and pulls out a metal walking frame. I am surprised when he takes it to the driver's side and opens the back door. He helps a little girl, matching black curls in a jaunty ponytail, climb out of the car.

The girl immediately sets forward, scraping the walking frame over the loose gravel, her frail body looking small in its enclosure. "Where is she? Where is she?"

The elderly lady tries to catch up. "Now, Molly, let's not forget our manners."

"Aw, Gran, she's just excited."

The moment he speaks, I recognize Dale, the perpetually absent biology student. But glossy black curls no longer covered by a beanie, and sinewy arms no longer covered in faded Goth black. In jeans and a t-shirt, Dale is barely recognizable as Dale.

He sees me as they approach, clearly surprised to see me here. "Oh, hey, Eden."

"Hi, Dale."

Orin passes me to greet our guests he obviously knew were coming; his hand brushes my back before he kneels before the little girl.

"Now, Molly, what do you know about taking care of cats?"

"Well, Dale took me to the library, and we've been reading books every day. And reading on the Internet, and talking to Uncle James in Minnesota cause he has five cats."

"That's a lot of research. Are you all ready?"

"Oh, yes. Her water is in the kitchen, and her kitty tray is in the laundry. It'll be my job to look after her." Molly's curls bounce as she skips within the confines of her walker. "We're gonna have tea parties and fashion shows, and I've already got her a stroller and special treats that smell kinda fishy, and I'm gonna read to her every night."

The need for oxygen finally stops Molly's excited never-ending sentence.

Orin smiles. "Oh, she loves to read."

"Did you hear that, Dale? She loves to read!"

"And how often do you need to feed her?"

Serious eyes hold Orin's. "Every day. Her bowl is in the kitchen, and her food is in the pantry on a shelf that I can reach."

"And what if you get sick or really, really tired?"

"Mum or Gran, even Dale, said they'd help out, didn't you?"

Molly's head zig zags between Dale and her grandmother. Dale chuckles, his hand coming to rest between Molly's fragile shoulders. "Sure will, curly girl."

Molly wrinkles her nose at the pet name before turning back to Orin. Her voice is quieter, practically solemn when she asks again, "Can I see her now?"

"I think that's a wonderful idea."

Orin leads the way into the cottage, and it shrinks the

moment four adults and one child enters. In the lounge, Aria sits in the middle of the dining room table, like she knew she was about to receive guests. Molly sees her instantly, a little gasp sucking in then failing to come out.

Aria stands, languorously stretching for her audience. She gracefully leaps from the table and instinctively heads to her new owner. With the wisdom and gentleness of an animal, she weaves between Molly's ankles then rubs her head against the metal leg beside them.

"Gran, Dale, she likes my walker!" Molly sinks to her knees, hands coming out to caress ginger fur. You can tell the moment we all become invisible as the two become absorbed in each other; Molly whispering animatedly, Aria purring contentedly.

I retreat so Molly can have some time getting to know her new friend. Outside, Caesar and his two new best buddies race around the cottage to join me. I'm struck again by the lack of a fence, despite the domesticated zoo that lives here. I suppose this way lost, wounded animals can come when they need.

I kneel, fingers rustling between Caesar's ears. "Giving her some space, huh?"

It hadn't escaped me that they knew to stay away until Molly had gone inside. Behind me the door opens, and a moment later Dale joins me in the sunshine.

He jams his hands into his jean pockets, shoulders relaxed as he smiles at me. "So, hope the family emergency is under control."

My lips try to smile back. It seems Mrs. Marple still managed to relay what little information she had. At least now that I've found someone who looks like me, the family part is plausible. "Yeah, I'll be back for exams."

I stand, hang-on-a-second bursting through my mind. "You've been to school?"

Dale grins, and with those black curls glinting in the sun, the grey of his shirt, he suddenly looks kinda carefree. For the few times I've seen him, it's a look he's never worn. "Yeah, every day for two weeks."

I give an impressed whistle.

"Yeah, it's an alternative universe. Me going to school, you and Noah not."

At the mention of his name, my eyes shoot to the grass, the green stripes blurring as I frantically search for self-control. But then I look back at Dale. "Noah hasn't been to school?"

"Nah. Biology is kinda lonely. And pretty confusing. I can't keep up, even with Mr. D's pace."

I smile, our ancient teacher talks, and walks, as if he's in permanent slow motion. "Chapter seven of the text is your best place to start."

"Thanks, dude, will do." I smile again, despite the clothes and hair, the essence of Dale remains. He heads to the car, pulling a pet carrier from the back seat.

Caesar leans into my leg, and I pat his furry head as curiosity has me asking. "Why the change?"

Dale stops, then resumes, slamming the car door. He puts the carrier down on the cracked concrete pathway, and stands to face me. "Dude, have you ever had a pivotal moment? A change or bust moment?"

Like seeing a guy turn into a horse-sized wolf then attack your lab partner? Or maybe letting the one who built your world go...

I swallow, knowing this pain will always be with me. "Yeah."

"That what you're doing is actually the opposite of what you should have been doing?"

I don't get a chance to respond, Dale is staring down the street, not seeing a thing. "Like maybe what you were really doing was running away?"

I clasp my arms around me, pulling up a smile as Dale turns

back to me. "That's not an easy change to make. You should be proud of yourself."

Squeals of laughter tinkle from inside the walls behind us, Molly's happy, girly voice not far behind. "Look, Orin, she's like a scarf!"

Dale gives a one shoulder shrug, those curls tilting to the side then bouncing back. "I was letting more than just myself down."

Watching Dale and his family leave, Molly's arm protectively wrapped around the cat carrier she insisted was buckled up, lights a first flicker of warmth that gives me hope that life can be bearable.

I settle with Orin back on the grass. "Molly and Aria look like they'll be happy."

"We heal, we move on."

I frown, knowing Orin is no longer talking about the cat. "I am. More importantly, I'm letting him do that."

Orin angles his head in silent question.

I stroke a piece of grass beside me, pale green base to dark green tip. It's a quiet tone, a painful pitch, that tells Orin Noah and I have bonded. That he didn't tell me. And why.

With arms around Caesar I whisper, "Now you know."

Orin also seems interested in the blades of green by his leg, almost imitating my posture, probably digesting that Noah would have had to choose me over his pack, a life becoming a limbo between human and Were. That I could never have asked him to give up being the Alpha, a future without the legacy of children.

Head down, eyes focused on the stubby emerald, he asks quietly, "Have you not learned you are far more than you ever imagined?"

I feel my elbow give out, and I quickly sit up. "What?"

"You are part Fae, the beings that are more connected to

nature than anyone else. You are the daughter of a king." I look away, not sure I've accepted that yet, or whether it makes a difference. "You are the girl who turned a Were through nothing but a connection."

And a good dose of fear. "Why are we going over this?"

Orin gives up pretending he was interested in his lawn. Those earthy green eyes look at me. "There is self-sacrifice, and then there is putting others first because you believe you are less."

Stunned, I can't find a response. What is more important than Noah being the Alpha of his pack?

"Why would Noah choose you? Before calling the animals, long before you knew you are the Changeling daughter of a king?" Orin's eyes grasp mine then spear straight through me. "Why would you be the one who changed him?"

I frown; I've loved Orin's tendency to be unpredictable until now, but all of a sudden this conversation feels dangerously out of control. "That's a puzzle I haven't been able to solve."

"I have. Tara and Mitch have. Noah knew long before any of us."

As Orin's words refuse to be ignored, my heart begins a painful staccato in my chest. What is the point of all this? Is he trying to break me more than I already am?

I try to look away, but Orin's gaze doesn't let me. It's a traction beam of green and significance. "What could happen if you believed they would choose you? That this is possible?"

Caesar is looking at me, doggy eyebrows raised. Not you, too. His mouth opens in a grin, canine tongue lolling unapologetically. Ramifications start to pile and gain weight.

I flop forward, head in his fur, muffling my words. "I've done it again, haven't I?"

Unfortunately, Orin can still hear me. "Run scared, underestimated yourself and what you could mean to someone else?"

I look up at my brother. "I was thinking of the first, but thanks for the list."

Orin smiles that serene smile of his. "Or lacked faith in a connection that has defied boundaries?"

"Have you finished?"

"I believe so."

I wait. But Orin doesn't contribute anything else. I look from him to Caesar. They are both watching me, 'what now?' expressions on their face.

Orin's question is still hanging in my mind. Like it's grown claws or burrs or roots or something. What would happen if I believed?

I shoot to my feet and head for the car. Orin and Caesar stay on the lawn, but somehow, I can feel their approval.

What could happen if I believed this was possible?

Once at the end of the street I stop. I suppose the Phelan home, the one with frowning Adam, is the most logical place to start. I close my eyes, calming...centering. I don't know if I can find Noah the same way he finds me.

But it's time to find out.

NOAH

I'm so caught up in my pity party that I don't feel her until she's practically on top of the Precept Rock.

A split second before I see her across the Glade I feel it fill me—the breath of life, a shaft of light reanimating my body. A bit like oxygen, you know theoretically you can't live without it, but it's not until you experience its loss that you realize how essential it is. How much it hurts when it's gone.

But my lungs are loving it. They suck in hard, trying to get a taste of wildflowers, hoping to draw her in quicker.

Eden walks slowly, hesitantly, toward me. I open my mouth to find my lips aren't cooperating. I try to move, to find my legs have lost the connection to my brain. She stops a few feet away, questions swirling in the forest green of her eyes.

My answer is the one thing I should have done months ago. With Eden standing there, beautiful and fragile and finally here, I grab the hem of my shirt and pull it over my head...let it fall to the ground.

And lose the ability to breathe and wait at the same time. I choose to wait.

Eden steps forward then frowns. She falters, her hand

coming up to touch behind her ear in that I way I haven't seen in ages. She pulls in a breath and steps again before losing momentum once more. Twice more she steps, stops then starts again. Three lifetimes pass until she's standing before me.

Arms that want to hold her stay by my side. I just watch and wait, let her assimilate what I've known for months. Those forest green eyes find mine, so luminous surrounded by pine, an aching mix of disbelief, confusion, questions...hope.

Her bottom lip slips beneath her teeth as one hand comes up and hovers so close, so close. I don't step forward, no matter how much I'm craving that touch. The warmth builds in the millimeters between her palm and my skin, my breath stops and soars at the same time. Then, her tentative, hot fingers brush over my chest. Over our mark. My knees consider crumbling, and hope breaks free as sweet sensation sparks and spreads. It's a barely bearable torture I never want to end.

"When?" she whispers.

I swallow past the shattered glass shards clogging my throat. "When Dad was shot...and you came."

Painful, poignant eyes look up. "How?"

"We were prophesized thousands of years ago." Man, I want to touch her. "We've been centuries in the making, Eden."

"Why?"

I finally move, stepping forward, pushing her trembling fingers firmly onto my skin. I trace her cheek, my hand touching what I've been bleeding to touch again. "Because no one has loved, adored, wanted, or needed anyone as much as I love and adore, want and need you, Eden."

Eden's face twists, emotions competing and wrestling for space. Every one of them I feel. Love. Adoration. Want. Need. "I know."

At last, with nothing between us, no shirt, no secrets, I pull her in, so tight like I'm trying to brand her with our mark, and kiss her. It's a sweet kiss. A profound kiss. A tentative touching of lips that reaffirms and reignites.

It's a kiss I pour my heart into, only to find hers meeting mine in the place our souls connect. Lips grasp, mouths gasp. The love, the aching honesty eclipses everything. The sensation of one hand skimming up my arm over my bare shoulder to grip my hair is heaven. The one that stays warm and protective over the mark that will soon tell everyone she's mine is the one that wrenches a groan from me.

This is what we should have been. This is what we will be.

Eden pulls back, that sweet, kiss-softened look I will treasure when we're eighty. "I knew you were keeping a secret, and I realized what it was when you changed in the forest, after that Were attacked us."

The day we returned. The day I was going to tell her. "Why didn't you tell me?"

"I thought you were choosing me over your pack, and I wasn't willing for you to do that." Eden's eyes drop to my collarbone. "But I think, beneath it all, I was scared of losing you." She looks up then asks the question that's been haunting her eyes since she arrived, the one that has made this moment so achingly painful. "Why didn't you tell me?"

"I was petrified of losing you."

She studies me for long moments, and I let her. I leave everything open and exposed, my skin to her touch, my heart to her scrutiny. What I've always wanted is, for us to be her decision.

And then she smiles. A wonderful blossoming of light that starts in her eyes and ends with my future. "We should have had more faith."

It's a good thing I'm a two-in-one package. One body couldn't hold all the love I feel for this girl. It turns out, even that's not enough because it overflows and spills. I pick Eden up, twirling her, spinning in the love that surrounds us. Her laughter squeezes my heart; her palms on my bare shoulders prompts another surge of emotion and spinning.

We slow and Eden slides down, her palm once again returning to our mark. Her smile is breathtaking as she shakes her head. "We did the impossible."

She hasn't realized...I turn her toward the granite slab that's been sitting patiently beside us, waiting to be acknowledged. "Yes, we've broken the one rule that couldn't be broken."

She looks to the Precept Rock. "Oh."

"Actually, I think we've broken every rule on the Rock."

Her rose red lips whisper the last line. *He who is above the law is the law.* I feel her body stiffen as realization streaks through hard and fast. "That means you're the—"

"It means we are."

I watch as that bolt of lightning creates flashes of meaning, rumbles of implication. Eden's bottom lip disappears back under her teeth. "Oh."

I loosen my arms, knowing this was always the risk I faced. What that slithering, crawling feeling has always been. Fear. Slimy, terrified fear.

She runs light fingers over my cheek. "Noah, I would follow you even if it meant ruling the world."

"Oh, Eden, don't you realize?" I say my words slowly, so she understands. "It's your smile that lifts me, your heart that moves me, your love that leads me."

Eden's eyes smile and shimmer, and I drown in the emotion I see there. Her hand slides back down, over our mark. "Then we do this together."

"Together." I breathe. I pull back, admittedly not far, but needing to be certain. For her to be certain. "Are you sure?"

Those tilted green eyes soften some more, crinkling around the edges. "Noah," she breathes before pulling me down for another kiss. It's a deep kiss, one of commitment and certainty.

It's lips as sure as the beating of our hearts, a hand that only presses more firmly on my chest.

Every cell in my body smiles. "I love your yeses."

"I love you, Noah."

I rest my forehead on hers, captivated by forest green and willing to live there for the remainder of my days.

"It looks like we're going to Council."

I wonder if going to Council will be as nerve wracking as returning to the Phelan household after these weeks of absence. From the moment I met them, Beth has had uncondi- tional acceptance as perfected as Orin. Adam, on the other hand, has spent large amounts of time practicing distance and distrust.

Walking up the path, Noah grabs my hand, nervousness already zinging in his body. We both stare straight ahead at the door we approach. This step will be the first in claiming Prime Alpha.

We take the final step to the porch; the front door is closed and blank. One small step for Eden, one giant step for Weredom.

What would you do if you believed this was possible? Orin's words rise up, the question that was the catalyst to going to the Glade. I suck some air into my lungs, pretending it's some magi- cal, calming tonic, and I hold it for a second. Who knows why I was chosen? But I was.

I squeeze the nervous hand clasping mine. "Let's own this," I say, my voice almost confident.

Noah looks at me, and that grin of his, the one that says, 'I love you,' blazes across his handsome face. I'm prepping my hostess-with-the-mostess face when a squeal sounds, barely dampened by the timber slab between us and Tara.

"It's her!" The door flies open and releases an excited ball of red. "Oh my goodness, oh my great aunt, oh my giddy galloping goat." I'm swallowed by Tara's body, the one that seems to multiply just by the power of her emotion, in an enthusiastic hug. "Where have you been? Council is two days away. Do you know what sweat does to my fair complexion?"

I open my smiling mouth with an answer I haven't formulated yet.

"Tara, why don't you let her in?" Beth's voice wafts from the hallway.

Tara releases me and I enter, only to be enveloped by Beth. "Hi, Beth."

"Welcome back, Eden."

Warmth swells in my throat. I know the next in the receiving line is Mitch, already armed for another hug. As I'm swallowed by brawny arms, he leans in beside my ear. "I'm glad my thick-skulled twin didn't completely screw up."

As I keep going I hear a distinct 'oomph' behind me, suggesting Noah just communicated what he thought of that comment.

I blush a little; this almost feels like coming home. Except Adam is last, and I can't tell if the high of this beautiful welcome is about to plummet and crash.

Adam stands last in line; his face is serious, the weight of what he is about to say weighing heavily on his brow. "Eden. Forgive an old fool for not seeing what was blindingly obvious?"

"Adam. Your family, and the Phelans, couldn't have a better person protecting them."

For the first time in my life, I get a Dad hug. It's big and warm and beautiful. I wrap my arms around this powerful torso, awkward, grateful, enjoying every moment.

I pull back, and Adam smiles. "I don't know why I didn't see it sooner, but I'm glad it's you."

The certainty, the absence of surprise from the ones behind me, has me turning to Noah. His hand comes up to rub his head sheepishly. "They all know."

"Right." Being the last to know is not a good feeling.

Mitch grabs Tara's hand and walks past us. He elbows Noah on the way through. "Only three quarters screwed up."

Noah scowls, but doesn't reply.

Beth slips an arm around my shoulder and begins propelling me toward the dining area. "I think I still have an eggplant in the fridge."

I feel Noah's hand tense around my own. "Mom, you need to be here for this conversation. Why don't we order in?"

Beth's brown eyes look to me. "Would you mind, Eden?"

The insistent pressure on my hand doesn't need our connection to communicate its meaning. "That sounds great, Beth."

Noah's hand relaxes in relief.

Beth smiles. "Thai Lotus it is!"

We all head to the dining table as Beth grabs her phone. Even Tara's bubbly personality has been muted by the seriousness of what we're about to discuss. We all take our seats at the table. This is the first time I've ever had take-out at the Phelan house, telling me exactly how serious this conversation is going to be.

Adam leans forward, hands clasping on the table. "So, what's the plan?"

Tara fidgets beside Mitch. "Seth's gone."

Noah looks to me to see what I think of that. I nod. "I know."

"You know?"

"I ran into him at Wyoming State."

Tara bangs her fist on the table. "What a stupid time to disappear. Coward."

I lean back a little. "He's probably gathering supporters."

Everyone turns to me, but for some reason, my usual nervousness doesn't surface. Adam's finger is on his bottom lip as he nods slowly. "That makes sense."

Noah leans forward. "It's also concerning. We know there are Weres out there that are dissatisfied with the way things are."

Mitch joins his twin. "They don't see a point in hiding."

Beth's face is rumpled with worried lines. "Seth's going to give them a reason not to."

Noah turns to me. "What do you know?"

I frown, trying to recollect those hazy moments. I'd spent more time focusing on not feeling and not thinking rather than deciphering the meaning behind Seth's words. "I'm not sure. We were at the memorial for his mother."

Beth nods. "She was an inspiring woman. It was a tragic loss for Weres and humans when she was killed."

"I think Seth was really close to her." Beth nods again, sadness straining her eyes. I focus on the table, trying to dredge up details from those fuzzy moments. "We spoke about her involvement in the wolf reintroduction, the importance of wolves in the reserve"—I look up wide-eyed to the Weres around me—"about their role in enforcing balance."

Silence moves around the table. The implications of those words weighing it down, keeping it there.

Noah moves, emotions lifting him out of his seat. "Seth's right."

All four heads—Adam, Beth, Mitch, and Tara—turn to Noah. I wait, sensing the excitement that has just begun morphing within him.

"It's time Weres made a difference. And the Earth that we have two feet and four paws planted on is our responsibility. The natural world and the human world are one and the same. We embody that."

For the first time I sit forward, leaning toward Noah. "Yes, he's just going about it the wrong way."

Noah's summer eyes are intense, serious, exhilarated. "It's the wolves' presence that maintains the balance. That's the connection between it all."

I want to leap into those sky blue pools. "That's what the Prime Prophecy is all about."

Two hands clapping snaps us out of our bubble. Noah and I separate. Over the course of the conversation we'd leaned away from the table, turning to face each other, leaned toward each toward the other. Tara bounces in her seat, a testament to her dancing toes.

Adam smiles as he repeats his original question. "So, what's the plan?"

Beneath the table our hands find each other. Our connection pulses with the drive to do this. We face the Phelan and Channon Alphas before us, the emotions slowly morphing to determination.

Noah rubs his lower lip, completely unaware he just mimicked his father. "We let Seth hijack Council, find out what his plan is, then surprise the crap out of him."

Mitch crosses his arms. "Seth won't accept this easily."

Tara sinks a little in her seat, finally looking like her real height. "And he'll have supporters."

Adam nods. "It's going to take some people time to adjust to a human Alpha."

In other words, not everyone is going to be happy to see me. Feelings of not belonging clamber up my consciousness, threatening the stirring emotions that were just there.

"They'll love her once they see what this will mean."

I shoot Tara a grateful glance, and although I'm not sure I

can mimic her optimism, knowing I'll have my own supporters is enough to squash the doubts. If I am chosen for this, I need to start believing it. And acting it.

Mitch nods, and I don't know how his own finger isn't doing the thoughtful stroke. "Eden will have to come in once Seth has said his piece."

Tara has finally stopping jiggling. "You're right. Her presence is going to cause a stir. We need to hear Seth's plans first." She turns darkened hazel eyes to me. "I wish I could wait with you."

I look around the table. Everyone here needs to be there; they're all Alphas. What an intimidating thought. I didn't even have to enter the Phelan house alone, and I knew at least one of them would be glad to see me.

I open my mouth to say I'll enter on my own, figuring now is as good a time as any to start this confidence-built-on-faith thing.

"I'll go with her."

We all turn to find Dana coming down the hallway. Five shocked Were faces register they never heard her enter, and I realize how absorbed in the conversation they must have been. I wonder if they're all asking themselves how long she's been there.

Dana takes two more steps into the room. "I'll wait with Eden in the carpark. Give me a signal, and we'll come in."

Tara beams at her sister. "Fantabulous idea."

There's not the same level of enthusiasm beaming from Noah. "Okay." He draws the word out slowly, a little reluctantly.

Dana grins like they've laid down a gauntlet. "Not to mention I'm a bit partial to a grand entrance."

My stomach quivers a little. Angry Seth and his collection of followers. Disbelieving and distrustful Alphas. A human, her royal Changeling blood a secret, claiming her place as the Alpha mate. How does one fake confidence in the face of that?

No one around the table sees when Noah goes stiller than still. But I feel it; I see it. I look up to find him watching me, asking me a question. He can feel my nervousness; he knows what I'm being asked. His emotions tightly reined, he's confirming this is what I want.

I turn back to the table, disengaging from the intensity of his gaze. There's only one way I can answer his question. "Let's own this."

Noah nods, and deep inside I feel his smile. "We already do."

OUTSIDE, the boughs of Grandfather Douglas blocking the almost-full moon, Noah holds me like goodbye doesn't want to pass his lips. With my hands wrapped around him, my head resting on his shoulder, I don't really want to hear it.

His lips brush my hair. "Where were you staying?"

"Orin's, on the other side of Cheyenne."

"No wonder I couldn't feel you."

I press my cheek more firmly onto his heated skin. "I also, ah, switched off for a while."

"That explains it. I've never felt anything worse, and I've had the pleasure of changing from human to giganta-wolf without warning."

I glance up, his handsome face all angles and planes in the gloom. "I think I was protecting myself. And then staying away seemed better for both of us."

"You've been protecting me as much as I've been protecting you."

I feel irony twist my lips. "With the same results."

We sink into each other's arms again, holding tightly, banishing the distance that's been living between us for too long.

I feel his head tilt down as he leans back a little. "How are you doing?"

It's almost redundant that he asked, but I give it voice anyway. "I'm pretty nervous, actually."

"Me, too."

I pull him in tighter, wishing there wasn't something about to happen that's going to test our bond. "To be completely honest, I'm bordering on terrified."

Noah's breath brushes my hair in a gust before he rests his cheek on my head. "Me, too."

NOAH

The Glade looks like any other time we've had a Council. The guardian pines stand straight and somber, silent sentries unruffled by what is about to happen. Mom and Dad greet each Were as they enter, me on their right, Tara and Mitch on their left, smiling and handshaking right along with them.

Who am I kidding? This looks like nothing any Were has seen before. There are Weres everywhere, far more than the Glade has ever housed before. Mostly Alphas and their heirs, they are tense and serious. This is the second Council in as many months. The knowledge that something significant is happening today is practically bannered across the trees.

They have no idea.

Tara takes her place by the Precept Rock, Mitch on her other side. The few Weres that were mumbling below the hushed atmosphere fall silent. Everyone looks around, wondering how we can be about to start.

But Tara squares her shoulders. She's not going to let a little thing like the absence of the defendant hold up this trial. "We are here to judge the actions of Seth Channon. Seth has"—I almost hear Tara's teeth grind, holding back the word 'repeatedly'—"disobeyed his Alpha. He has exposed our secret." Tara looks around the Glade. "And he has attacked a fellow Were."

Just as Tara finishes her sentence, Seth enters the Glade. He walks, that arrogant swagger that has my teeth gritting, to center stage. He stands and waits, adjusting the cuffs on his jacket sleeves. Not only does it look incongruous that a Were is wearing a jacket, but the casual Wyoming State blazer is an obvious statement on how seriously he is taking this.

Tara ignores his insolence, his brazen contempt. Without waiting for him to reach the center of the Glade she continues. "Today we pass sentence on his disrespect and indifference for our laws." Seth reaches the center and turns to Tara. I don't know how she doesn't banish his butt there and then. "Before you are judged for your actions, Seth, do you have anything you want to say in your defense?"

I would bet every last cheesecake on this planet he does.

Seth turns on the spot, a slow pirouette in the middle of the Glade. "Weres have done nothing but hide. We sit back and watch everything we love, that we should be protecting, be slowly destroyed."

I feel the moment Eden arrives, the addition of the extra layer of nervousness gurgling in my gut. For some reason, as Seth continues to take in the crowd, it settles me.

"When wolves were removed from the reserve it degraded, trees were lost, some species almost went extinct. Sound familiar?"

The crowd of Alphas is silent, listening, making the connection.

"The appearance of the last Precept tells us what I already knew. It is time. Time to exert our place as the dominant species. We will no longer waste our strength. Our unique abilities. And we will use them to do what wolves do right here."

There's silence—no agreements, but no objections. Tara and

Mitch stand by the rock that shows some of what Seth says is true. Except he's wrong, I feel the anger start to simmer but I take in a breath. Seth can say his words. I get to see who believes this supremacy trollop, and, once Eden arrives, he will be silenced. Finally.

Seth's voice continues to rise with his passion and conviction; he spins again, making sure none of his words miss the mark. "Wolves are the enforcers of nature, the ones responsible for balance."

Suddenly I feel the nervousness start to fade, disappear. I want to frown; I can't imagine Eden's had an unexpected burst of confidence. Another breath, and I tell myself I'm not worried.

As one fist slams into his palm, Seth delivers his bottom line. "Humans are doing this. Weres will stop them."

Some Weres shuffle, clearly uncomfortable with this concept. Others, the supporters, smile, shifting forward. One or two throw their fists up in the air. There are more of them than make me comfortable.

I look at Tara, who acknowledges me with the slightest incline of her head. With the signal sent I step forward; Seth has said enough.

As I step into the ring, Seth's eyes light up. Hazel pools of satisfaction track my movements as I approach him then stand before him. Just as I suspected, Seth wants a fight.

Little does he realize the consequences if we did.

"Seth's right, the world needs Weres."

Stunned surprise starts with Seth then arcs around the Glade. That wiped the smug smile off his dial.

"As those that stand with half of our being in the human world, the other in the animal world, we have a responsibility." I narrow my eyes at him, a sucker punch of my own winding up. "But Seth forgets we are living proof that the human world and the natural world is one and the same."

Seth's eyes flare and metal stings my nose. "All the more reason to take our place. Were's are not cowards. We do not hide." He steps forward, finding my personal space and invading it. "It's time we fought for what we believe in."

I stand there, voice dropping. "You're not only suggesting that we risk our identity and all the consequences of exposure, but that we put our lives on the line for this?"

Seth's hands bunch, two balls of anger at the end of his sleeves. "I would lose my life for this."

Just like his mother did. I turn from Seth, knowing Weres need to hear the alternative to this violent, bloody path.

"We are not purely predators. Seth's words speak of a desire for domination and blood. Unnecessary exposure and pain."

I look around the Glade, like I'm making sure they all get this. But what I'm really doing is searching. Where the heck is Eden? With a frown, I realize I almost can't feel her.

When I feel a shove; when the force has me stumbling forward a step, a handful of gasps sprinkle from the crowd. Fury has me spinning, turning to face him.

Seth straightens, I-want-Prime-Alpha stamped all over his face. "A war has already begun."

36

EDEN

here is Dana?
W
I pace the dusty parking lot beside the Glade. Fifteen steps from Noah's truck that I arrived in a short while ago to the trees on the opposite side. Nervous energy has my legs stretching and pacing. It only takes fourteen to get back.

The sound of an aging truck heralds a giant, blue metal nose entering the clearing. Dana parks the truck and clambers out. I walk over, arms crossing, uncrossing, then crossing again.

She smiles brightly, "Soz I'm late." She sounds so much like Tara that my heart rate calms a little. "You have to look your best if you're going to be center stage."

I look at Dana. She's wearing a pale green blouse over a cute denim skirt. I tighten my arms, fingers gripping the material of my top. I didn't even think of what I was wearing. Jeans had been sensible, my blue top comfortable. I tell myself it's too late now, wishing it wouldn't be riding high on my mind when I enter the Glade.

Dana links her arm through mine, pulling me away from the Glade entry. "Come on, Noah wanted us to wait back here."

What? I stop, only to find myself propelled forward again by the arm chained around mine. "But we're going the wrong way."

Dana flaps a hand over my forearm. "Didn't Noah tell you? There's another clearing back here. This way we're out of sight, and we come in the back way."

I suppose that makes sense.

Although it seems logical, I can't help but bite my lip. "He never mentioned it."

"He has had a lot on his mind."

"That's true."

"Come one, we don't have much time."

Dana doesn't seem to notice I continue to be a weight on her arm. She pulls me toward the little track I noticed the first time Noah brought me to the Glade. The one that heads away from the Glade. Within seconds we're swallowed by the forest, walking side by side down the pine-littered track.

I rub my arm like it's much cooler than it really is. "Do you have your phone?"

Dana pats her back pocket.

"Have you checked it?"

Dana rolls her eyes. "We'll hear it. It's got this cool ringtone that sounds like a crazy donkey." She looks at me from the corner of her eye. "Tara said you were a worry worm."

She said that? To Dana?

When the path turns, heading back in the direction of the Glade, the nervousness releases its grip on my chest. I need to get myself under control, being like this doesn't help anyone.

"It's just up ahead." Dana giggles, even covering her mouth to do it. "Actually, it's a bit of a Were make out spot. Mitch and Tara would have spent heaps of time here."

I wonder why I've never heard of it. When the path bends again, this time in the opposite direction, I no longer feel nervous. This feels wrong. I turn to Dana, tension pulling my brows down.

Dana clasps my hand, an excited smile keeping her forward momentum. "This is so amazing. Do you think you're ready?"

I shrug, trying to shake the feeling of foreboding this walk has spawned. "Not really. But I won't be alone."

"That's true." The change in tone has me glancing back at Dana, but she skips ahead, red hair bouncing, bare legs skipping over the pine-needle path. "It's just around this corner."

With that, she disappears around the bend.

The trees begin to thin, for some reason making me feel exposed. "I think we should turn back." There's no response from up ahead. "Dana?"

Silence is my answer.

I run the last few steps, reaching the edge of a clearing. When I hear a rustle, I spin one way then the other, to find nothing behind me. Dana is gone. *What is going on?* I turn to face the clearing, only to discover there is definitely something in front of me.

On the other side of the clearing, a wolf materializes from shadowy trunks. Not a wild wolf, but a massive Were. My eyes widen enough to see two more separate from the forest, one on my left, one on my right.

When an ominous rumble, an angry growling, vibrates behind me I have no choice but step forward into the clearing.

Into the space where four predatory Weres begin to close in.

37

NOAH

S eth takes off his jacket. That slow, deliberate movement is all for show—if we shift, our clothes come with us. My eyes track his movements. They don't need to scan the Glade to know Eden is not where she's supposed to be. Fury fights with fear in my chest, neither an emotion I can do anything about. Seth, with his plan for a new world order, thinks he wants a fight, thinks he can claim Prime Alpha.

Eden has just dropped off my radar. Again.

"Now I show the world what Weres will become." Seth kicks the jacket aside; it tumbles once before splaying out, the Wyoming State logo staring up at the sky.

The jacket.

"Nice jacket."

Dana all smiles and sincerity. "I totally forgot I had this on. A friend lent it to me..."

Seth smiles. "We always knew a Channon would be Prime Alpha."

We...

I shift, Seth changing, too, thinking he's about to get the fight he wants.

I turn.

Then run.

Because I've just left Eden with Kurt's daughter.

38

EDEN

The four wolves spread out, evenly spaced around me. They begin to circle, becoming a whirlpool inexorably drawing inwards. I spin, trying to keep them all in sight. Although they are moving slowly, I get dizzy trying to divide my frightened brain amongst their stealthy bodies.

Heads low, they keep up the deadly dance; saliva spills from one, hatred from another. Telling me what they are hungry for.

I stop, a trembling pivot point to the intent that is completely single minded. My fear scores off the Richter scale. It shakes entire hemispheres of my brain, making it hard to think.

I need Orin to tell me what to do. They are too angry, aggressive, goal driven. Frantically, I scan the tree line. This would be a good time for my father to appear.

Someone does appear from the trees, and even though it's Dana, a small bubble of hope rises. She moves forward into the clearing then stops, the circling wolves a protective line between her and me.

Dana watches me, a snarl on her lips, her hazel eyes hard.

I look away, the sliver of hope killed by that gaze. I focus on the massive beasts surrounding me, dredging up the melody. I see one's eyes widen, only to have his head drop lower, the snarl deepen.

"I know what you're trying to do. He told me."

He?

Dana's lip pulls up in a twisted smile. "These are not wild animals for you to pull their puppet strings. They're human minds in animal bodies."

A sinking feeling shows me she's right. Two wolves pad past in that slow focused dance inwards, teeth glinting as they smile. The other two never lose their determined focus.

I try a different tact. "Dana, you can turn this around. Call them off."

"They were so happy when you returned. The prodigal daughter."

What is she talking about?

"I was getting kinda tired of you stuffing up my plans. I had Seth at the movies, doing what we agreed, making this Council happen." She flicks her red hair in agitation. "All you had to do was stay away, and this could have been avoided."

"Dana, call this off." I hear the hint of pleading, the note of desperation in my voice. "You don't know what you're starting."

I can feel Noah drawing nearer, and he's angry and scared. Actually, Noah is heart-wrenchingly furious and desperately frightened, and when he arrives blood will be shed. Except no one here knows that if Noah draws blood Weres will become human.

Dana snorts. "Right now, Seth is claiming Prime Alpha."

Seth was a part of this? Although we were never friends, there was something about his sad soul that I could relate to. For some reason, it feels more of a betrayal than calculating Dana standing on the other side of four deadly Werewolves.

Dana sees my crushed face and smiles. "Yes, he had a soft spot for you, too. The fool was a nothing but a puppet. A zealous mind is easy to predict and manipulate." She shrugs. "With you gone, Noah can never claim Prime Alpha. Seth will eventually be dispatched"—Dana's arms spread out wide, like she's welcoming victory—"and the rightful Channon Alpha will take his place."

Kurt.

How did we not consider that he was behind all of this? He would be the one with the power to convince four young wolves searching for purpose to attack a human. To expose their secret. To kill.

I step forward, but the snarling and growling has me stepping right back. "You'll start a war."

"You took my place. You took him." Her face clouds, hands clenching. "And you're not even one of us!"

Behind me, a deep growl reverberates through me, spiking my shivering pulse. I don't need to turn around to know the wolves are getting impatient.

Dana takes a step back. "We get our revenge, and once my father is Prime Alpha, the Phelans will need us. Noah will need me."

This is no time to be shocked at the ridiculousness of her plan. "Kurt told you this?"

"I know this." Dana raises her voice, anger now apparent in her tone and tight pose.

"Dana, think about it. Noah would never choose being an Alpha without me."

As I say it, I know it's true. It's as a pair that we have strength.

But it's the truth that finally snaps Dana. It's the power of denial that has her screaming, "Do it!"

It's the wolf on my left that finally breaks rank. It vaults toward me, snarling teeth and growling grey. I can feel his intent, and it gives me a split second to step to the side. Seeing my deflection, his head twists, those glistening teeth snapping at me, tearing my shirt. I stumble, hands and knees hitting the ground hard. I push myself upright as fast as I can, wiping my hair from my face, leaving a sticky smear across my cheek. I look down to see crimson blood seeping from my palm. I look up to see satisfaction gleaming in the wolf's eyes.

With Dana gone, I try again. *You can make a different choice.*

I only have a second to think when two decide to jump together. I see the one to my left glance behind me, feel the moment the decision is made. I stand still until the last second.

I wait until the two projectiles are about to intersect at the point where I'm standing then vault to the right. I jolt when one muscled missile brushes my shoulder. I pull away, knowing it only takes one tooth or claw for pain and damage to be inflicted.

One Were lands on his feet, feet grappling with the ground in an attempt to stop. The other hits the ground, one leg collapsing, gouging the soil on his side for the last few feet. He slows to a stop at the feet of his pack members.

As he stands, his three comrades contract around him. I'm now faced with a monochrome wall of wolf, four Weres that have just decided to work as one. With the coppery stickiness drying on my cheek, my mind scrambles frantically for a solution. Collaboration isn't going to work with these animals. They have the strength of the wild, but the intent of the conscious. Their need for violence is vibrating through their bodies.

With Noah so close, the wolves so much closer, I straighten. I face them. I make a decision.

With courage I don't feel, I know what I need to do to prevent a blood bath.

39

NOAH

The scene, broken by trees, grows closer, more terrifyingly real. What I see freezes my heart and shoots hot, furious adrenalin through my veins. Flashes of Eden in the middle of a clearing, four wolves, big and burly, fanning out to surround her. I can't destroy the distance between Eden and me fast enough. Before I've left the trees, I roar, a sound that is deafening, even to my ears.

There are four of them, Channon scum, and they circle Eden, the trap progressively getting smaller. Snapping, snarling, growling, scaring the living crap out of me. One pounces forward, and when Eden doesn't move, my heart does, straight up my throat, where its frantic pounding chokes me, each pulse triggering the need to scream, run, vomit. My mind plays out sickening scenes of when they reach mauling distance.

It's the wolf behind her that is most heart-freezing. He's stopped moving; all he does is stare. There's no way to tell if he's listening...or scheming.

Noah, stop!

I ignore the counterintuitive command. I'm a freight train

with a target. A meteor on a mission. Nothing can stop me from reaching those Werewolves and annihilating them.

Noah, please.

I falter, actually slow a little. What is she talking about?

I can do this.

She wants me to watch? She wants me to stand by as the driving force for every beat of my heart is surrounded by predatory killing machines? Why doesn't she just ask me to take a flamethrower to the lifeline to every hope, dream, and breath I take?

You need to let me do this.

As my paws slow, my heart rate skyrockets.

She's asking me to believe in her.

So, I stop. Every fiber of muscle straining with the need to scatter the Channon scum like vermin, with every micro-particle wanting to be beside her, I stop.

And watch the most petrifying scene I've ever witnessed.

Faith has never been so impossible.

That's when I finally hear it. What the Weres surrounding Eden are hearing. Why they haven't attacked yet.

You will not hurt me. Weres are more than this.

The wolves pace, crisscrossing as they take several steps one way then the other. They've stopped closing in, now in a holding pattern. To prove it, they halt simultaneously, no less angry, but no longer moving. They're listening.

This is not what Weres are about. You do not hurt the vulnerable.

Eden practically grows before my shocked, proud eyes.

"What are you doing? Attack her!"

Dana, with Eden and the wolves between us, screeches, hands fisted in her hair. She watches everything unravel in slow, painful glory.

One then two wolves glance over their shoulders at Dana. Eden steps forward, actually moving toward the animals that could still kill her. I can feel her fear, tightly contained within steely determination. Layered with focus.

That's what courage looks like.

"Yes, you are more than human, but far more than predators, too."

The wolves all turn to face Eden.

"You are more than the sum of your strength and power."

Eden extends a hand. "You will not hurt me."

The wolves stop.

And before my eyes, they drop.

Four sets of legs bend, chests and bellies hit the ground. Heads drop in shame.

She finally looks up and sees what I already sensed. The Alphas, the pack representatives and their families, have all arrived in time to witness the impossible. Weres premeditatedly planning to attack a human. A girl commanding them.

The power of words showing us what Prime Alpha will be.

Eden stands so still and tall it makes my chest hurt. No one knows the proud, tall girl before them is trembling inside, scared and overwhelmed.

I'm glad I won't have to walk past their scummy, submissive hides to get to her. I can't guarantee I still won't unleash every petrifying moment I've just had to sit back and watch.

It's time to be with my mate.

40

EDEN

My knees would like to give out now. I turn on jelly legs, finally facing Noah. The one that I asked the impossible of—to not fight my fight. To not protect me.

There's no higher level of trust.

The four traitors stay in their place, submissive and resigned, like they won't be moving until I tell them to. Noah moves toward me, his wolf eyes glancing at their prone position behind me. I'm glad he won't have to pass them to get to me; I had very clear images of what he wanted to do to them.

I turn my back on them. Right now, I just want to be held, for someone else to be my legs. I need my wolf, my bonded mate.

Noah walks steadily toward me, the weight and reality of what just happened sinking and lifting in those summer sky eyes. I know the 'wow' is coming even before he thinks it.

A few feet away, his eyes widen, locking on a place over my shoulder. They fill with fear then fury. Suddenly, Noah runs, a blur of blazing white, coming straight toward me.

"Look out!"

It's Seth's voice that has me spinning to see what's propelled Noah like a detonating explosive. Dana, a red wolf, violence dark and hot in her eyes, is only paces behind me. Her trajectory, her eyes, set on me.

I step back, everything slowing down so I can see it in stark detail. Noah, fur pushed back by his own propulsion, claws spearing into the soil, eyes full of determination, is just a few feet to my right. I turn to see Dana vault up, surge forward, that mad fury I saw in Kurt—my death, her objective.

I look back to Noah, the fear he won't get there in time pounds in both our hearts.

I crumple when she ploughs into me, the weight of her hatred slamming me into the ground. The red fur that pins me down muffles Noah's roar; I can't see anything past the teeth, white and dripping, that arc down to my chest.

Rather than the terror that wants to dominate my last moments, I think of Noah. I close my eyes, pulling around me the love that I'm glad I lived for.

When I register the impact, I don't feel the tearing and the agony I was braced for. Relief surges through me then confusion. I blink up at the blue sky that just opened up.

My brain takes long seconds to process what happens next. A wolf drives Dana into the ground beside me, but not the one I anticipated. The white one I expected to see is there a split second later.

Noah doesn't get a chance to change his trajectory, the mouth that was open, ready to defend me, twists at the last moment. His teeth never connect with the chocolate wolf that covers Dana, but the claws bared and ready to subdue do. The yelp that impales the sky is not that of a female wolf. The wound that opens, the blood that stains Noah's fur, belongs to the one that just saved my life.

As Noah rights himself, so does Seth. But he stumbles then drops to his knees. Wide hazel eyes open in shock as he irrevocably, irreversibly turns human.

Kneeling, Seth glances at the gash on his bare torso. His hands, dirty and trembling, rise to his chest, bypassing the bleeding gash and hiking higher. His fingers leave three streaks of soil across his skin.

On the bare skin that no longer holds a wolf tattoo.

I rise, ignoring the aftershocks of adrenalin that quiver through my muscles, moving toward him.

Seth looks up and sees me approaching, Noah moving to join me. I can't tell if the anguish I feel is mine or his...or maybe Seth's. He puts his hand up, a plea to stop neither of us deny. In one graceful move he pushes and stands, holding his shoulders square and proud.

He looks to Noah, and with the same slow dignity, bows his head once. Then his hazel eyes turn to mine.

"It looks like we all just became part of the fabric you were weaving all along."

I blink the tears from my eyes. It's a high price to pay for a lesson to be learned.

His eyes fall to the ground behind me, and Noah and I turn to see Dana, dirty but unscathed, standing just a few feet away.

Noah turns and starts a stealthy, angry walk toward her. Thanks to her, the Prime Alpha has just proved what he is capable of.

Dana morphs to human, an instant submission.

41

NOAH

I stand over her, anger filling my lungs like bellows. I have to consciously remind them to expel it. Dana's terrified eyes jump between me, the white wolf, and Seth, the now human. She scans the clearing, no doubt looking for her four aiders and abettors. When wide, pale eyes dart back to me, I know the cowards are gone. Meaning she's alone. I snarl, showing the weapons capable of wreaking havoc.

Dana cringes. "No, please."

Eden is next to me, pity warring with anger.

I morph, this time choosing to lose my shirt in the shift. My chest is breathing heavily, moving the mark that says it all up and down in rapid movements.

I already have Seth's humanity on my conscience. I won't have two.

"I'm not giving your father another reason for hatred and revenge. Go back and tell him what you've seen. Tell him this ends now."

Dana scuttles back, red hair a frazzled mess around her pale face. Once she's gained some distance, she stands. Eden slips her hand into mine. Dana hesitates, watching our bodies connect.

My free hand clenches. "You can leave Were, or you can leave human. You choose."

Dana runs. Loss and humiliation are her companions as she streaks across the clearing, never stopping to look back when she enters the trees. The minute she's within their shadowy protections she shifts. A light red wolf powers away.

I turn to Eden, hands I can't stop from shaking coming up to cup her face. My fingers in the wild tangle of her hair, my heart allowing itself to beat again as I feel her breath brushing my face, I stare at her. Knowing what I need right now, she pushes up and her lips touch mine, capturing everything that just happened and letting me know we can face it.

I pull away so I can look at her, and the touch, the silent communication of love and confidence, lets me know what we need to do next. We turn, hands clasped, and face the Weres that have seen it all.

Despite the crowd facing us, there is silence. The whole clearing has become a no man's land of sound. Like everyone's thinking so hard they forgot to breathe.

Eden looks up at me. "Now?"

I nod. "Now."

With a heavy-light heart, with the comfort of our love, Eden and I raise our chins and our hopes and say what is practically redundant.

"We are Prime Alpha."

42

EDEN

I've had a full month to prepare for my Bonding. A month that has taken so long a snail could have overtaken it. All because it's a month I've been bonded to Noah...unofficially. What a passion-filled, heart-lightening month it's been, nothing but the truth between us, a whole future before us. There were days I wanted to personally pick up the snail-dragging time and bring it to this day.

Sitting in my blue and green room, Diamond brushes against my leg, and I wonder how I'll get through these last few hours. I lean down to scratch under his chin, and he begins to purr. He looks at me, ear tattered, that one eye seeming to say, 'probably the same way you got through the past four weeks.' Busy.

I've been there to watching Seth as he's had to adapt to being nothing but human. He seems to sense we have more in common than ever before. Although he doesn't know we're both pseudo-humans amongst the Weres, there's an understanding that we belong, but are forever different.

We'd met again at this mother's memorial.

"Are you going to talk to Emily?"

"I don't know. I may not be able to have kids after all."

"There's a difference between not wanting and not being able to have children. Maybe it's only the first that Emily couldn't live with."

Seth had nodded, eyes on his mother's plaque. When he'd looked up again, he'd been smiling. "I'm not the only one who could be having kids."

My stunned open mouth never had a chance to recover and retort before Seth had winked, turned, and left.

That conversation prompted a trip to the obnoxious Dr. Welch. Blushing and stammering, I'd managed to get the contraceptive pill.

I've spent a lot of time strengthening the bond with my brother. I remember Orin greeting me when I'd returned from the Glade. He'd hugged me, and our Fae connection, amplified by touch, had conveyed all the shock, the sadness, the indescribable happiness about what was to come.

I'd stepped back. "I wish you could be there."

"In some ways, I will be."

Looking at my brother, at his enigmatic smile, I knew he wouldn't explain what that meant. "Oh, and we can command them."

His smile had grown wider. "I know. We've just never needed to." He'd grasped me in another fierce hug. "But I'm glad you did."

I'd been there for my bestie, comforting Tara now that Dana is gone, no doubt wherever Kurt is. I suspect our first task as Prime Alpha will be to locate them. Prime Alpha. A role and responsibility that, despite it all, comes at me too fast. The same month that has gone so fast it's made my head reel.

When Noah had left Orin's this morning I'd held on a little too long. He'd grinned, summer sky eyes twinkling like the sun, making no effort to move. "Are you all packed for...after? I've found the most amazing spot."

My breath had picked up, my body temp had skyrocketed. I'd only managed to breathe one word. "Yes."

I'm not sure if a honeymoon happens after a Were wedding but with graduation looming, who knows what with Prime Alpha—I think no one knows to be honest—we only get one night. But our first night together as officially bonded mates will be fitting. In the forest, a pine canopy, the protection of the trees, Mother Earth's green mattress.

Noah's kiss was long and lingering. "It's going to be perfect."

I'd leaned in for another, a touch of lips that affirms so much has passed, but promises there's so much to come. "It will blow perfection out of the forest."

The three dogs barking pulls me from my musings. Caesar and his friends herald the arrival of a car. Telling me it's time.

Thankfully I'd had cyclone Tara to organize the logistics of the Prime Alpha Bonding. Invites had been by phone call only. Beth and Tara had stubby pointer fingers by the time they'd finished punching out all the numbers. Thankfully the Glade, nature's cathedral, is already decked in spring glory. That just left the dress.

Tara enters, her cheeks matching her hair, a white dress bag draped over her arm. She'd insisted it would stay a secret, probably knowing part of me didn't want to know.

She blows a kiss to Orin as she sails past straight to my room. His smile, those matching forest eyes are full of mischief as he watches me follow her, walking gingerly, like I'm expecting tulle and frills to envelop me the moment I enter.

Inside, Tara's already unzipped the bag. She removes the dress, takes it from its hanger, and passes it to me with the biggest smile I've seen yet. The ivory material slides into my hands.

"I like it." It's impossible to keep the surprise from my voice.

"Isn't it stupendously fabulous? It had to be Were, Fae, and human seeing as all three basically meet at Eden."

I grasp the cap sleeves, the light silk waterfalling over my fingers. The sheer presence of sleeves shows I'm human—at a bonding, any Were would proudly display their marks. I stroke the fine embroidery climbing up the skirt. Vines and fragile flowers adorn the hem, slender tendrils reaching up to the waist. That would be the Fae part. I look closely, searching for the Were part. Along the waist sits a narrow satin band and embroidered along it are silhouettes of a wolf, head thrown up in howl. The Werewolf tattoo.

I turn it around so I can fully appreciate its simple beauty. "Ah, where's the back?"

Tara giggles, skips with her hands under her chin. "Surprise!"

"Tara, there is no back." A triangle of satin is missing, starting at the shoulders, ending just above the waist.

"Your hair will hide it. No one will know." She wriggles her brows. "Noah will."

I flush, mostly out of embarrassment, a little because I like the idea. A hidden, exposed piece of skin only Noah will discover.

"And here are the shoes."

Relief has me smiling as Tara passes me two ivory ballet slippers. Eden in heels on grass is a recipe for eating lawn.

Nervousness and excitement compete for domination, and I can't tell who is going to win. One moment one takes the lead, raising my pulse, wringing my hands. Until the other overtakes, squeezing out a few more thousand beats per minute, twisting my hands into sweaty knots.

Tara chatters as she does my hair, paints my face. All I catch are fragments—this Bonding will become the first Were wonder of the world...and I mean awesome, capitals, underlined, bold, in size gigantor font...Venus and Aphrodite are gonna want to claw your eyes out...I think we'll go for 'secret garden' eyes.

I resist rolling my eyes; we've already had this chat. This is going to be the most anti-climactic bonding ever. There'll be no marks glowing and changing—I don't have one, and Noah's has already done that. The only reason it'll be unforgettable is because it'll be anxious Eden in front of every influential Were you can imagine. That Eden doesn't, can't remember dance steps, lines, the valuable art of walking without tripping on a hem.

Tara and Orin are there when I exit my room, dressed and ready. Their faces make me blush, a little embarrassed, secretly pleased. Neither of them say a thing for long moments.

And then Tara breaks the silence. "I'm considering bonding with you myself, Eden."

My laughter breaks the heavy moment, and I'm glad for some lightness.

"I'll go get the car." Efficient as always, Tara is out the door.

I look to Orin, who smiles the smile of the proud. He steps forward and brings something from behind his back. My eyes widen as I take in the fragile wreath of blooms he holds up to me.

"Orin, it's beautiful."

The most prolific flowers I recognize—white columbines, just like the one Noah gave me, their star shape giving the garland a crown-like feel. But they are sprinkled amongst ones I don't know. That I haven't seen around here.

"This is our gift for you, Eden."

The hand that was reaching out to touch the fragile, pale petals stops. *Our*...Orin's eyes tell me why I don't recognize the remaining white flowers. That they came from very far away.

"We would all be there if we could."

Orin steps forward and as he places the woven threads of my Fae heritage and the one that stole my heart on my head; I feel my eyes sting with moisture. When his lips press on my forehead, the blessing is complete.

"Thank you, Orin."

The sound of an impatient horn smashes the moment to smithereens. We hug as we both laugh. "Now go forth and bond, little sister."

For a moment, all I feel is shimmering, blazing happiness, and I quickly kiss my brother's cheek before I'm out the door.

On my way to my bonding.

Tara and her truck bring me to the Glade early, so I can take my position at the West end. Noah will enter from the East. Deep in the woods, several rows of trees between me and the Glade, I can't see how many Weres are arriving. But soon I hear them. With each new group of voices, I hear the Glade shrink, crowding my ears, crowding my throat.

Nervousness triumphantly sports a gold medal.

Tara, glowing in a peach strapless dress, fusses around me.

Then I feel it. Noah's presence, his anticipation. I realize he's been hoping, looking forward to this day longer than I have. This was a horizon he was hoping to reach far longer than me.

And under the sun that is Noah, the nervousness evaporates. There is no longer a contest. Anticipation builds to excitement then grows to impatience.

Just as the music starts.

43

NOAH

E den is...
    Eden is...

It sure would be good to finish a sentence right now. But there's only one word that's a vortex in my mind. W.O.W.

Eden is stunning. The dress, a waterfall of pure alabaster, slips and slides over her curves. Dark hair down her back cascades like Niagara Falls. Forest green eyes defying the law of physics with the amount of emotion they contain.

The moment we exited the trees a hush blanketed the crowd, and considering how many Weres are here, that's a feat. My mark, the wolf tattoo married beside the circle containing a five-pointed star, bold across my chest explains part of the silence. The rest, the majority, is totally owned by the phenomenon walking toward me.

The music, played by Dad, Mitch, Grandpa Ben, is the familiar lilting chords I've heard since I was a child. They tumble and glide around us, filling the already overflowing air. But this time, everything diverges from anything I've ever experienced. This time bears no resemblance to anything I've ever felt. The music more meaningful. The emotions more raw.

This time, it's Eden, walking toward me, faith in her eyes. She doesn't falter. Not. Once. I don't think the Prime Alpha is supposed to run across the Glade, grab his mate-to-be and kiss her until oxygen is a life-threatening necessity...and then keep going.

Instead, I let the rhythm count out my steps, moving in the straight line that will bring us to meet in the middle. Nothing could stop the forward motion that takes me, beat by beat, toward Eden. My mate. The straightforward movement nothing like the journey that got us here. Which is okay. It's a journey that means Eden never falters as she approaches the most intimidating calling anyone could ask of her, one where I learned to walk beside her.

When we meet in the center, the music stops, arresting the silence.

I grasp her hand, aching fingers finally touching what they've been yearning to hold. As we connect, the audience, the Glade, the whole world dissolves and disappears. Like the moment we met, before the trials and the hard won, barely survived, lessons, I look into profoundly connected green eyes and stop, floored by the same certainty that something is changing, rearranging, realigning into something I want to be part of. Eden and I create a whole new universe in the space between us, in the love within us.

How the heck is a guy supposed to speak with this much emotion clogging his throat? Luckily, these are words I've wanted to say for a long time. In truth, there are no words I want to say more. No words I want to hear more.

With the conviction of love, I start. "In your hands..."

"I place my trust." My heart tightens with the truth in Eden's words. Her free hand comes up to tenderly stroke my cheek. "In your eyes..."

Man, I want to kiss her. "I found my home." I place my palm over her heart. "In your heart..."

"I found my love." Eden's voice is gilded in honesty, a little choked with tears. Her hand comes up to mirror mine, resting over the mark that already knew this was true. "In your spirit..."

My chest expands, my voice gains conviction. "I found my mate."

Together, our eyes locked, our hearts beating beneath each other's palm, we say the words that will make this binding. Complete. Forever.

"I give you my body, so that two become one.

I give you my soul, till our life shall be done."

As we stand there, I can feel the new, rightful whole take root from the seed that was sown so long ago. All of a sudden, I'm scared to kiss her. This has been centuries in the making; it's expanding, swelling into something overwhelming. Can someone be crushed by this much love and adoration and implications?

Eden smiles, the most ethereal and beautiful thing I have ever seen. She knows; she feels it blooming. "I want it all." She mouths, barely breathing the words.

I grin as I lean down. It's a light kiss, and it's the breath of a beginning, the life about to come, that I taste in those rose red lips.

The music starts again, the distinctive notes of the final dance flood the Glade. The medieval notes multiply, intensify the emotions barely under control.

I tuck one arm behind my back as Eden does the same. We're both smiling as we begin the first steps as bonded mates.

44

TARA

S eeing my guy bestie and my girl bestie tie the knot is the most amazing, tear-yanking thing I've ever seen.

Eden, the girl with beautiful as her baseline, glows. It's like her nervousness never existed. Probably because right now, we don't exist. Noah looks like a guy who's been through a trial by furnace. The hardest trial—where you almost lose everything and the one where you find out what's really important, the ones where if you take up fate's challenge you end up with the greatest reward. Something along the lines of everything your heart ever wanted, and something your mind could never have imagined.

Standing there with my pack, I hear a shuffling behind me. I spin, high alert still easily tripped after last month's happenings. There's nothing. Actually, there's more than I expected. I squint, amongst the trunks hundreds of eyes— furred, scaled, low to the ground, taller than makes you comfortable—are watching alongside the biggest Were turn out in history.

Great Scot, Noah's ark has come to see his bonding.

I can't help an impressed nod. Some of these would be prey to us or the predator standing next to them, but they don't care.

Noah and Eden fold their arms behind their backs and begin to move. With the rhythm of the music guiding them, they step back, to the side, then in. Opposite shoulders brush as they turn half a step then step away, moving in a slow circle.

I'm glad Eden is too completely captivated to remember that Noah's mark won't change. It was the thing she spoke of the least, which means it worried her the most. But I don't think it'll be a problem. If I thought she had eyes only for Noah before, I'm pretty sure right now she wouldn't look away even if her father turned up. With a salted caramel cheesecake.

The music picks up, and so do the lovebirds. They step, slide, then reunite. Even the animals behind me can tell that's their favorite part. Then I see it, like it kinda crept up on me. Like I never saw it coming. Although Noah's mark doesn't change, it stays black on his chest, the two glow like the Aurora Borealis, a shimmering halo of love and happiness. I grab Mitch's hand, and we glance at each other.

Something is building, you can feel the air being sucked into the center like a whirlpool, maybe a cyclone. The notes, that Celtic-Baroque music, pick up tempo. Noah and Eden match the rhythm; they brush, touch, separate, turn. It feels like two nuclear reactors have developed a magnetic force field and are inevitably, quite voluntarily, being drawn into each other.

The silk of Eden's dress billows; that heavy mass of hair that took forty minutes to straighten divides and reunites around her. She dances like she's always been one of us (which I could have told you was true months ago). Noah's steps are so full of meaning you almost want to look away. I. Don't. Think. So. I take a quick peek around. No one else considers blinking right now.

Although the air is so thick it practically weighs a ton, the tempo picks up, and so do the lovebirds, sucking the weighted air into their magnetic pull.

This is gonna be one monster mushroom cloud.

As the music crests then dies, Eden throws herself at Noah, the smile the size of the equator on her face. Noah's arms are already open, ready, and they instantly close around the person destined to be in them.

The moment they touch an orb of light, all the kinetic energy they've been accumulating, arcs out in a circle. A sonic boom of emotion, a herald of the future, leaves the two hearts where it was born. It grows across the Glade, streaking through everyone assembled, dispersing into the trees. The sensation of light and love flashes through me and everyone lucky enough to be here. As it hits the vegetation, a mass of birds, it looks like all of Wyoming's avian population, lifts for the sky. Taking all that potential and spreading it to the world.

I look at Mitch, wondering if my face matches his dumb-struck expression. Lamest bonding ever my tuckus.

The aftermath leaves behind a hush and a stillness; shock has frozen everyone's tongue. Noah would love to know I've been rendered mute. Not that I'll ever tell him.

Noah and Eden never left the ground, but they look like they've just returned to Earth.

A round of applause roars so loud, if every feathered friend hadn't already startled to the sky, the thunder of hands slapping hands with such enthusiasm would have done it. Beth is crying, so is Aunt Mavis, but with a lot less grace. Mitch's chest has tripled with pride. Behind me, two palms clap with the force of faith. I turn to find Seth rejoicing with the rest of us. The one who has lost the most; even I, who carries the pain of a scorned father and a sister's betrayal, still have my identity. Seth nods— he's lucky he doesn't wink—then turns back to my ecstatic besties.

Even the rumble of hundreds of hands going red from clap-ping doesn't invade the bubble Eden and Noah have created. Noah leans down, the intent to kiss a banner on his face. To be honest, I have to give them some credit, they've kissed once since this Bonding started, and that was a peck that would be legal in a church. I've spent enough time with these two (like five minutes) to know it's killing them. I thought Mitch and I were joined at the lips.

Their kiss is one that you know you should look away from but have no intention to. Hopping horse puckey, I don't know how they manage to make it look so sweet and tender and so laden with just-wait-till-tonight all at once. I'm relieved, maybe a bit disappointed, when they keep their hands where they are. I almost applaud them again. And to be honest, it's probably a good thing that Noah hasn't found the great big patch of skin without the barrier of silk at Eden's back.

Hands held, they turn and face the crowd. Weres upon Weres upon Weres. Even if you don't know what these two have been through to be together, that much love in the Glade will have your mouth tipping up and your eyes misting over.

Most are smiling. The love between these two eclipses any Bonding they've seen so far.

Some are a little more serious. A couple have their arms crossed. The question, the one that's whispering through my mind and probably the rest of the smiling crowd, is probably clamoring a little louder in their heads.

A question I can't shake.

A question I can't answer.

What now?

THE END

Ready for the next installment in the Prime Prophecy series?
Check out PROPHECY FULFILLED!

PROPHECY FULFILLED

A divided Were nation. A hidden Fae heritage.

Newly crowned Prime Alpha pair, Noah and Eden are preparing for the destiny they have been chosen for. When the final Precept appears, three words etched in stone that change everything, they know their fated connection is about to be tested as never before.

Because the need to conquer is exactly what the prophecy is asking for.

As packs splinter, as the Fae reveal their secrets, and as a new threat to the Glade seems unstoppable, Eden and Noah are about to discover the Prime Prophecy is even bigger than they imagined.

For the Prophecy will dictate the future of all – Were, Fae and human alike – by showing that the power of uniting is far greater than choosing to stand alone.

Don't miss this stunning finale to the award-winning and best-selling Prime Prophecy series.

Available at all online paperback stockists or order directly from your local bookstore.

HAVE YOU READ THE PRIME PROPHECY PREQUEL?

As an exclusive for my subscribers,
you can download it for free!!

Tara grew up playing and laughing with her two best friends. Life is uncomplicated and carefree...until she falls for one of them. The wrong one.

Because Tara is the first born of her pack, and with the title comes responsibility - the expectation that she will bond with an Alpha heir to strengthen her pack's standing...and Mitch was born seven minutes too late.

Tara's heart is torn when a deep connection with Mitch is awakened and she discovers the potential for so much more than friendship. But her mind knows what she must choose.

When the impossible strikes Mitch's family, when their

sacred Glade is threatened, Tara is forced to decide — her heart or her pack?

USA Today Best-Selling author, Tamar Sloan, brings you the prequel of the breathtaking and best-selling Prime Prophecy series. Discover where a love destined to leave a legacy all began!

CLICK HERE TO DOWNLOAD FOR FREE!

ALSO BY TAMAR SLOAN

KEEPERS OF THE GRAIL

The legendary Holy Grail is real.

Yet everything known about it is a lie.

KEEPERS OF THE CHALICE

A vampire. A huntress.

A cure that will change everything.

KEEPERS OF THE LIGHT

Angels and demons have battled for millennia.

Their inevitable war has begun.

KEEPERS OF EXCALIBUR

A fated love. A cursed wolf.

A supernatural war only they can stop.

DESTINED DEMIGODS

Love that defies the gods.

Powers that define destiny.

ELEMENTAL GAMES

Elemental powers. Deadly Games.

No escape.

THE SOVEREIGN CODE

Humans saved bees from extinction...and created the deadliest threat we've seen yet.

THE THAW CHRONICLES

Only the chosen shall breed.

ZODIAC GUARDIANS

Twelve teens. One task.

Save the Universe.

ABOUT THE AUTHOR

Tamar hasn't decided whether she's primarily a psychologist who loves writing, or a writer with a lifelong drive to make a difference. She must have been someone pretty awesome in a previous life (past life regression indicates a Care Bear), because she gets to do both. She divides her time between helping families and writing emotion driven YA stories set in amazing imaginary worlds that surprise even her.

The driving force for all of Tamar's writing is sharing and connecting. In truth, connecting with others is why she writes. She loves to hear from readers. Find her on all the usual social media channels or her website, www.tamarsloan.com where can download one of her books for free.

(Seriously, I LOVE hearing from you guys!)

www.ingramcontent.com/pod-product-compliance
Lightning Source LLC
Chambersburg PA
CBHW031547240626
47153CB00002B/416

* 9 7 8 0 6 4 8 0 9 2 3 4 6 *